LAST BREATH

SALLY RIGBY

Edited by Emma Mitchell of @ Creating Perfection.

Cover Design by Stuart Bache of Books Covered

GET ANOTHER BOOK FOR FREE!

To instantly receive the free novella, **The Night Shift**, featuring Whitney when she was a Detective Sergeant, ten years ago, sign up for Sally Rigby's free author newsletter at www.sallyrigby.com

Chapter One

Detective Chief Inspector Whitney Walker frowned at the computer screen. Should she start with the overtime figures and review expenditure in line with their objectives, or address how well her team had been doing against their key performance indicators? All of which needed completing by the end of the month, and she had to force herself to do. It wasn't that she didn't see the point of all the reporting and analysis. Of course she did. But they weren't her favourite jobs. She much preferred to be out in the field, planning and monitoring the front-line operations and working with her team.

Recently, her boss, Detective Superintendent Jamieson, had been struggling with issues at home, and so had asked her to deputise for him at various functions, and to comment on reports which he'd been tasked to do. She had to admit, her reasons for helping weren't exactly selfless. She didn't want his commitment questioned as it could lead to him being passed over for promotion. No way would she sit back and let that happen. As far as she was concerned, the sooner he moved on the better. He'd come into the force on the fast track scheme and was intent on making his way to the top in record time. They butted heads most of the time, and she'd be more than happy to see him on his way.

The phone on her desk rang. 'Walker.'

'It's Matt, guv,' her detective sergeant replied.

'This better be important. I'd allocated the morning to get through my admin and didn't want disturbing.'

'Sorry, guv, but I think you'll agree this is an exception. A woman's been found murdered in her house in Pennington Grove.'

She tensed. Not another murder. Every city had their fair share, but sometimes she felt they were being given someone else's allocation on top of their own.

'What else do we know?'

'She was found by her cleaner … bound and gagged, and she appears to have been strangled. But we won't know for certain until we have confirmation from the pathologist.'

'Right. We'll go there straight away. Make sure pathology and scenes of crime officers have been informed.'

She ended the call and closed the document she'd been working on, pleased to have an excuse to park it for a while. After throwing on her jacket, she picked up her handbag from the back of the chair.

'Ready?' she asked once she'd walked into the incident room to collect Matt.

'Yes, guv. Pathologist and SOCO are on their way.'

They drove to the address which was in a smart area of the city, and when they arrived a uniformed officer was stationed by the wrought-iron gate.

'Were you first on the scene?' she said to the officer, who she recognised as PC Timms.

'Yes, guv. PC Carson and I were on duty close by when the call came in at nine o'clock this morning.'

Whitney glanced at her watch, it was already nine forty-five.

'Who found the body?'

'The cleaner. Sandy Griffiths.'

'Where is she now?' Whitney asked.

'Inside with Carson.'

'Do we have a name for the victim?'

'Yes, it's Mrs Celia Churchill,' the officer replied.

'Where did she find the body?'

'In her bedroom.'

'Is the pathologist here yet?'

'No, guv.'

'Okay, you stay here and keep the crime scene log, while we go inside and interview the cleaner. SOCO are on their way.'

They walked up the long drive to a three-storey, red-brick monstrosity with annexes to either side, one of which included a triple garage.

The front door was open and they entered a large, square reception hall with stone flooring and a huge set of French doors at the rear which looked out onto the mani-cured back garden. Broken glass was scattered over the floor. The entry point?

'Wow, this must be worth millions,' Matt said, his eyes wide.

'And some,' Whitney said. 'Let's go and find the clean-er.' They headed down a short corridor in the direction of voices and entered a large open-plan kitchen which had a sitting area in one corner overlooking the garden, and a large dining table in the other. Sitting on the sofa was a woman in her fifties and next to her, on an easy chair, was PC Carson. He stood as soon as they came over.

'I'm Detective Chief Inspector Whitney Walker and this is Detective Sergeant Price. I understand you found Mrs Churchill,' she said to the cleaner.

'Yes. It was awful.' Her face crumpled.

'Would you be up to answering some questions?' Whitney asked gently.

The woman nodded.

Whitney turned to PC Carson. 'You can leave us now. Go and stand with PC Timms at the front gate. We're waiting for the pathologist and SOCO to arrive.'

'Yes, guv,' he said.

'Please can you tell me what happened?' Whitney said, sitting on a chair opposite.

Sandy Griffiths stared at her, a glazed look in her eyes. She swallowed hard. 'I came in at half-past eight, as usual. Everywhere was quiet. Sometimes Mrs Churchill is in bed, and sometimes she's out when I get here. I have my own key. I went upstairs to see whether she was there, so I could change the sheets, and—' She gulped and tears rolled down her cheeks.

There was a box of tissues on the coffee table in front of them, and Whitney slid it over to her.

'Would you like a cup of sweet tea? It will help with the shock.'

'Yes, please.'

'Matt could you do the honours. A cup of sweet tea for Sandy, and I'll have a coffee. Do you mind if I call you Sandy?'

'No. That's what everyone calls me.'

'This is a lovely house. Have you worked for Mrs Churchill long?' Whitney decided to take a different approach to ascertaining the facts, so it wasn't so painful.

'I've been here for five years.' She gave a weak smile.

'And what are your duties?'

4

'I come in three times a week… on a Monday, Wednesday, and Friday. I do the cleaning, the laundry, and any other jobs Mrs Churchill needs doing.' She buried her head in her hands. 'I can't believe she's gone. It just doesn't seem real.'

'What about the garden?'

'There's a gardener who comes in once a week.'

Whitney pulled out a notepad from her pocket and started jotting down some details.

'When you arrived this morning, did anything seem out of the ordinary?'

Sandy sat upright and sucked in a loud breath. 'No. My first job is always to tidy up the kitchen. Mrs Churchill had been out to a charity gala last night, so there were no dinner plates or pans to wash. All it needed was a general wipe around.'

'I thought you said you went upstairs to see if Mrs Churchill was there and to change the sheets?' Whitney clarified.

'Usually I do the kitchen first, but today I went to see if she'd gone out so I could get the washing on straight away.'

'What are your hours?'

'Eight-thirty to two-thirty, though sometimes I stay later if Mrs Churchill is entertaining, to help her get everything ready.'

'Are you up to talking to me about what happened when you went into the bedroom and found Mrs Churchill?' Whitney asked, anxious to move on.

'Yes,' Sandy said with a sniff.

'Was the bedroom door open or closed?'

'It was open. Definitely.' Sandy nodded.

'When you saw that, what did you think?'

'That she was out, because when she's in bed the door is shut.'

'Did you notice whether her car had gone?' Whitney asked.

'No, I didn't, because she keeps it in the garage, and I don't go in there.'

'If she was to go out at this time of day, where would it be?'

'She'd go out early if she was going to London, shopping. Or sometimes she'd go to an exercise class, but she hasn't recently because she twisted her knee and was waiting for it to recover before she went again.'

'So, this morning you saw the door was open and, because you assumed Mrs Churchill wasn't there, you went into the room with a view to stripping the bed,' Whitney said, continuing to write notes.

'Yes. I was going to take the sheets and towels and wash them,' Sandy said.

'Can you talk me through what happened next?'

'I think so,' Sandy faltered, her face pale.

'I know it's going to be hard, but just take it steady.' Whitney gave an encouraging nod.

'I walked in and the curtains were drawn, which I thought was odd because usually she opens them once she's up and dressed, and ready to go out. I headed over to the window and opened them. I turned to go over to the bed and then I saw her.' Her hand flew up to her chest. 'She was lying there in her nightie with her eyes open and staring up at the ceiling. Her ankles were tied together and so were her hands. A pink scarf was tied around her neck. It was … It was…' Her voice cracked, and she began to sob.

Whitney moved from the chair and sat beside her. She rested her arm around Sandy's shoulders. 'You're doing really well. You've had a huge shock. Take some deep breaths. Is there anyone we can phone to take you home later?'

'My husband's at work. I'll be fine to drive myself.'

Matt came over holding two mugs. He leant forward until they were hovering above the table.

'Stop,' Sandy called out. 'We need coasters. Mrs Churchill is very particular about it.' She took two coasters from the stack in the centre of the table and put them down so that Matt could put the mugs down. 'Sorry, I didn't mean to shout,' she said, blushing.

'No problem,' Matt said. 'It's the same in our house.'

'Sandy, what did you do after finding Mrs Churchill?' Whitney asked.

'I screamed, but no one could hear me.' Her hands were clenched so tightly in her lap that her knuckles had gone white. 'I had to pull myself together. So, I used the phone by the side of the bed and dialled 999. After I'd told the operator how I'd found Mrs Churchill she calmed me down while they were getting the police to come. It's all a bit of a blur.' She shivered.

'You're doing very well,' Whitney said to reassure her. Her heart went out to the woman. Seeing any dead body was traumatic, but to find a murder victim was even worse. Whitney had grown a hard shell when it came to coping, but Sandy wouldn't have. 'What happened next?'

'The nice police officers arrived and brought me down here to wait for you. There was nothing else I could do.' She shook her head.

'You did everything you should've done,' Whitney said. 'A lot of people panic and can't even pick up the phone. I'd like to ask you some more questions about what's been happening recently at the house, if that's okay?'

'Yes.' Sandy nodded.

'Where's Mrs Churchill's husband?'

'They're divorced. It was very messy. They were only married for a short time. I'm surprised it lasted that long.'

Whitney started at the aggressive tone in the cleaner's voice. 'Can you explain what you mean?'

She sat upright in her chair and looked directly at Whitney. 'I don't know exactly what happened between them, but he was only in it for her money, that much was obvious. He was a lot younger than she was. She met him on a cruise and they got married quickly. I shouldn't speak ill of the dead but she had a very strange taste in men.'

'What's his name?'

'Jason Allen. I never liked him.'

Whitney wrote it down. Murders were usually committed by someone who knew the victim. He'd be one of the first they interviewed.

'Had she been married before?'

'Yes, but I'm not sure how many times. At least three, to my knowledge. I've only known two of them since I've been working here.'

'Does Mrs Churchill have any children?' Whitney asked.

'She has a daughter, Natasha, who lives in Bristol.'

'We'll need to inform her what's happened to her mother. Do you have her details?'

'No. You should find them on Mrs Churchill's phone. They phone and text regularly.'

'Has anybody been hanging around outside the house recently? Someone acting suspicious?' Whitney asked.

Sandy paused for a moment. 'Not as far as I know. It's usually a very quiet street.'

'What about the gardener? What's his name?'

'Dave. I don't know his surname or his number. He works on a Friday morning.'

Whitney pulled out her card and gave it to her. 'You've been really helpful, thank you. If you think of anything that might help us, please let me know. You can call me on this number any time.'

'Can I go home now?' Sandy asked.

'If you could just wait for our scenes of crime officers to arrive before you leave, so they can take your finger-prints, that would be helpful. We need them to eliminate you from our enquiries. Which reminds me, when you were in the bedroom … did you touch anything else other than the curtains and the phone? Did you touch Mrs Churchill at all?'

'No.' Sandy shook her head. 'That's what they asked me when I phoned the emergency services.'

'Well done. That makes our life easier. I'll leave you with DS Price for now.'

She took a large swallow of coffee, replaced the mug on the coaster, and left the room as she wanted to view the crime scene before the pathologist arrived.

Chapter Two

Whitney made her way to the reception hall so she could go upstairs. Before she could get there, Dr Claire Dexter, the pathologist, turned up. Claire was the best pathologist in the county, if not the country. But she was extremely particular when doing her job, and she wouldn't want Whitney getting in the way.

'Hello, Claire. How are you?'

'Early starts aren't my thing. Why this body couldn't have been found later in the day, I don't know.'

Whitney smiled. Claire, as usual, was wearing her unique blend of outlandish clothes. She hadn't yet put on her coveralls, so her green and white striped, wide-legged trousers were on show, as was the navy and white polka-dot blouse, tied with a bow at the neck. Her short red hair looked like it hadn't seen a brush that morning, and in her ears she wore a pair of red plastic hoop earrings. Claire was one on her own when it came to fashion choices.

'I haven't yet been up to the crime scene. I'll come with you,' Whitney said.

'Providing you make sure to keep out of my way.'

They walked up the open light wooden staircase to the next floor and along the wide hall until arriving at a door with a yellow cordon across it. Claire placed her bag on the floor and pulled out some white coveralls and disposable gloves, which she put on. Whitney also put on some gloves.

'I'm going in first,' Claire said.

'That's fine, I'll follow.'

The room was huge and in the centre was a four-poster king-size bed. There were two doors off the bedroom, both of which were open, one leading to an en suite bathroom, and the other to a walk-in wardrobe.

Whitney looked over at the victim. She was, as the cleaner had described, still in her nightwear and bound. She was also gagged. Around the woman's neck was a pink chiffon scarf.

Claire took out her camera, strode over to the bed, and started taking photographs of the body.

'Strangulation, would you say?' Whitney asked.

'You know better than to ask me that. I'm not drawing any conclusions until I have the body back at the lab, and can do my tests. All I will say is the scarf is tied tightly around her neck, and there are ligature marks. But that doesn't mean that's what killed her. I'll tell you more once I've completed my investigations.'

Whitney moved over to the dressing table. Sitting on top was an antique silver brush and comb set. Also there were photographs of the victim standing next to a younger version of herself. Her daughter? Celia Churchill was a very attractive woman, slim with blonde hair, large eyes, and an angular jawline. Her daughter was the same. She picked up the photo and put it in an evidence bag. She then went into the walk-in wardrobe and gasped. Rows and rows of clothes were lined up, according to the season, and at the back, taking up the whole wall, were racks of shoes. More than she'd ever seen.

'There must be over two hundred pairs of shoes in here. Crazy,' she called out to Claire.

'An Imelda Marcos emulator,' Claire said.

'Who?' Whitney frowned.

'Imelda Marcos. She was First Lady of the Philippines during the sixties and seventies. She was famous for her collection of shoes. You must have heard of her,' Claire said.

'No, I haven't.'

'You're probably too young to remember,' the pathologist said.

Was she? She'd bet George, the forensic psychologist she worked with, would know. Despite being a few years younger.

She left the wardrobe and headed into the bathroom which was also huge. There was a double walk-in shower, and in the centre stood a large white free-standing bath with Victorian legs, and gold taps. Beside the sink were several candles and bottles of bubble bath. Everything was spotlessly clean.

'Sandy Griffiths is an exceptional cleaner,' she said, leaving the bathroom and walking back into the bedroom. 'Not a speck of dust anywhere.'

'I'll take your word for it, I haven't looked,' Claire said.

'Time of death?'

'Judging by the state of the body, in terms of temperature, lividity, and rigor she's been dead for at least eight hours, and no more than thirty-six. I can be more precise once I've done further tests.'

'Any signs of a struggle?'

'If I tell you, will you stop asking me questions and let

me get on with my work?' Claire lowered her camera and stared directly at her.

'Promise,' Whitney said.

'It appears there may have been, which I'm deducing from the fact there's a rip in the nightdress. I can't be certain until the body is back at the lab and I can look for trace evidence. Now, that's all I'm telling you, so leave me alone.'

'When will you have you something for us?' Whitney pressed.

'When I do.'

'What about if I come and see you tomorrow morning? Will that give you enough time?'

'Possibly,' Claire said.

'That's sorted then. You can expect to see me tomorrow morning.'

'With your partner in crime?' Claire asked.

'If you mean George, I don't know. She doesn't know about this murder, yet. The university is being difficult about her having so much time off to work with us. I don't know why because she's still doing what she's trained to do, being a forensic psychologist.'

'Yes, but this is Lenchester University. They're far more into theory than its application in the real world,' Claire said.

'How would I know that? I didn't go to university.'

She didn't usually mind her lack of a university education, though occasionally it got to her. But it wasn't to be. When she was seventeen she'd got pregnant with her daughter Tiffany and that had changed everything. She didn't regret it. She wouldn't swap her daughter for the world. Tiffany was studying Engineering Science at university. She was the first person in the family to go, and Whitney couldn't be prouder.

'Well, I'll see you, on your own or with George, tomorrow,' Claire said.

Whitney left the bedroom and took a look around the rest of the first floor. There were another three bedrooms all with en suites, plus an additional family bathroom. She walked up the stairs to the top floor and discovered two more bedrooms, again with en suites.

Seven bathrooms to clean. How on earth did Sandy manage? Then again, if the victim lived alone, it was only an issue when there were guests. She returned to the ground floor to look around further. She came across the study. A big antique desk sat in the centre of the room. There were patio doors leading out to the garden.

On the desk was a laptop which she put into an evidence bag. She tried the drawers, but they were locked. Maybe the key was in the victim's handbag. She couldn't recall whether there was one in the bedroom, so she went back to check.

'What are you doing here?' Claire barked as she walked in.

'I wanted to check whether the victim's bag is in here.'

'I haven't seen it.'

'I'll ask the cleaner.'

She returned downstairs and into the kitchen where Sandy was still seated.

'Can you tell me where Mrs Churchill kept her handbag?'

'Never in the same place twice. Have you tried the drawing room?'

'No, I haven't. Please take me,' Whitney said.

'I'm meant to be having my fingerprints taken.'

'Don't worry, they can be taken when you get back.'

When they reached the reception hall, the SOCO guys were talking with Matt. She nodded to them and followed

Sandy into the annexe. The drawing room was large with a fireplace in the centre of the longest wall, and three ivory and white striped sofas surrounding it. There were floor-to-ceiling curtains on both sets of windows.

'How did you manage to keep this place clean?' Whitney asked.

'Mrs Churchill is very tidy and it's usually just her. If she has guests, I do extra hours and my sister comes in to help.' The cleaner looked by the side of the sofa closest to the fireplace. 'Here it is.'

She handed Whitney the handbag and she looked inside. There weren't any keys. Damn.

'Do you know where Mrs Churchill kept the key to the desk in her office?'

'There's a drawer in the kitchen where she kept lots of odds and ends. It could be there.'

'Okay, let's go and look. How are you feeling now?'

'I'm not sure. It all seems like a bad dream. I'll be glad to get home. Now I don't have a job I'm not sure what we'll do. I know that sounds awful, but we need my money. I haven't received my pay from last week yet.'

'It's natural for you to worry. We'll be contacting her daughter, at which time I'll let her know you're concerned,' Whitney said.

When they arrived back at the kitchen, Sandy went over to the kitchen units and opened one of the drawers. 'Have a look in here.'

There were a number of keys in one corner and Whitney picked up one which looked as though it might belong to the desk. A good place to keep it, in plain sight.

The kitchen door opened, and one of the scenes of crime officers walked in.

'Hi, Colin. I'll leave you to take Mrs Griffiths' finger-prints,' Whitney said.

'No problem,' the officer said.

She went back to the study and tried the key. It worked. The drawers were just as tidy as everywhere else. It didn't look as though anything had been disturbed. In the large middle one was a calculator, a small box of paperclips, a pencil sharpener, a roll of adhesive tape, and an envelope with *Celia* handwritten on the front. She opened it and pulled out a single sheet of writing paper. The letter was dated several months previously.

I'm begging you, please don't do this to me. Think of what we had. What we could have. It was one silly mistake and I promise it won't happen again. I need you. Your life won't be the same without me.

JA

The husband? Had he cheated on her? Was the last sentence a veiled threat?

She left the study and saw Matt waiting by the front door, peering at the screen on his phone. She showed him the letter. 'We need to get back to the station and gather the team.'

Chapter Three

George scanned the university café to see if she could see Whitney's daughter. It had been a while since they'd met up for coffee and she was looking forward to catching up with her. She'd had a soft spot for Tiffany ever since a year ago when she'd been abducted by a pair of psychotic twins who'd attended Lenchester University and had been murdering female students. George had been a part of the rescue team who'd saved her life.

It had affected Tiffany greatly, and because she hadn't wanted to worry her mother, who had enough on her plate with her own mother and brother, she'd confided in George instead. George had insisted she attend counselling, and that had proved to be the turning point. After a few months, Tiffany had become less withdrawn and better able to go out on her own and return to having a social life.

They were still waiting for the twins' trial to take place. According to Whitney, cases like theirs could take up to eighteen months to get to court, so they could be waiting for a further six. Tiffany would need a great deal of support at that time. Whitney, too. Having to relive the nightmare would be traumatic for both of them. George would help them as best she could.

She glanced at her watch. They weren't due to meet for another five minutes, so she decided to get herself a drink and find somewhere to sit. The café wasn't too busy and there was a vacant table by the window. It was nice to take a break, as this was the busiest time of year for her. She had all the new first years to contend with, although as they were now halfway through the first term of the academic year, they were mainly licked into shape. She was very strict regarding attendance, punctuality, and handing in assignments, as she believed sloppiness in everyday life would lead to sloppiness in their studies.

She'd also decided to allocate more time to her research, in particular writing up her findings relating to working with the police. She'd already written one paper which had been well-received, based on the case involving Tiffany and the twins, but now she wanted to go into more depth, and examine in greater detail the application of theory to solving crimes in a more general sense. She'd been invited to present at a joint symposium being held by the Metropolitan Police and the government, and was looking forward to it. Not least because it would get her head of department off her back. There had been concern about the amount of time she'd been spending working with the police, rather than being at the university. She'd already been passed over for promotion because of it, and although initially that annoyed her, she was now okay about it.

'Hey, George.' Tiffany appeared holding a bottle of water.

'Hello.' She smiled. It was good to see her looking so happy.

'How's it going?' Tiffany asked as she sat.

'Very well. I've settled into the new term and I'm enjoying the students. I've got a very capable bunch. What about you? It gets harder once you hit the third year, doesn't it?'

Tiffany frowned. 'It's all okay and I'm coping with the extra work. You're right, though, it does seem to have stepped up a gear … There's erm … something I want to speak to you about. In confidence. I don't want you to tell Mum.'

'If you want to confide in me that's perfectly fine.' George took a sip of coffee while she waited. She didn't like keeping things from Whitney, but she wouldn't betray a private conversation.

'You're going to think I'm crazy, but I'm not. It's something I really want to do.' Tiffany paused and chewed her lip.

'I've never known you to do anything crazy before, so I'm sure it isn't. Tell me,' George encouraged.

'I want to drop out of university.'

George's jaw dropped. She hadn't expected that.

'Why? You've been doing so well with your studies. Don't you enjoy being here?'

'I might come back, but at the moment I want to go to Australia with a friend of mine. I wanted to discuss it with you first, to find out my options.'

How was she meant to handle this? Whitney would be mortified if Tiffany dropped out. She was so proud of her daughter's achievements. Should she discourage Tiffany? No. It wasn't her role to do that. She wanted advice, not coercion.

'When you say "options", what do you mean?' George asked.

'If I leave at the end of this term and go away for a year, possibly two, will I be able to complete my course when I return? Could I join where I left off, or will I have to start my third year again? Will they accept me back? Will they be angry with me for leaving?' The words tumbled out of Tiffany's mouth.

'Let's take this one step at a time,' George said, trying to get her head around the effects Tiffany leaving would have on Whitney. 'Why do you want to travel now and not when you've completed your course?' It seemed the most obvious question to ask.

'Because my course is four years long and I'm only halfway through. My heart is set on going now. This is the best time of year to travel there because it's summer. I can apply for a Working Holiday Visa, which lasts twelve months, and make an application for a second one while I'm out there and extend my stay for a further year. I want to see the world. I haven't been anywhere, or seen anything, other than Lenchester.'

Whitney had told her that in Tiffany's formative years there hadn't been a lot of money, and they'd never travelled abroad in the same way George had done with her family when she was young. She could understand how, for Tiffany, the thought of experiencing another country and its culture would be attractive.

'I know you're anxious to see the world, and I don't blame you. There's a lot out there. But there are things to consider before you make the decision to drop out. First, there's no guarantee they'll allow you to complete your course, you may have to apply again.' She wasn't prepared to sugar-coat it.

'Can't I just defer my third and fourth year?'

'It's not that simple. You'd have to discuss it with your tutors and see if they would be prepared to hold open a place for you. And that will depend on how you've done in your studies so far. Whether you could come back into the second term of the third year, I suspect not. I imagine you'd have to complete the whole of the third and fourth years. You'll need to speak to the university admissions department, as well as your tutors, and explain your reasons for wanting to leave now, and convince them it's the best thing for you to do.'

'What happens if they say no to me coming back?' Tiffany asked, frowning.

'You'll have to apply through UCAS to go to a different university, but there's no guarantee you'll be offered a place. You really should speak to your mum,' George said, hoping she could persuade Tiffany to include Whitney in this.

'I don't want to. Not yet. I wanted to speak to you first and then make a firm decision.'

George's heart sank. She didn't want to come between the two of them. Whitney's daughter was the centre of her life, along with her mother and brother who were now in care homes. If Tiffany left, how would Whitney cope?

'I really believe you should be discussing it with her.'

'How can I? You know how proud she is of me going to university. I'm the first person in the family to go. What's she going to think if I tell her I might be leaving?'

'She'll be upset. But even more so to know you'd confided in me instead of her. She's going to find out eventually, so why not now? If she knows you're definitely coming back and returning to university, then she'll likely be more accepting.'

'I'm not sure. It's always been the two of us against the world. That's what she says all the time. I'm dreading telling her I want things to change.' Tiffany fidgeted nervously in her chair.

'Two years will go quickly. Or you might even decide to return home sooner.'

'Unless I love the place so much I apply to stay.'

'That's an option, but isn't easy. There are strict immigration regulations. But you won't know whether it's something you want to do until you've experienced the country. Who's the friend you're planning to go with?'

'It's Phoebe. She's on my course.'

'She's dropping out as well?'

'She was going to leave anyway as she's not happy with the course. That's why she decided to go travelling, and wants me to go with her.'

'That seems very selfish. Just because she's leaving, doesn't mean she should insist you do, too.'

'It's not like that. It was me who suggested going with her. She's been trying to persuade me to stay at uni. But I don't want to. We'd have an awesome time travelling together.'

'What about the twins' trial? You'll most likely be called to give evidence.'

Tiffany's jaw tensed. 'I'll come back for it. We don't even know when it's going to be. I'm not going to hang around and wait.'

It appeared Tiffany's mind was made up, but George didn't want her to go into anything without having thought it through properly.

'Before you make any drastic decisions, I really think you should contact the admissions department and see what your options are. You don't have to make any commitment regarding leaving until you're sure.'

'Could you do that for me?' Tiffany asked.

'No, I can't.' George shook her head. 'It's something you have to do for yourself. If you're old enough to travel across the world, then you're certainly old enough to sort out leaving the university.' She had no intention of making it easy for the girl.

'Sorry, you're right.' Tiffany averted her eyes. 'I'll go to see them and find out what I can do.'

'Then you need to talk to your mother. She can't be the last to know. She deserves to be included in your decision-making. In the past, you've never done anything without consulting her.'

'I know that. I just wanted to speak to you first. Promise me you won't say anything to her. I don't want to mention it until I've spoken to the admissions department and final decisions have been made.'

'What will you say if she asks you not to go?' George asked.

'She won't do that,' Tiffany said.

'You're probably right. But she's going to hate you going. I anticipate it will affect her greatly.'

Tiffany twisted the silver ring she was wearing on her little finger. 'I know, but she won't try to hold me back if travelling is what I really want to do. I think her main issue will be with me leaving university.'

'Have you decided on a date for leaving?'

'We'd like to leave the country mid-December, before the flights get more expensive because of Christmas.'

How on earth was Whitney going to come to terms with it in such a short time?

'That's in a month. You're not giving your mother much time to adjust, especially as you're not planning on telling her immediately,' George said.

'It's the best time to go. We want to travel a little first before looking for jobs.'

'Have you enough money?' George asked, a thought entering her head.

'I have some savings, which will cover my fare and some to spare. It might be tight until I can get a job, but that's fine. We'll manage. I'm not going to ask Mum for any help because she can't afford it.'

'I'll give you some money towards your trip. You'll be away for your twenty-first birthday and I was planning to give you some for that.'

'Are you sure? That's amazing. Thank you so much.' She jumped up from her seat and gave George a hug.

'You're welcome. I'd rather you had enough money to keep you going. I don't want to be worrying that you're running out. In the meantime, hurry up and speak to your mother.'

'I will. Just not yet. Let me look into leaving here first, so I can present her with the whole picture.'

George's phone rang and she glanced at the screen. 'It's her.'

Tiffany grimaced. 'Okay. I'm going now. Promise … not a word.' She did a zip sign in front of her lips, then waved and left.

'Whitney.'

'You're not going to believe this. There's been a murder. A woman was found strangled in her bed. I'm waiting for Claire's report. When can you get here?'

'I can't this morning. I've got classes.'

'What about this afternoon?'

'Okay. I can be there at two.'

'Is everything all right?' Whitney asked, the concern in her voice evident.

'Yes, why?'

'Well, for a start you haven't even asked about the body, which is what you usually do, and you sound a bit distant.'

'Everything's fine.'

'Are you sure? You know you can tell me anything.'

'I've already told you, nothing's wrong. Why do you always have to read something into everything?'

'Okay. Okay. I only asked. Excuse me for being concerned.'

'I'm running late for class. I'll see you later.'

George ended the call, feeling like shit. She had to pull herself together. She didn't want Whitney to suspect she was hiding something from her.

Chapter Four

Whitney opened the incident room door and was bombarded by the sound of phones ringing, computer keyboards tapping, and the team talking. All of her team were in, working. It was a large room with twenty desks and computer screens facing each other in pairs. She walked to the far side where they had a big board. In the centre she wrote the name "Celia Churchill".

'Listen up, everyone,' she said, calling her team to attention. The chatter continued. The problem with being so short was she often got overlooked. She dragged back a chair and climbed onto the desk. 'May I have your attention,' she shouted.

Everything went quiet and her team stared in her direction.

'I've just come from Pennington Grove where a woman was murdered. Her name is Celia Churchill, and she was found by her cleaner. She'd been bound, gagged, and strangled with a scarf. We're waiting for confirmation from Dr Dexter of the exact cause and time of death. I interviewed the cleaner and she reported that the victim lived alone, and she'd recently been divorced from her latest husband. To her knowledge, he was at least husband number three.'

'Was she rich?' Frank, her older detective constable asked.

'What makes you ask that, Frank?' Doug asked.

'Pennington Grove, and at least three husbands. She's got to be,' he said.

'We haven't yet looked into her finances, which is what we'll be doing today. Though the house was massive,' Whitney said.

'What colour was the scarf?' Frank asked.

'It was pink,' Whitney replied, frowning. 'Why?'

'Is it one of those flimsy see-through types? I can't think of the name. You know what I mean, it—'

'Do you mean chiffon?' Whitney interrupted.

'Yes, that's it. Was it pink chiffon?' Frank asked.

'You haven't lost one, have you?' Doug asked, laughing.

Other members of the team joined in with the laughter.

'Very funny,' Frank said, rolling his eyes. 'Was it?'

'Yes,' Whitney said.

'And she was bound and gagged?' Frank continued.

'Yes,' Whitney said.

'Was there any sexual interference?'

'No, there didn't appear to be, but we have to wait for Claire. Why? Come on, get to the point, Frank.' Her jaw tightened with impatience.

'It sounds like the Lenchester Strangler from the 1980s. Do you remember him?'

Several people let out a soft gasp.

'Not really. I was only a child then,' Whitney said. 'Tell us what you know.'

Surely he couldn't be right about the strangler returning. If he was … she didn't want to go there.

'During the night, he'd go into the houses of women who lived alone. He tied them up in their beds and strangled them with a pink chiffon scarf. It was his calling card.'

'And he was never caught?' Whitney said.

'We thought we knew who it was, but nothing could be proved.'

'When did it stop?' Doug asked.

'The man who we thought was responsible killed his wife and was sent to prison. The murders stopped after he was taken off the streets, which proved we were right in believing it was him. It would've been around thirty-five years ago, in the mid-80s,' Frank said.

'Let me get this straight,' Whitney said. 'Once your suspect was found guilty of murdering his wife, you no longer worked on the other deaths? They were left unsolved?'

'I don't know if further investigations were made. I wasn't involved in any,' Frank said.

She shook her head in disbelief. Call that police work? It wouldn't happen on her watch.

'Who else was on the case with you?'

'The DS was Don Mason.'

Whitney's eyes widened. 'Are you sure?'

Don Mason was her old boss. He'd never have given up on a case just because a suspect was charged with another crime. Never. She'd call him once the briefing was over to find out more.

'How many murders were committed?' Whitney asked, forcing herself to focus and not get distracted on how negligent the police had been.

'It was a long time ago, guv. I believe maybe four or five. Could've been more. We'd need to check.'

'Who was this man? If he's out of prison, he could've started up again,' she said.

'I can't remember his name. He'd be in his eighties now, so I doubt it would be him.'

'Right, Frank. I want to know everything there is about the Lenchester Strangler, including how many deaths, where they occurred, how much detail was given to the public. Was it made known that a pink chiffon scarf was used? Were any details kept quiet? The usual,' Whitney said.

'You know, the more I think about it, we did publicise the pink scarf, but the murderer also took a trophy, and we didn't tell the public about that,' Frank said.

'Can you remember exactly what was taken?'

Frank was silent for a while. 'Sorry, guv, I can't. I hadn't been in the department long and was more on the fringes of the case.'

'Let's find out what we can and have a look at what physical evidence we have in the store. Forensics has come a long way since then, so there might be something we can DNA test which will point us to who the murderer was all those years ago. I also want to know everything you can find out about the person who was originally thought to be the Lenchester Strangler. Nice work, Frank.'

'Thanks, guv.' He puffed his chest out.

She should praise him more often, it was just he didn't always warrant it. Though she couldn't fault his loyalty to her, and that counted for a lot in her book.

'Ellie. Use the self-service kiosk to look through our victim's phone and extract the daughter's details. She lives in Bristol. We need to let her know what's happened to her mother. Make it a priority.'

'Yes, guv.'

'After that, see if you can find anywhere locally which sells pink chiffon scarves.'

'Leave it with me,' Ellie said.

'Doug, as Frank's busy, you can check the CCTV footage around the area. We don't have an exact time of death, yet, but it was within thirty-six hours so take the last forty-eight to be safe. Trace any cars coming in the direction of Pennington Grove and then leaving a while later.'

'Yes, guv,' Doug said.

'Sue, I want you to do a background check on Celia Churchill. Friends, social media, finances. Look into the daughter, too. We need everything you can find.'

'Yes, guv,' Sue said.

'Matt, give Sue a hand. But first I need contact details for her latest ex-husband. Jason Allen. The split was acrimonious. I suspect from the letter I found that he cheated on her. He needs to be interviewed straight away.'

'I'm on it,' Matt said.

'Our victim led quite a colourful life, so this could be a one-off murder, by someone with a grudge who imitated the Lenchester Strangler, or we could be facing another serial killer.'

The room hushed, and Whitney's jaw went tight.

Her mind whirled. It was imperative they found out about the previous murders. Records weren't computerised back then, and all the information would be in hard copy files somewhere. They needed to know what trophy was taken because if this was a copycat then that would tell them about the link between the original killer and this one. Then there was Don Mason's input. She had to speak to him now. She wouldn't be able to concentrate until she'd found out exactly what had happened.

She left the incident room and went into her office. Her hand hovered over the phone before she could bring herself to call. She couldn't bear it if he turned out not to be the man she thought he was.

'Hello, this is Don and Katie.' The warm, deep tone of her ex-boss's voice echoed in her ear. Damn. Her call had gone to voicemail. He was out. 'Sorry, we're unable to speak to you. We're currently cruising down the Nile and can't be contacted until our return.' He had to be kidding. Of all the times to be on holiday, now wasn't one of them. 'You can leave a message or call back after Sunday twenty-fourth November. Bye for now.'

'Hello, Don, it's Whitney,' she said, putting on a bright voice. 'I need to speak to you about a case you worked on during the 1980s. The Lenchester Strangler. I'll give you a call after the twenty-fourth and arrange to see you then. I hope you're having a wonderful time.'

She remembered he'd always talked about watching the sun as it rose over the pyramids. The holiday of a life-time he'd called it. Said it was the first thing he'd be saving for after retirement. Except why did he have to go now, when she needed him?

She groaned and thumped her desk in frustration. There was no choice but to wait for his return. In the meantime, she'd have to force herself to stop thinking that he'd let her down by doing a crap job and get on with the case. Once she could discuss it with him, she'd have all the facts.

She headed back into the incident room.

'Guv, I've got details for the daughter,' Ellie said, as she walked in.

'That was quick. Text it to me.'

She contacted Bristol police and arranged for them to visit the daughter straight away and give her the news. Then she left the room and went to Jamieson's office, as she needed to discuss the press conference.

His door was open and for a change it was quiet. Usually he was on the phone. She knocked gently and walked in. He was staring intently at his computer screen.

He glanced up and seemed surprised to see her. 'Walker, what do you want?'

'I came to see you about the murder,' Whitney said.

'What murder?' he said.

Was he serious? How could he not know?

'Earlier this morning a woman was found bound, gagged, and strangled.'

'I haven't checked the dailies yet, as I've been busy with this.' He nodded at his screen, but she had no idea what he meant.

'She was discovered first thing this morning by her cleaner.'

'Do we have any suspects?'

'Too early to say. The murder is very similar to those committed by the Lenchester Strangler in the 1980s.'

He frowned. 'I remember. My old dad had a strange fascination with the case, and used to bore us senseless at the dinner table discussing it.'

'We're requisitioning all the old files and looking into the previous murders. DC Frank Taylor worked in the department at the time, but his recollection of the case is a little sketchy. It's unlikely to be the same person because the original suspect is now in his eighties. We think it might be a copycat. A trophy was taken that wasn't publicised in the press at the time, but until we have Dr Dexter's report we don't know if that's the case in this instance,' Whitney said.

'We need a press conference,' he said.

'That's why I'm here. I'd rather we waited until Dr Dexter has done the autopsy. Then we'll have something concrete to release to the media. We also don't know if this is a one-off or if there are more to come.'

'Let's hope it's a one-off … we've had an *abundance* of serial killers recently. I wonder what the collective noun is.' He laughed at his joke.

What had got into him? 'I've no idea, sir.'

'Mind you, the fact that we've solved all the cases will look very good on my application.' He averted his gaze. 'You didn't hear that,' he said quickly.

Had finally her wishes been granted? Was he leaving?

'Are you going for another job?'

'Now I've let it slip, I'll tell you. But if I hear that anyone else knows, then you'll find yourself confined to the office and won't be SIO on any future cases.'

Was he threatening her? She wasn't going to tell anyone. He should know she'd do everything in her power to help him on his way.

'You can trust me to keep it to myself. As you know, I've already been discreet regarding the extra work I've had to do for you recently.'

'I realise that, and I'm extremely grateful. There's a position at the Met and I've been given the nod to apply.'

'Is it a Detective Chief Superintendent position?' she asked, since that was the next level.

'Yes, it is. It also includes special advisory responsibilities to the government.'

'So you'll be working with the Prime Minister?'

'I'm not sure, but it will involve liaising with government ministers and having an input into policing policy. It's a good position, and perfectly suited to my abilities.'

She couldn't comment on whether his abilities were suitable, but what she did know was if it kept him out of the operational side of things it would be for the best, because he was a paper-pusher extraordinaire. When it came to the day-to-day workings of the force he was a pain in the arse. If he did get the job she'd be jumping for joy.

'When would you be leaving?' she asked.

'The closing date for applications is next week and then there's the selection process, which can take several months. They want someone by the middle of next year. The current postholder is retiring.'

She'd hoped he'd be gone within a few weeks. But she could wait six months, if it meant she'd finally be rid of him.

'I hope you get the position, sir. Rest assured, I won't let anyone know about it.'

'Thank you, Walker. I know we haven't always seen eye to eye, because although you're very good at your job, you can lack forward thinking in terms of how we should be policing.'

Typical. A compliment on the one hand and then straight away he was on his usual twenty-first century policing methods crap, because he thought she lacked the ability to apply them.

'I don't want to get into a dispute with you, sir. You continue with your application, and I'll carry on solving the case.'

'We can't sit on this for too long. I accept that you wish to wait for the pathologist's report and also to find out more about the original Lenchester Strangler, but we really need a press conference soon and no later than Wednesday. That gives you two days.'

'Leave it with me. Currently, the only person to know the nature of the death is the cleaner who found the victim. I'll make sure we speak to her and explain she's not to say anything.'

'Is Dr Cavendish coming in to help? If it is the

Lenchester Strangler, or a copycat, we could certainly do with her expertise.'

'She'll be here this afternoon, after her classes are over.'

'Good. Does the victim have any family?'

'She has a daughter living in Bristol. The force down there is letting her know. I'll be contacting her later to arrange an interview.'

'Okay, you can go now. Keep me posted.' He dismissed her with his usual flick of the hand.

She left the office and walked casually down the corridor until out of sight of his office, and then she punched the air. She couldn't believe her luck. Finally, she was going to be rid of him, because surely he'd get the position if he'd been given the nod to apply.

Chapter Five

George headed into the police station a few minutes before two, as arranged, determined to act normal and not as she had done earlier. She'd been so concerned about accidentally breaking her confidence with Tiffany that she'd lost her cool and caused a problem between herself and Whitney. Although, the officer had texted her later and mentioned the Lenchester Strangler so hopefully it would be okay between them.

She drew in a breath, plastered on a smile, and opened the door to the incident room. Whitney was standing at the board talking to Matt. She strode over.

'Good afternoon,' she said to them both in the most cheerful voice she could muster. She felt ridiculous, Whitney was bound to notice her discomfort.

'Hi, George. I was just talking to Matt about Jason Allen, Celia Churchill's ex-husband. I was waiting for you to come in so we could interview him. We've looked into his business and it isn't doing well. In fact, since the divorce it's taken a nosedive. We need to know why.'

'Maybe the victim had a financial stake in it, which she took out following their split?' George suggested.

'That's what we'll find out. I also found a letter in her drawer. Here's a copy.' Whitney took it from the desk and handed it to her.

'Interesting use of language,' she muttered. 'A combination of begging and threatening.'

'Exactly what I thought. I'll be asking him what he meant by her life not being the same without him.'

'I doubt he'll tell you it was a death threat,' George said.

'I know, but you'll be able to gauge his response when I pose the question.'

'Of course,' she replied. 'When do you want to leave?'

'Now. If he's not at work, we'll go to his house. Okay with you?' Whitney said.

'Absolutely,' George said, as Matt excused himself and left, holding his phone to his ear.

'You're sounding a lot better than earlier,' Whitney said, as they left the incident room for the car park.

'I did say I was fine and there was nothing to concern yourself about,' George said.

'You know you can talk to me, if there's anything wrong. That's what friends are for.'

'I'll remember that, if ever I have something I want to discuss,' she replied.

Whitney laughed, then gave her an apologetic smile. 'Sorry. You're so formal, it makes me laugh sometimes. I don't mean anything by it. You understand that, don't you?'

'I do. My car?' she asked, knowing it would be a peace offering.

'If that's okay?' Whitney said.

'Of course.'

'Are you with me for the rest of the day or do you have to get back to work?' Whitney asked.

'I want to go into the office later this afternoon, but that's all. I have no more lectures or tutorials today.'

'Good. I need you with me.'

'I've been on the Internet checking out the Lenchester Strangler after you mentioned him. Six unsolved murders. Women frightened to spend time alone, even in their own homes. And no one convicted.' Her brow furrowed.

'Don't remind me. I'm not happy about that.'

'At least the murders stopped,' George said.

'Yes, but that doesn't mean the culprit should get away with it. What about closure for the victims' families?' Whitney clenched her fists.

They drove to JA Distribution in the Thorplands Industrial Estate which was on the outskirts of the city. The offices were beside a large warehouse.

'We're here to see Jason Allen,' Whitney said to the young woman sitting at the reception desk.

'Is he expecting you?' she asked.

'No,' Whitney replied.

'He doesn't see anyone without an appointment,' she said.

'Detective Chief Inspector Walker and this is Dr Cavendish, we're here on police business.' Whitney held out her warrant card for the woman to see.

'If you'd like to take a seat over there,' the woman said pointing to a seating area with some low leather chairs and a coffee table. 'I'll let him know you're here. Can I tell him what it's about?'

'No,' Whitney said.

They sat down and George picked up one of the company's brochures from the table, and flicked through it.

'According to this, over three quarters of consumers act

on promotional leaflets they receive. I find that hard to believe,' she said.

'Me, too. I can't stand all the junk mail that comes through the letter box. It drives me insane. Such a waste of paper.'

After several minutes, a tall, good-looking man who looked to be in his early forties appeared. He had short dark hair and was wearing a navy suit with a white shirt and red and green striped tie.

'I'm Jason Allen. How can I help you?' he said.

'We're here on a police matter and would like to speak to you in private,' Whitney said.

'We can go to my office.'

They followed him down the corridor and into a large office with a window overlooking the car park. It was modern and furnished in light oak. He gestured for them to sit in the chairs around a small table next to the window.

'We'd like to discuss your relationship with Celia Churchill,' Whitney said.

A dark shadow crossed his face 'I have nothing to say about that woman.'

'Mrs Churchill was found dead this morning, and we're investigating her death as suspicious.'

'She's dead?' His eyes widened.

Too wide? Was he genuinely shocked?

'Yes. What were you doing last night and into this morning?' Whitney asked, going straight in with the question.

George nodded her approval. He didn't have the chance to compose himself. It was the best way of getting at the truth and why Whitney was so good at her job.

'You can't possibly believe I would have anything to do with her death?' he said.

'We investigate all avenues. We know there were issues during your divorce,' Whitney said.

'*Issues*. Is that what you call it?' He pursed his lips. 'More like being thrown under the bus. After everything I'd done for her. But, just because we had problems doesn't mean I'm guilty of her murder.' He couldn't meet Whitney's eyes.

He was hiding something. Whether it was anything to do with the murder George couldn't tell.

'Please answer the question. What were you doing last night and into this morning?' Whitney pushed.

'I'm not answering any more questions without my solicitor present,' he said.

Panic? Giving himself time to prepare? Whatever, his response was interesting. They'd hardly begun the questioning. There had to be a reason for him to terminate the interview so soon.

'That's your prerogative,' Whitney said. 'I suggest you contact them now and arrange to meet us at the station immediately.'

He phoned and made the arrangement for an hour's time. 'You're lucky she was free, because usually she's very busy. Do I have to come with you or may I go in my own car?'

'We'll meet you there,' Whitney said.

They left the building and returned to George's car.

'What did you make of him?' Whitney asked.

'Difficult to tell. He made an attempt to appear shocked at her death, but didn't ask anything about it. Most people would want to know what had happened. And he was very quick to say that he wouldn't speak to us without a solicitor present. Too quick. His demeanour certainly indicated he was hiding something,' George said.

'We don't know the full extent of what happened

between them, so obviously he's going to be worried. It shouldn't have come as a surprise to him that he would be one of our suspects,' Whitney said.

'Agreed.'

'We've got an hour, so let's go back to the station and see if the team have anything more for us,' Whitney suggested.

∽

'We'll interview him together,' Whitney said, once they'd been informed that Jason Allen had arrived with his solicitor.

'Don't you want me outside watching?' George said.

'No, it's fine for us to be together, as we were earlier. But remember my rules. I ask the questions, you observe,' Whitney reminded her.

George seemed to be more like her old self, although there was still something that Whitney couldn't put her finger on. She was being more reserved. It was almost like the twelve months they'd known each other had disappeared and they were back to how they were when they'd first met.

In the interview room, Allen was talking animatedly to his solicitor, but he stopped as soon as they entered.

Whitney placed her files on the table and then pressed the recording equipment. 'Interview on Monday, November eleventh. Those present: Detective Chief Inspector Walker, Dr Cavendish. Please state your names for the tape,' she said nodding at the other two.

'Jason Allen.'

'Yvette Dunn, Mr Allen's solicitor.'

'Mr Allen, please confirm that you are here voluntarily, and you understand you're not under arrest.'

'I confirm,' he said.

'As you're aware, we're investigating the death of your ex-wife, Celia Churchill. When we spoke to you earlier, you were not prepared to tell us where you were last night, into the early hours of this morning. I'm asking you again to please answer the question.'

Allen leaned in and spoke quietly to his solicitor. 'No comment,' he said.

'Why no comment? You're here to help us with our enquiries. Even though you were divorced, surely you'd want us to find out who was responsible for the death of your ex-wife?' Whitney asked.

'No comment,' he repeated.

'We've been informed your divorce from Mrs Churchill was messy,' she said.

'Messy,' he snapped. 'It was more than messy. She took everything from me. I was left with nothing, despite all the time I spent with her. Escorting her everywhere. Being a dutiful husband.'

'But you were cheating on her, and that's what prompted the divorce. How could you call that dutiful?' Whitney arched an eyebrow.

'You don't know what she was like to live with. So possessive. She wouldn't let me go anywhere or do anything on my own. She always tried to get involved in everything I did. It drove me insane. I wasn't allowed a minute to myself.'

'Yet you found time to have an affair,' Whitney said.

'With someone who worked for me. Being at work was the only time I was away from Celia's clutches, and even then she'd call to check up on me. For what I put up with, I deserved more than being treated like a piece of shit and given nothing,' he said.

He'd gone from *no comment* to spilling everything. She should've started with the divorce.

'You were left with your company.'

'Only because it was in my name. She invested in it as a wedding gift.'

'I understand it's not doing too well,' Whitney said.

'How do you know that?' he said in a sharp voice.

'Because we do our research.'

'We have a cash flow problem, but we'll get through it. Before we split, Celia was going to loan me some money for the business, but there were certain provisos which I wasn't happy with,' he said.

'What were they?' Whitney said.

'She wanted to be a partner, and that's why I hesitated. Quite frankly, it's a good job I did, otherwise I'd have probably lost the business as well in the divorce.'

'Would it be a fair assessment to say you harboured a great deal of resentment towards Mrs Churchill?' Whitney asked.

'What do you think? Anyone would after being treated the way I was.' His top lip curled.

'Did you give this letter to Mrs Churchill?' She slid the copy towards him and he picked it up.

'Yes.'

'What did you mean by the words *"your life won't be the same without me"*?'

'I don't understand.'

'Were you threatening her?' Whitney pushed.

'No.'

'You've already displayed a great deal of anger towards Mrs Churchill, so you can understand why we might think that.'

'Well, you're wrong.' He glared at her.

Her instincts were on full alert. What was he hiding?

'I'd like to ask you again. What were you doing last night?'

'I was home on my own.'

Finally, he'd answered.

'Can anyone vouch for you?' Whitney asked.

'Not really.'

He averted his gaze. Something wasn't right.

'When you say "*not really*" is that because you were out during that time?' Whitney pushed.

He glanced at his solicitor. 'I might as well tell you, because you're going to find out sooner or later. I was out drinking and got home around eleven-thirty.'

'Where were you drinking?'

'At the King's Head pub with friends.'

'Write down the names of these friends,' Whitney said, sliding her notebook towards him.

He wrote down two names and passed it back to her.

'After you got home, what happened?' she asked.

'I had to go out again because I'd run out of cigarettes. I went to the twenty-four-hour petrol station and bought myself some.'

'Were you driving?' she asked.

'Um…' he hesitated.

'Just answer the question. We're not going to charge you with driving while under the influence now … it's over twelve hours later,' Whitney said.

'Yes, I drove there. I picked up some cigarettes and returned home.'

'What was the name of the garage?'

They could easily check out his story using the CCTV footage from there.

'It was the one on Stockton Road,' he said.

'What time did you arrive home?' she asked.

'I'm not sure. Probably somewhere between twelve-fifteen and twelve-thirty. I don't remember exactly,' he said.

'Then what did you do?' she asked.

'I crashed out on my bed, fully clothed. I woke up when the alarm went off at six, and then I got up, had a shower and dressed for work. No one can vouch for me, before you ask, because I was alone the whole time.'

'You haven't asked once what was the cause of Celia's death,' Whitney said.

'Because I don't want to know,' he said, a little too quickly.

'I find that hard to believe,' Whitney said.

'Did you already know she was dead when we saw you earlier?' George asked.

Whitney cast a glance in her direction. For two reasons. First, she shouldn't have been asking a question. Second, it was actually a good one. Why hadn't she thought of it?

'Yes, I did.'

'Who told you?' Whitney asked.

'I heard from the cleaner's son.' He averted his gaze and stared down at the table.

'How do you know him?'

'He works for me, in the warehouse.'

'So why did you act surprised when we spoke to you about it?' Whitney asked.

'Because he told me in confidence, that's all. There was nothing devious about it.'

'Devious? That's a funny word to use.'

'Is it? All I meant…' He paused. 'It was just a figure of speech.'

Was he involved? Did the cleaner's son have something to do with the murder?

'We'd like to search your house,' Whitney said.

There could be something incriminating there. He'd

admitted to being out when the murder was possibly committed, which was sufficient grounds for a warrant to be granted. Though for expediency, getting his permission would be preferable.

'If I say no?' he asked.

'We'll get a warrant. It is entirely up to you.'

'I'm guilty of nothing, other than the fact I don't care that she's dead.' He stared at her, a belligerent look on his face. It was like dealing with an arrogant teenager.

'We would still like to search your house,' Whitney said.

'Flat, you mean,' he spat. 'I can't afford a house. Not until I get back on my feet.'

'Are you giving us permission?' Whitney pushed.

'Do what you like,' he said. 'You won't find anything there.' He took some keys from his pocket and threw them across the table. Whitney slammed her hand on top of them before they shot onto the floor.

'Interview suspended,' Whitney said, as she picked up the keys.

She left the room with George. 'I'll take these up to Matt so he can search the flat. Good call, by the way, asking if he already knew about the murder. We'll speak to the cleaner's son.'

'It was the only reason I could think of as to why he didn't ask how she died. Considering he hated her so much,' George said.

'That doesn't make him guilty, though,' Whitney said.

'He was hard to read, as there was so much anger towards the victim because of the divorce, and the fact his business is in a slump.'

'We'll keep him here while his flat is being searched. It shouldn't take long as it isn't far from here.'

'If you don't need me, I'll go back to work,' George said.

'Okay. I'm going to see Claire in the morning. Are you free then?'

'I should be able to pop out.'

'Meet me there at ten.'

She stared at George's retreating back. Something was amiss. She'd get to the bottom of it sooner or later. For now, she had to get back to the incident room.

'Listen up, everyone. I've just left Celia Churchill's ex-husband, Jason Allen, in the interview room. Matt, take Doug and search his flat. Here are the keys. Ellie will give you his address.' She handed them to him.

'Yes, guv,' Matt said.

'Allen's movements around the time of the murder need to be checked. He admitted to being out for some of it. Frank, I want you to examine the CCTV footage around Stockton Road petrol station between eleven-thirty and twelve-thirty, last night.'

'Yes, guv,' the older officer said.

She often gave him the CCTV footage to check as he enjoyed doing it. Most likely because it meant he could sit comfortably behind his desk rather than being out in the field.

'Sue, contact the King's Head pub and confirm he was there all evening. Check with the friends he said he was with, too. I'll text you their details.'

'Yes, guv.'

'Ellie, get in touch with Sandy Griffiths. I want to speak to her son. Get them both in, now. Allen already knew of his ex-wife's death and I want to know why.'

'Guv?' Matt said, as he came into her office after she'd called him in.

'The cleaner and her son will be here soon. I want you with me.'

'Okay.'

'Has Jason Allen left?'

After nothing had been found at his flat, she'd instructed Matt to let him go home.

'Yes.'

'Good. We may still want to search his business premises, when—' Her phone rang. 'Walker.'

'Sandy and Luke Griffiths are here, in interview room three,' one of the officers on the front desk said.

'Thanks. We'll be down shortly.' She ended the call. 'They're here.'

In the interview room Sandy was sitting with a young man who looked to be in his mid-teens. He was wiry, with straight, light brown hair which came to his shoulders.

'Hello, Sandy. You must be Luke. I'm Detective Chief Inspector Walker and this is Detective Sergeant Price.'

'They told me it was urgent, and we had to come to see you,' Sandy said.

'Yes. Luke, I understand you told Jason Allen about Mrs Churchill's death.'

Colour leached from Sandy's face, as she turned to face her son. 'You did what? Why? You were told in confidence. I didn't expect you to blab to everyone.'

'I thought he should know. He was married to her,' Luke said, a defiant tone in his voice.

'It wasn't for you to make that decision.' Sandy turned to Whitney. 'I'm so sorry. I was upset when I went home, and Luke was there which is why I told him. I had no idea he'd tell anyone. I swore him to secrecy. Please believe me. I know how you wanted it to be kept quiet. I've told no one else, apart from my husband, and he won't say anything.'

'Apology accepted, Sandy. But you, Luke. This is a

police investigation and your actions could have damaged it.'

'I don't see how.' He scowled at her.

'Show some respect,' Sandy said, glaring at him.

'In murder investigations the first few days are very important. We control the dissemination of information. How well do you know Jason Allen?'

'I work for him,' Luke said.

'Doing what?'

'Operating a forklift. Stacking shelves, moving boxes.'

'Mrs Churchill arranged it for him after he left school and couldn't get a job,' Sandy said.

'How did Jason Allen react when you told him about Mrs Churchill's death? Did he appear surprised? Shocked? Upset?'

Luke glanced at his mother. 'Tell the truth,' she said.

'He said it served her right, and that he, for one, wouldn't mourn her loss.'

'So he wasn't upset by it. But when you first told him, did he appear surprised?'

'Yes. Then he laughed.'

'Laughed?' Sandy said. 'That's disgusting, and so disrespectful.'

'Not everyone idolised her like you did, Mum,' Luke said.

'I don't care. The poor woman was murdered. No one deserves that sort of response.'

'I'm only telling what happened, you can't blame me.'

'Luke, what were your movements last night?' Whitney asked, interrupting the conversation.

'I was at home.'

'Can anyone vouch for you?'

'I can,' Sandy said.

'So you can't lay the blame on me,' Luke said.

'I'm warning you,' Sandy said, eyes blazing. 'I'm sorry, Chief Inspector. I didn't bring him up to be like this.'

'It's okay, Sandy. You can go now, Luke. But we may wish to speak to you again. And if you're ever in a similar situation again, remember to do as requested and keep it to yourself.'

'Thank you,' Sandy said. 'He'll do as he's told from now on.'

The cleaner and her son left the station and Whitney returned to the incident room with Matt.

'Well, that didn't help much,' he said.

'Apart from reinforcing my opinion that Jason Allen is a nasty piece of work. But whether that makes him a murderer, we don't know yet.'

Chapter Six

George pushed open the door to the morgue and walked down the corridor. She tightened her hands into fists and released them. Having to keep Tiffany's secret had thrown her way off balance. She was known for often saying the wrong things in social situations, and this wasn't helping.

As she reached the office, she could hear Claire and Whitney talking.

'If she's not here soon, I'll start without her,' the pathologist said, sounding impatient.

'We arranged to meet at ten, and it's only five minutes to, so let's give her a bit longer,' Whitney replied.

'You know, I'm very busy. This isn't the only post-mortem I'm working on. Contrary to your expectations, I can't drop everything and be at your beck and call whenever you see fit.'

'No need for alarm … I'm here,' George said as she entered the office area where Claire, and the other pathologists, had their desks.

'Good. Let's get cracking,' Claire said, not even bothering to say hello.

They followed her into the main lab to where the body was laid out on one of the stainless-steel tables. Claire reached for the overhead light and illuminated the body.

'Can you now confirm it was strangulation?' Whitney asked.

'Give me a chance,' Claire said as she drew back the sheet covering the body. 'Yes, the victim was strangled.'

'What are the signs?' George asked as she peered at the body.

'Do you see how swollen and grey it is here?' Claire pointed at the facial area.

'Yes.' George nodded.

'That's because of the fluid which has collected in the tissues. It's a direct indicator of someone being strangled. Also, the victim's tongue and larynx were enlarged which is another indication.'

'What an awful way to go.' Whitney said, grimacing. 'Gasping for breath and unable to do anything about it. I couldn't think of anything worse.'

'Actually, it's not as bad as you think, because the victim would have lost consciousness within a few seconds. After that they wouldn't feel a thing. Which is good, seeing as most strangulations involve much more pressure than is actually necessary, causing all sorts of extra damage. As was the case in this instance, and why I found blood in the neck muscles,' Claire said.

'It's good to know she didn't suffer for too long. We believe this could be a Lenchester Strangler copycat. Do you remember those murders from the 1980s, Claire?' Whitney asked.

'No. I haven't heard of them. I would have only been in primary school. I'll research into them, though.'

'Can you tell whether the victim was strangled by hand and then the scarf tied around the neck, or whether the scarf was actually used to strangle her?' George asked.

'I wondered that, too,' Whitney said. 'A chiffon scarf seems too flimsy to cause such extensive damage.'

'Believe me, it's plenty strong enough,' Claire said. 'The marks around the neck indicate the scarf was used. The dark brown band with the red band either side, shows us the width of the scarf when it was pulled tight.'

'Presumably, if the strangulation had been done by hand, there would be finger and thumb bruising around the neck,' George said.

'Exactly,' Claire said. 'And there's no evidence of that.'

'What are those tiny specks in the ligature marks?' George pointed to flecks in the red band around the victim's neck.

'That's caused by the chiffon's meshlike weave, because it was pulled so tight,' Claire said.

'Are there any signs of a struggle?' George asked.

'Her nightdress was ripped around the underarm area, as I discussed with Whitney, yesterday, which suggests a struggle took place. Additionally, there were some abrasions and bruising on her hands indicating she fought her attacker, in an attempt to push him away.'

'You believe the offender to be male?' Whitney asked.

'I always say *he*. You should know that. It saves saying *he/she*. I don't like to use the word *they* unless I believe there to be two or more assailants … it's confusing.'

'Any trace evidence?' Whitney asked.

'Under the victim's fingernails I found traces of polymer microparticles.'

'What's that?' Whitney frowned.

'It's a fibre found in latex.'

'Meaning the offender wore disposable gloves,' George said.

'And, therefore, no DNA,' Whitney added.

'No. Nothing,' Claire said.

'Any sexual interference?' Whitney asked.

'No evidence of sexual intercourse having taken place, or any abrasions in the genital region,' Claire said.

'Do we know whether she'd been drugged?' George asked.

'I've sent her bloods to toxicology, but as far as I can tell she hadn't. There would have been no need for sedation if she'd been unconscious within a few seconds.'

'Have you been able to narrow down the time of death?' Whitney asked.

'Yes. Between midnight and four o'clock on Monday morning.'

'Do we know how the killer got in?' George asked.

'Not relevant to me,' Claire said.

'I believe, through French doors in the hall. SOCO's report shouldn't be too much longer which I expect will confirm it. I'll let you know when we have it,' Whitney said.

'I do have something else interesting for you,' Claire said.

'What?' Whitney said.

'The victim's last meal included pheasant egg, truffles, and a rich chocolate dessert. Washed down with a great deal of red wine.'

'According to her cleaner, she went to a charity event on Sunday. We need to find out more about it. Do you have anything else for us? If not, we'll get going,' Whitney said.

'Yes. I believe the killer took a trophy from the victim. Look.' Claire lifted up a section of hair and underneath there was a gap where a piece had been cut off.

'That's very interesting,' Whitney said. 'We know the

Lenchester Strangler also took something from his victims, and we're waiting to find out what it was. If it was hair, that confirms our link. Also, the trophy wasn't divulged in the media, so if it is a copycat they would have had inside knowledge of the police investigation.'

'It doesn't necessarily mean they were members of the police force. It could be a family member or friend of an officer,' George said.

'True. Thirty years ago things weren't kept so discreetly as they are now. But at least we have something to work with. Is that it, Claire? Anything else for us?' Whitney asked.

'The bindings used to tie the victim were cable ties,' Claire said.

'Can you trace them?'

'I'll let you know once we've investigated.'

'Maybe we'll get lucky,' Whitney said.

'I don't believe in luck.' Claire rolled her eyes. 'You'll have my report once I hear back from toxicology. You can go now.'

'We'll see you again soon,' George said.

'Why did you say that?' Whitney asked. 'Do you think we're going to be having more murders?'

'It was just a figure of speech. I have no idea whether this is a one-off or whether we are to expect more.'

'Well, you shouldn't have said it, because it jinxes it.'

George didn't rise to the "jinx" comment as it was something Whitney often accused her of doing.

'Perhaps you could finish deliberating in the corridor and leave me to get on,' Claire said, scowling at them.

'We're going,' Whitney said.

They left the lab together and headed down the corridor in silence.

'You're still acting strange, are you sure there's nothing wrong?' Whitney asked.

'Everything's fine. It was yesterday, and it still is today.' She hoped that would assuage Whitney's increasing concern.

'It doesn't seem fine. Has something happened with Ross? Are you having problems?'

If only it was that simple. That she could handle and divulge to Whitney.

'No, there's nothing wrong between us.'

'Well, what is it then? I know you're not into endless talking, but you're being very distant, even for you.'

George tensed. Usually she admired how good Whitney was at her job, but right now it was problematic. But she couldn't say anything. It wouldn't be fair to Tiffany.

'There's nothing wrong with me, and there's nothing wrong with Ross. Everything is satisfactory, so give it a rest.' She instantly regretted how aggressive she'd sounded, because it wasn't Whitney's fault.

'If you want to be like that, then suit yourself.'

'I'm sorry. I didn't mean to snap, I'm just busy at work, that's all.' It was the only thing she could think of saying.

'Apology accepted. Let's grab a coffee.'

Whitney's phone rang before George had time to answer.

'Walker.' She paused. 'We'll go straight away.' She ended the call.

'Where to now?' George asked.

'Celia Churchill's daughter, Natasha Bedford, is waiting at her mother's house. Are you able to come with me to speak to her?'

'Tell me the address and I'll meet you there.'

She was grateful they'd come in separate cars. She

didn't fancy a long journey with Whitney, because once her friend had something on her mind she wouldn't give up. She'd keep pushing until George accidentally dropped Tiffany in it.

'We could leave my car here and go in yours. Or drop mine back at the station, first?' Whitney suggested.

'I'd rather we went separately … I have to go back to work after. I've got a few things on this afternoon that I have to deal with.'

'If I didn't know better, I'd say you were deliberately trying to avoid me. You're acting very strange, even for you. Are you sure there's nothing wrong?' Whitney said.

George's body tensed. 'How many times do I have to tell you? There's nothing wrong. I've just got to get back to work. You know the hassle I've had in the past about me spending too much time away from my desk.'

'I thought that had all been sorted,' Whitney said.

'It has, but I don't want to push my luck. If there are further murders, I'm going to have to spend more time out of the office, so I think it's best for me to come with you to visit the victim's daughter and then go back to work.'

'Okay, that sounds like a plan. I don't want to get you into any more trouble.'

'I'll meet you at the victim's house.'

'Okay. It's about a twenty-minute drive. You'll fit right in there … it's an extremely posh house.'

George brushed aside Whitney's comment, and when they reached the end of the corridor, they went out into the car park and parted ways.

Chapter Seven

As Whitney drove, her thoughts focussed on George's behaviour when they were at the morgue with Claire. George had a number of strange characteristics and could be abrupt. She hated small talk and often missed social cues that other people wouldn't. But this was different. She was being distant and holding back. One thing about the psychologist was, she always said what she thought, and wasn't intimidated by anyone. It made her behaviour even more puzzling.

Had she done something to upset her friend? No. If she had, George would've mentioned it. Whitney frowned. What if it was about Ross? When George found out her ex was cheating on her, she didn't mention it to her. Though that was when they'd first got to know each other. It was different now.

She turned into Pennington Grove and to Celia Churchill's house. The wrought-iron gate was open, and she drove up the long drive and parked in front of the house. A uniformed officer was outside. George had already arrived and was standing beside her car.

'I suppose you put your foot down, as usual,' Whitney said, laughing.

George was a petrolhead and driving one of her pleasures, especially going fast.

'I kept within the speed limit.'

'I was only joking.' George gave her a funny look. 'Oh, never mind. It doesn't matter.' She went over to the officer on duty. 'We're meeting Natasha Bedford here. Do you know where she is?'

'Yes, guv. She went for a walk with another woman.'

'Is SOCO still here?'

'Yes.'

'Didn't they come yesterday?' George asked.

'It's a big house, they've come back today to finish off,' Whitney said.

'Okay.'

'Who's here from SOCO?' Whitney asked the officer.

'Colin and Jenny,' the officer replied.

The front door opened and both of them appeared, wearing their usual attire of white coveralls.

'Hello. We were just talking about you,' Whitney said.

'We've finished if you want to go inside,' Colin said.

'What can you tell me?' Whitney asked.

'The bedroom where the murder took place was exceptionally clean. No fingerprints other than the victim's and the cleaner.'

'Wiped down?'

'Doesn't appear to be, or we might have found smears. My guess is the offender wore gloves,' Colin said.

'Point of entry?' she asked, to confirm her suspicions.

'The French doors in the hall. We found a partial footprint in the garden and from it we concluded it belonged to someone with size ten feet. Pretty average.'

'It could have been the gardener. We'll check.'

The sound of footsteps on the drive distracted her. She glanced across and saw Sandy Griffiths walking up the drive with another woman. Natasha? She was in her early thirties, with blonde, shoulder-length hair, and was dressed in a pair of dark brown trousers with a beige blazer and cream silk shirt under it.

Whitney hurried over to meet them. 'Natasha Bedford?' she asked, to confirm.

'Yes.'

'I'm Detective Chief Inspector Walker. I'm very sorry for your loss.'

'Thank you.'

'Hello, Sandy. I didn't expect to see you,' Whitney said.

'I asked her to meet me here,' Natasha said. 'I'd like Sandy to stay on until we decide what to do with the property.'

'It's the least I can do,' Sandy said, relief evident in her eyes.

'Our scenes of crime officers have finished so we can go back into the house.' She led them over to where George was standing. 'This is Dr Cavendish, she's working with us on the case.'

They entered the house and stood in the hallway.

'Would you like me to make you all a coffee? If I'm allowed in the kitchen?' Sandy said.

'Yes, you can go in there, now. Milk, no sugar for me, please,' Whitney said.

'Likewise,' George said.

'Make that three,' Natasha said.

'Before you go, Sandy, I'd like a quick word,' Whitney said.

'I'll wait for you in the drawing room.' Natasha headed off, leaving the three of them.

'You mentioned an event Mrs Churchill attended on Sunday evening. Do you know more about it?'

'Yes. It was the annual ball for a charity she supported. The invitation was in the kitchen. I'll check if it's still there,' Sandy said.

'Thank you, that would be very helpful. I also wanted to ask if you knew whether she was currently dating anyone?'

'Not that I know of, but she didn't confide in me very often. Apart from to say that she was off men in general after the ex-husband.'

'Did she take anyone to the ball?' Whitney asked.

'No. She said she was looking forward to going alone so she could mingle with whoever she wanted and not worry about a sulking partner feeling left out.'

'Was she referring to her ex-husband?' Whitney asked.

'I assumed so, but I can't be certain,' Sandy said.

'Thank you for your help,' Whitney said.

'I'm sorry again for what happened with Luke. I couldn't sleep last night for worrying about it.'

'It's not your fault, you weren't to know what he'd do,' Whitney said gently.

'That's beside the point. He should've known better.'

'This way to the drawing room,' Whitney said to George, after Sandy had left them. 'What do you think of the house?'

'It's large, ostentatious, and crass. I much prefer period properties,' George replied tersely.

'Say it like you mean it,' Whitney said, laughing. 'You might not like the house, but look out here.' She led George over to a large floor-to-ceiling window overlooking an expanse of perfect lawn, with overhanging trees and a sweeping garden. 'I dare you to tell me you don't like that,' she said.

'It's very well landscaped and designed. But to me it lacks character.' George shrugged.

'What is it with you? You're being negative about the house, and garden, and being generally miserable.'

The psychologist was always on an even keel. If anything, Whitney was the one who could be temperamental. She had to get to the bottom of it.

'Because *nothing* is wrong. I'm entitled to have my opinion on the house and garden, even if it isn't favourable. Let's talk with the victim's daughter, because I have to go back to work.' George's jaw was tight and her arms were folded. Even Whitney knew that meant she was putting up a barrier and it was best to back off.

'I get your point, and won't mention it again. Back to the task in hand. Take note of anything you think might be of interest and that will help us.'

'As I always do,' George said.

They walked into the annexe and through the open door of the drawing room where Natasha was seated on one of the sofas. Her face was a tight mask and her eyes flickered for a moment before she collected herself.

'Please, sit down,' Natasha said.

George and Whitney sat on the sofa opposite.

'Do you feel up to answering some questions?' Whitney asked.

'Yes, of course. I want to find out what happened.' She appeared fully in control. An act?

'When was the last time you saw your mother?' Whitney asked.

'We spoke on the phone a week ago. We were arranging a time she could visit us in Bristol.'

'Did she visit often?' Whitney asked.

'She was always very busy at some event or other, so

not as frequently as we would have liked. The children always enjoyed her stays.'

'How many children do you have?' Whitney asked.

'Three. A boy aged seven and twin girls, aged five.'

'I understand your father was your mother's first husband,' Whitney said.

'Yes. He was a lot older than her, and died when I was only two years old. He left her all his money hence why she was able to live the way she did.'

'She'd had several husbands since, I believe?' Whitney said.

'She had just got rid of husband number five, thank goodness. He was an absolute shit,' Natasha said, raw emotion showing for the first time.

'Could you explain a bit more?' Whitney asked.

'A cruise ship romance. I didn't like him from the first time we were introduced. He isn't much older than me and was clearly only after her money.'

'How do you know?' Whitney asked.

'Let's just say, before they married, he was all over her. It was embarrassing, the way he was always stroking her arm, or kissing her. That all stopped once they were married. The last time I saw them together, when she left the room he made a pass at me. As if I'd be attracted to a jumped-up nobody like that.'

'What did you do?'

'I threatened to tell my mother, and he denied doing it. Said I'd misinterpreted his actions.'

'Did you tell her?' Whitney asked.

'No. I didn't want to hurt her. I figured she'd find out what he was like soon enough. And she did.'

'Why did she divorce him?' Whitney asked, assuming that was what Natasha was referring to.

'She hired a private detective and found out he'd been cheating on her. She'd suspected and wanted it confirmed. She divorced him, and he didn't get a penny, even though he tried his hardest. His company was the only thing he was able to keep after the divorce. Mother made sure no one could get their hands on her money.' Natasha gave a wry smile.

'Your mother didn't take his name?'

'No. Churchill was my father's surname and she never changed it.'

'Have you been in contact with him since the divorce?' Whitney asked.

'No. Absolutely not.'

'Do you know whether everything is left to you in the will?' Whitney asked.

Natasha's eyes widened and she stared directly at Whitney. 'I can't believe you're asking such a question. My mother has only just died. I have no idea what's in her will.' She pulled out a tissue from her bag and wiped her eyes.

Whitney couldn't tell whether it was for effect, or whether it was genuine because so far she'd remained very calm and collected.

'Can you tell me what you were doing yesterday, between the hours of midnight and four in the morning?' Whitney asked.

'I was at home in bed,' Natasha said.

'Can anyone vouch for you?'

'Yes. My husband was lying next to me, and my children were in their bedrooms. Why are you asking?'

'We want to eliminate you from our enquiries. Do you know of anyone who might wish to harm your mother?' Whitney asked.

'No. Some people may have found her a bit full on, because she wasn't backwards in coming forwards, and at times she could be quite loud, especially after she'd had a drink or two, but I don't believe that's reason enough for her to be murdered.'

'When you last spoke, did she mention anything about having fallen out with someone, or anyone acting suspiciously around her?' Whitney asked.

'No. As I said, the last time we spoke it was to arrange a time for her to come and stay with us. For all her ostentatiousness, when she was with my children she was totally different and they loved her. She was much more relaxed with them than she'd ever been with me. It was like she could be herself and not put on a show.'

'Yes, grandparents can be very different with their grandchildren than they are with their own children. I think it's because they can hand them back and don't have the responsibility,' Whitney said.

Next to her George flinched.

'I've brought your coffee,' Sandy said as she walked into the room carrying a tray which she placed on the low mahogany table. 'And here's the invitation to the charity ball.' She handed it to Whitney, who pulled an evidence bag from her pocket and dropped it inside.

'Thank you, Sandy,' Natasha said.

'Did your mother do anything different from usual during the last week or two?' Whitney wrapped her hands around her china mug and inhaled the aroma, just about managing to refrain from groaning in ecstasy. One good thing about being with posh people was they had great coffee.

'What do you mean?' Natasha said.

'Did she visit any new places, or spend time with people she didn't usually? Anything that was different from her usual routine?' Whitney said.

'I honestly don't know. She always kept herself busy

because she didn't like her own company. She was particularly excited about some new art she'd bought recently.'

'Was she a collector?' George asked.

'Yes. She would often buy pieces of art or sculptures. There's a bronze sculpture of a horse in the garden which she bought last year.'

'Where is this new art? The one she was excited about,' Whitney asked.

'It could be in here. She tended to rotate her pieces. Anything new would start off in the drawing room because this was where she'd spend most of her time when she was home, and she enjoyed looking at it, until she bought the next thing.'

'Would you recognise any new pieces if you saw them?' Whitney asked.

'I'm not sure.'

'Shall we have a look around?' Whitney stood and studied the three gold-framed paintings on the wall in front of her. The others followed suit.

'This is new,' Natasha said, pointing to a painting which looked to Whitney like someone had thrown a number of different brightly coloured pots of paint onto a canvas. 'But I've no idea when she bought it. I'm fairly certain it wasn't here the last time I visited.'

'When was that?' Whitney asked, squinting to see if she could make out what it was meant to be.

'Maybe three months. This is new, too,' Natasha said, pointing to a painting equally puzzling, only it was all greys and blacks. 'Other than that, the rest I've seen before.'

'What can you tell us about your mother's other husbands?' Whitney asked, after she'd taken photos of the pieces with her phone. 'We know your father died, and the latest one she'd just divorced, what about the other three?'

'Husband number two was Daniel Reese. He was a

doctor. I really liked him but the marriage only lasted three years before they divorced. He now lives in Australia with his second wife. Husband number three stuck around for five years. I'm not sure what happened between them because Mother was very cagey. He was younger than her, and the last I heard he was working in Guernsey. I didn't have much to do with him because when they married I'd just left for university. Husband four was her accountant, and he died of a heart attack after they'd been together for just a year.'

'Did you always live here while you were growing up?' Whitney asked.

'Mother had this house built twenty years ago, before that we lived on the other side of the city.'

'Do you have any questions for us?' Whitney said.

'Yes. I want to know more about what happened and how she died. I only know what Sandy's told me.'

'We have had confirmation from the pathologist that she was strangled during the night.'

Natasha winced. 'I'd been on at her for ages to get a burglar alarm, but she wouldn't because she said she'd forget to set it, or lose the number and not be able to get into the house. She'd always felt safe here.' She paused, and tears filled her eyes, which she blinked away. 'How did the murderer get in?'

'Through the French door in the hall, and then upstairs to your mother's bedroom.'

Natasha grabbed the back of the sofa, her knuckles white and her face drained of colour.

'Why don't you sit down and rest for a while,' Whitney said, taking the woman by the arm and escorting her. 'You've had a huge shock.'

'I've been trying to keep it together, the stiff upper lip and all that, which we were taught at boarding school. But this is so awful. I can't believe I'll never see my mother again.' She bowed her head and dragged in some deep breaths.

'Is there someone we can call to be with you? Your husband? Friends?' Whitney asked, gently.

'No. I'm going to stay here for a few days, if that's okay? Sandy will be here.'

'Yes, that's fine. We'll be in touch once we have more information.'

'What about the funeral?' Natasha asked.

'We have to wait until the post-mortem is complete and the coroner has agreed for your mother to be returned to you. I'm sorry I can't be more specific,' Whitney said.

'I understand,' Natasha said.

They left and once outside, Whitney turned to George. 'I'm going back to the incident room, now. Are you still going to work?'

'Yes,' George said in a flat voice.

'Are you free tomorrow?' She hated the stilted nature of their conversation.

'I can be.'

'Good. Be at the station first thing. We need your input.'

Chapter Eight

Whitney headed to George who was sitting at one of the empty desks in the incident room, her eyes fixed on the computer screen. She glanced at her watch. It wasn't even eight.

'What are you doing here?' she asked.

'You said for me to be here first thing. I'm checking my work emails, if that's okay?'

'Yes, of course it is. Thanks for coming in.'

'You're welcome.'

She frowned. Why were they sounding so formal? She pushed the thought to the back of her mind. There were more important things to concentrate on.

'Attention everyone,' she said as she headed towards the board which had very little information on it. 'We're now forty-eight hours into the investigation and things are moving too slowly for my liking. Frank, you were looking into the original Lenchester Strangler. What information do you have for us?'

'His name is Harold Skinner. He's now eighty, and five years ago was released from prison after serving thirty years for his wife's murder. He lives in Featherstone Manor care home,' Frank said.

'I've heard of it. It's really expensive. How can he afford it after thirty years in prison?' she said, tensing.

Featherstone Manor had the reputation of being the most luxurious private care home in the county. Her own mother was in a care home, which was excellent, but not in the same league. Yet here was a murderer, who'd been incarcerated for thirty years, affording the best. How fair was that?

'Hidden money?' Frank suggested.

'Look into his finances. Actually, no. Ellie, you do it.' The young officer was one of the best researchers Whitney had ever come across. She'd had to fight long and hard to keep Ellie on the team when she was initially seconded to them, as her previous department wanted her back, but it was worth it.

'Yes, guv,' Ellie said.

'Any joy finding out where pink chiffon scarves can be purchased?'

'They're everywhere guv. Once we get the one used back from the pathologist, I'll see about narrowing it down.'

'Thanks. What about the trophies, Frank? Did you find out what they were?'

'Yes,' Frank said. 'The same as our current victim. A lock of hair. Always from underneath, so it wasn't immediately visible.'

Whitney's heart pumped in her chest. A definite link. 'Text me the full address of the care home. George and I will pay him a visit.'

Thirty minutes later, George drove up the long gravel drive and parked outside the large stone house in the idyllic village of Willington.

'Very impressive,' Whitney said.

'It's a fine example of a classic Georgian building,' George said.

'How do you know?'

She should be used to George's extensive knowledge by now, but it still never ceased to astound her. Intimidate her, almost.

'The style of the building. It's square and symmetrical. Also the panelled door in the centre of the house and the two pillars at the entrance. Take a look at the windows, as they're another clue. At the top they're smaller, only six-paned, whereas the main floors have twelve larger panels.'

Whitney stared at the windows and could see what George meant.

'Every day is a learning experience when I'm with you.' She grinned, and George laughed.

They walked into a large entrance hall with high ceilings, decorated with a lovely ceiling rose, and headed to the reception desk. Sitting there was a woman in a dark blue uniform. She had a name badge with *Beth, Care Assistant*.

'Good morning, Beth. I'm Detective Chief Inspector Walker,' Whitney said holding out her warrant card. 'We'd like to speak to Harold Skinner.'

'You'll find him in the day room, but I doubt you'll get much out of him today.'

'Is he ill?' Whitney asked.

'He's got dementia and isn't having a good day.'

Whitney exchanged a glance with George. If they'd got a copycat strangler on their hands, Skinner wouldn't be able to help them much. Not that she'd expected him to admit to the original crimes, but he might have let something slip.

'We'll go and see him, anyway. Where's the day room?'

'I'll take you,' Beth said.

She led them down the corridor and into a big room on the left, which had high-backed, rolled armed, leather chairs, and two floral fabric sofas. There were ten people sitting in silence. A television was blaring out from one corner of the room.

Beth took them over to where an elderly man was seated, his head bowed slightly.

'Harold, you've got visitors.'

He looked up and stared at them but didn't say a word.

'Is there somewhere we can speak in private?' Whitney asked the care assistant.

'You can go into the conservatory.'

'Can he walk?' Whitney asked.

'Yes, I can,' Harold said, glaring at them. He stood and Beth handed him his stick which was beside his chair on the floor.

'Come on, Harold,' Beth said to him, slipping her arm through his. 'We're going somewhere quieter where you can talk.'

They followed them through the glass double doors on one side of the day room, into a large conservatory which overlooked the landscaped gardens.

'Please leave us alone,' Whitney said to Beth, once they'd all sat down on the cane furniture. Harold on a chair and George and Whitney on a two-seater sofa.

'It might be better if I stay. He can be a little awkward,' Beth said.

'We'll be fine, thank you,' Whitney said.

'Okay. I'll be around if you need me.'

Once she'd left Whitney turned to the old man.

'Harold, my name is Detective Chief Inspector Walker. I want to speak to you about the Lenchester Strangler.'

His face remained expressionless.

'Harold?' Whitney said.

He blinked and looked at her but didn't speak.

'We want to talk to you about some murders that were carried out in the 1980s. Do you understand?' She enunciated every word clearly.

'Yes, please,' he said.

'What?' Whitney said.

'I'm Harold. Would you like a cup of tea?'

'No, thank you. But we would like to ask about the Lenchester Strangler. Do you remember?'

'Yes, my name is Harold. I live here. I used to live in prison,' he replied, staring directly at her.

'Why were you in prison?' Whitney asked, trying a different tack.

'I don't remember.' His voice was stilted. He looked from Whitney to George. 'Who are you?'

'I'm Dr Cavendish.'

'I don't need a doctor. I'm not sick.'

'I'm not that sort of doctor. I'm a forensic psychologist and I work with the police,' George said.

'I can't remember why I was in prison.'

'You murdered your wife,' Whitney said.

'I'm not married, but I've been in prison. I don't know why.'

Whitney sighed. They were getting nowhere fast. She hated that she was feeling compassionate towards him, a murderer. But his condition was much the same as her mum's and the hopelessness of it gnawed at her heart. 'We need to ask you about the Lenchester Strangler,' she said, softly. 'He committed several murders in the 1980s and you were suspected of being him.'

'I don't know what you're talking about. Does anyone want a cup of tea?' he asked.

'No, thank you. We're investigating a murder which was identical to those carried out in the 1980s,' Whitney said. 'We think someone might be copying the original strangler and we want to find out from you as much as we can about the previous murders.'

'What murders?' he said.

'The victim had a pink chiffon scarf tied around her neck,' George said.

'I like pink,' he said.

'This is a beautiful home. How can you afford it, after being in prison for so long? Where did the money come from?' Whitney asked.

'I want the toilet,' he said.

Whitney exchanged a glance with George, who shrugged. It was clearly a waste of time.

'I'll fetch Beth,' Whitney said.

She left the conservatory and found Beth in the day room, talking with one of the residents.

'Harold would like the toilet,' she said.

Beth walked away from the resident. 'He's only just been. I expect it's his way of wanting to end the conversation. Did you get anything of value from him?'

'No. This is a very upmarket home, how are Harold's fees paid?'

'He privately funds his care. Money is never an issue if we need to buy anything for him.'

'Does he have many visitors?' Whitney asked.

'I haven't seen any, but I'm fairly new. He seems like a nice old man. He does tend to spend a lot of time alone in his room. His choice. You need to speak to the manager if you want to know more. She's in her office which is behind the reception desk.' She pushed open the conservatory door. 'Come on, Harold, let me take you to the toilet.'

He got up and she escorted him out.

'I had a quick word with the carer,' Whitney said, once they were alone. 'Money's no object and, as far as she knows, he doesn't have any visitors. We'll go and see the manager to find out more. Did you notice anything from our conversation with him?'

'There was a tiny flicker of recognition in his eyes at the mention of the scarf. I suspect he was putting on the extent of his dementia, so he didn't have to answer any questions. He just couldn't hide that slight acknowledgement.'

'Interesting, but nothing we can do about it. We'll look into his family. I'll get Ellie onto it, when we get back.'

'We really need to focus on the copycat aspect of it. Who would have sufficient knowledge of the previous crimes to be able to copy them? Even with copycats, it's never identical. We should investigate any differences, however small. It's hard with only one murder, though,' George said.

'I'll get the team onto it.'

They headed to the manager's office and Whitney knocked on the door.

'Come in,' a voice called.

Seated behind a desk was a woman who looked to be in her fifties, with grey hair cut in a short bob.

'Detective Chief Inspector Walker and this is Dr Cavendish,' Whitney said, holding out her warrant card. 'We've been to speak to Harold Skinner, and we'd like to ask you about him.'

'I'm Rosemary Driscoll, the manager. Please take a seat.' She gestured to the two seats in front of her desk. 'How can I help?'

'I understand Harold pays for his own care and there's no contribution from social services,' Whitney said.

'Yes, that's correct.'

'Do you know where the money comes from?'

'His account is paid four-weekly by direct debit. That's all I know. There's never been any issue with his payments.'

'Do you know of his background?' Whitney asked.

'I'm aware he was in prison before moving in here.'

'Did him being an ex-con bother you? Especially in an upmarket place like this.'

'It wasn't until his social worker told us that we found out, and by then he was already here. It's not an ideal situation but, because of his illness and its prognosis, after discussing it with my senior staff members, we decided to let him continue being cared for here. It hasn't proved to be an issue.'

'Beth informed me that he rarely has visitors. Can you confirm?'

'Yes, that's correct. When he first moved in, he had visits from a social worker. To my knowledge, apart from his parole officer, there haven't been others. If you check the visitor book on the reception desk that will confirm it.'

'Providing the visitors sign in.'

'Most people do, but sometimes they don't. He could have received visitors that we were unaware of. Having said that, it wouldn't happen often, because we'd notice.'

'Thank you for your time. We'll take a look at the visitor book before we leave.'

They checked and found the manager to be right. There were no entries relating to Skinner, apart from the parole officer who last visited three months ago.

'Let's get back to the station as I need to arrange the press conference,' Whitney said.

'If you don't need me, I'll go back into work after I've dropped you off, as I've got some things to sort out, too.'

'I assumed you didn't have any lectures and tutorials today,' Whitney said.

'I don't, but that doesn't mean I don't have other things to do. I have my research, marking, and preparation. My work doesn't just comprise being with students,' George said.

'It's okay, I was only saying.' Whitney gave her a sideways glance. 'Are you around tomorrow?'

'I'm busy at work but call me if anything comes up that you want my opinion on.'

'If I didn't know better, I'd say you were avoiding me,' Whitney said, before she could stop herself.

'Of course I'm not,' George said, perhaps a little too quickly. 'Unfortunately, we need more murders in order for me to build up a credible profile. Especially as we have no idea of motive.'

Whitney winced. More murders were the last things she wanted. 'I'll be in touch if there's anything to tell you.'

Chapter Nine

So far, so good. I thought it would be harder than it actually was. Yes, she struggled a little, but she was never in any danger of escaping, and restraining her was easy.

Too easy.

I'd have liked more aggression on her part. It would have spiced things up a bit.

But I still got a kick from replicating the old murders.

I made sure to get it exactly right, even down to taking a lock of hair from the correct place. I did that when she was still alive, just to see her reaction when I approached her with the scissors in my hand. She couldn't move because of the ties, but her uncontrollable shaking and staring eyes gave away her fear.

The adrenaline rush when I pulled the scarf tightly around her neck and I watched her eyes bulge, was incredible.

As the last breath left her body, my heart pumped so hard it almost burst from my chest. I had total control.

Now I understand how killing can become addictive.

And so easy to orchestrate.

It took hardly any time at all to find out what she did and where she went. She was so predictable. Can you believe, no security on her home? It was like being given free rein in a sweet shop.

So, that's one down, and the rest to go.

When will I commit the next murder?

Very soon.

Four victims lined up. Ready and waiting.

If they knew what was in store for them, that their lives were coming to an abrupt end, maybe they'd do something useful or interesting, instead of the boring, pointless activities I've observed.

The police will never discover who I am because they don't have the skills and knowledge. I'm far cleverer than they are. But it's still going to be fun, watching them try. They're a bunch of tossers, and I have no time for them.

It's almost worth doing it just to see their incompetence.

Almost.

The pink scarf, tight on my hands is all I'll need.

Soon. Very soon. That innocuous object will enable me to commit the ultimate act.

Murder.

Chapter Ten

Whitney hurried to Jamieson's office. There was only twenty minutes before the press conference, and she hadn't yet had time to brief him on what else they'd learnt. She didn't expect him to field any of the questions, as he usually left it to her. She believed it was because he didn't want to be caught out and made to look a fool. Well, that was her theory based on the fact that everything he did had a motive behind it. He invariably covered his back before hers. She should be used to it by now.

Or was she being supersensitive? He brought that out in her. But with a bit of luck not for too much longer.

She entered his office as he was putting on his jacket. Small creases ran out around his eyes and his skin looked tired. He'd aged. Not surprising after all the issues he'd had with his daughter and being a single parent since his wife had left.

'What's happened since we last spoke?' he asked as he fastened the silver buttons.

'We brought in the ex-husband for questioning and searched his flat. We have nothing on him, apart from he doesn't have an alibi for some of the time when the victim was most likely killed. He was seen purchasing cigarettes at a petrol station around midnight and, after leaving, heading in the direction of his home. We've also been to visit the old man suspected of being the Lenchester Strangler in the 1980s.'

'Surely you don't think it's him?'

'No. He's in his eighties and has dementia. But if it is a copycat, the offender had details regarding the trophy that weren't released to the public. It's likely someone who—'

'Who worked on the case?' Jamieson asked, interrupting.

'It's not necessarily going to be a police officer. It could be someone who knew about the trophy. Any number of people would have had that knowledge.' She wasn't prepared to have Don Mason's reputation tarnished. Once she'd been to see him she'd have a clearer picture of what had happened.

'What was taken?' Jamieson asked.

'A lock of hair,' she said.

'How original.' His lips turned up into a patronising smirk.

What was he expecting?

'It is what it is. Are you ready to go now?' she asked.

'Yes and let's make it snappy. I want to leave early.'

'How's it going with your daughter?' she asked as they left his office and headed down the corridor.

He stopped dead in his tracks and glowered at her. 'My family issues are between you and me. I hope you haven't mentioned them to anyone.'

'Of course I haven't,' she said frowning.

'I'd rather we didn't talk about this outside of my office.'

'I only brought it up because there was no one else

around. I'll make sure not to do so again.' She gritted her teeth.

'Things are going a little better, as you've asked,' he said, ignoring her response.

'I thought it might be, as you're not relying on me so much to do the extra work.'

Thanks goodness. And long may it continue.

'That's all we need say on the subject,' he said as they reached the corridor leading to the conference room, and again ignoring what she'd said.

Melissa from PR was waiting for them. They walked in and sat behind the long table. As usual, the room was full, with reporters at the front and TV camera crews at the back.

'Thank you for coming,' Melissa said, calling the room to attention. 'I would like to hand over to Detective Superintendent Jamieson and he will outline what information we have for you.'

'Good afternoon. We've called you in today to inform you that a woman in her sixties, living in the Pennington Grove area, has been murdered.' A ripple of sound echoed around the room, as reporters commented to each other. 'We would like anyone who was in the area between the hours of midnight and four on Monday morning to contact the station,' Jamieson continued, once the sound had died down.

'What's the name of the victim?' a reporter called out.

'I'll pass you over to Detective Chief Inspector Walker for further details.'

Whitney took the mic. 'At the moment we're not releasing the victim's name, out of respect for her family. To reiterate what Detective Superintendent Jamieson said, we'd like anyone who was in the vicinity, or who has any information, to contact us.'

'What was the cause of death?' another reporter asked.

'The victim was strangled,' Whitney said.

'Was a pink chiffon scarf used?' a female voice in the front row called out.

Whitney stiffened. How the hell did she know? That information hadn't been released.

'I'm unable to discuss any of the details at this time as it may harm our investigation.'

'Do you suspect the Lenchester Strangler?' the reporter continued.

Whitney sucked in a sharp breath. The woman was only in her twenties, so either she was very well informed, or somebody had set her up for asking the questions.

'We're following several lines of enquiry at the moment,' Whitney replied.

'But you're not denying the similarities?' the reporter pushed.

'I'm neither confirming nor denying, as we haven't got to that point in our investigation.'

'The Lenchester Strangler wasn't ever caught. Do the police have any suspects?' the woman continued.

'Let's give someone else a turn. Any more questions?' Whitney scanned the room.

'What can you tell us about the Lenchester Strangler?' called someone else in the room.

Whitney glanced at Jamieson; his face was like thunder. They were on the back foot, rather than taking the lead.

'I'm not prepared to discuss anything to do with the Lenchester Strangler. If there are no other questions related directly to the case at hand, then thank you for coming in. We will keep you up-to-date with information once we have it.'

They left the conference room and walked in silence

until Melissa turned down a corridor, leaving Whitney and Jamieson alone.

'What was that all about?' He demanded, his eyes flashing with anger.

'Someone tipped them off,' she said.

'Who do you think that might be? Your team are fully informed, aren't they?'

'My team know better than to do that. Have *you* mentioned it to anyone?' she challenged.

'You're treading on dangerous ground, Walker.'

'We don't know who it is. It could've been a civilian who knows. Or someone in uniform who attended the murder site and let it slip. There are a number of ways it could have happened. But it wasn't pathology or anyone from my team, and I resent any implication that it was.'

'Now it's out, we can use it to our advantage.'

'How's that, sir?'

'If people know this murder is connected to the originals it will capture their interest and we should get plenty of calls and information from the public.'

'Yes, an inordinate number of tyre-kickers and time-wasters just waiting to jump on the bandwagon. This isn't going to help our investigation one bit. Thank goodness they didn't appear to know about the trophy,' she said.

'I'm going now. Keep me up to speed with everything and remember to impress on your team the need for complete discretion.' Jamieson turned and walked in the other direction.

Whitney childishly stuck her tongue out at his retreating back. He had to stick the knife in.

She marched back to the incident room, pushed open the door, and slammed it shut behind her.

Matt looked up from the file he'd been reading. 'What's wrong?'

'I'll tell you what's wrong. Somebody blabbed to the press and Jamieson implied it might be one of us.'

'That's ridiculous. No one here would say anything,' Matt said.

'Exactly what I told him. Whether he believed it or not is a totally different matter.'

'Does it hurt if they know?' Matt asked. He always saw both sides of the story.

'Well, apart from the fact we'll be inundated with calls, and the press will drag up everything they have on the original strangler's victims, which could get in the way of our investigation, then no. We know it's not going to be the original strangler. I suppose it was more a case of being wrong-footed by the journalist. But we do still have a leak.'

'It's not uncommon,' Matt said. 'Can you remember any case where aspects of the investigation haven't found themselves in the media? I can't, and I don't believe we should spend our time looking for this leak. We should be more concerned with finding the person who committed the murder, and the motive behind it. If it's just a copycat, with no motive, then we're looking for someone who may kill again. We don't want that.'

'You're right. We need to focus on that side of things, and I'll wind my neck in.' She laughed and then scanned the room to make sure no one could hear what she was about to say. 'By the way, I'm still waiting for your response regarding the inspector exams.'

She'd been on at him for the last twelve months to take them, but he'd been resistant.

'I'm still thinking about it,' Matt said.

He glanced away. There was something he wasn't telling her.

'When you first came here as a detective constable, I

remember you telling me you wanted to make inspector before the age of thirty-five. What's happened?'

'I'm not sure I want it now,' he said. 'I'm happy being your sergeant, and if I was to become inspector, it brings a whole new level of responsibility. We have too much going on at home for me to contemplate it.'

'Do you want to talk about it?' she asked.

'I don't like bringing my personal life into work, as you know.'

She nodded. They'd worked together for many years and she could count on the fingers of one hand the number of times she'd met his wife, Leigh, who was a nurse. 'You can still talk to me.'

He was silent, jaw tight, as if considering the offer. 'Okay,' he said, a relieved expression crossing his face.

'Let's go into my office, rather than staying out here.'

'Thanks.'

She strode through the incident room, with him following, until reaching her door.

'Now you can tell me,' she said gently, once they'd sat down.

'Leigh's been offered promotion to matron.'

'That's great. Congratulations.'

'It is, but we've also decided to go for IVF treatment.'

Guilt washed over Whitney. She had no idea they were struggling to have a family.

'It's a big step,' she said.

'Yes. If it does work, we can't have both of us in such demanding jobs. We've discussed it and decided Leigh will have the career advancement and I'll continue working as a sergeant.'

'Why didn't you tell me this sooner? I would've understood,' she said, hoping her disappointment didn't show.

'I didn't want to let you down. I know how keen you've been for me to go for it.'

'You're not letting me down. As long as you're happy with what you've got planned.'

'Very. If we have a baby, we'll have the support of both sets of grandparents, but I'll be the one mainly responsible.'

'I'm thrilled for you. And remember, if you need any time off to go for appointments then you only have to ask. You'll want to be with Leigh.'

'Thanks, guv. I appreciate it. I'm not telling the others. At least, not yet.'

'They won't hear anything from me. I'm sorry for having been on your back all the time about the exams.'

'You weren't to know,' Matt said.

'I'm glad I do now. You're the best sergeant anyone could ask for, and I know you're going to make a fantastic dad.'

He coloured slightly. 'We have our first appointment next week, but I'll make sure to be quick. I know it's tricky during an investigation.'

'You'll be as long as it takes. As good as you are, I'm sure we can manage without you for a couple of hours.'

'Thanks, guv.'

'In the meantime, we need to prepare ourselves for the onslaught of phone calls we're about to get. Make sure we have at least three people by the phone as it'll be ringing off the hook with people wanting to comment on the Lenchester Strangler.'

'Yes, guv. And thanks.'

Whitney pushed open the door to the home where her

mum now lived. There was a hive of activity as carers were taking residents to their rooms to get them ready for bed. She didn't usually come this late in the evening, but time had got away from her and she knew if she didn't visit now, she couldn't be sure when she'd next be able to come. She'd intended on bringing her brother, Rob, but there hadn't been time to collect him from the residential care home he was in.

She signed the visitor book and headed towards her mum's room. 'Hello, Meg,' she said to the care assistant, as she passed her. 'Is Mum in her bedroom?'

'Yes, she's been there since dinner. She didn't want to watch telly.'

'Thanks.'

She took the stairs to the first floor and as she got close, she could hear her mum talking to herself. Was that another stage in her illness?

Pushing open the door, she was surprised to see Tiffany there. Her mum wasn't alone, after all. 'What are you doing here? I thought you were with your friends at university.'

Her daughter blushed. 'I wanted a chat with Granny.'

'Hello, Mum,' Whitney said kissing her on the cheek. 'Have I interrupted something?'

Tiffany and her mum looked at each other, guilt etched on both their faces. What was that all about?

'No, of course not. I'm allowed to have my grand-daughter to visit, aren't I?' her mum said.

Whitney smiled. She was having a good day.

'You certainly are. I hadn't realised Tiffany was visiting today.'

'Actually, I've got to go. I've got an assignment to do.' Tiffany stood and gave her granny a hug.

'Okay, love,' Whitney said. 'I'll see you later, we can

chat then. It seems like ages since we've sat down and talked. I've been very busy at work. But I'm definitely going to be home soon, once I've left here.'

'Do you mind if we don't tonight? I don't want to stay up late as I'm going in early tomorrow.'

Was she fobbing her off? Since when did Tiffany do that? They had such a close relationship and talked as often as they could. It wasn't easy when work was demanding, so they took whatever opportunities they had. Or was she letting her imagination get the better of her?

'No, I don't mind. We'll catch up another time.'

Chapter Eleven

'Damn,' Whitney said as she replaced the phone. Another murder. Would George be available? She reached for her mobile and pressed speed-dial.

'Hello,' George said.

'What are you doing?'

'Working. Why?'

'Can you get away?'

'Umm…' George paused.

'Don't worry if it's too much trouble,' Whitney snapped, immediately regretting it. 'Sorry, I know you're busy.'

'It's not that.'

'What is it?' Whitney asked.

'Nothing. Has something happened?'

'Yes. Another murder. I'd hoped you'd be able to meet me at the scene.'

'I don't have anything on until this afternoon.'

'Great. I'll see you there. The address is—'

'Blast. I'd arranged a meeting with a colleague,' George interrupted.

'Can you cancel?'

There was a pause. 'Yes. I'm sure it will be fine. Leave it with me.'

'Meet me at 115 Winchester Gardens. It's two streets away from the first murder.'

She ended the call; glad George had agreed to come, but still convinced something wasn't quite right. Was George tired of spending so much time with her on cases? Whitney tended to forget the psychologist had a life away from the station and expected her to be available whenever she was needed.

She left her office and went into the incident room, where the team was working.

'Listen up, everyone. We've had a second murder. I'm meeting Dr Cavendish there. In the meantime, Matt, I want you to go to Celia Churchill's house and see if the gardener turns up, as today is his day for working. There was no number for him on her contact list. His name is Dave. He works in the morning. Take a statement from him. Don't forget to find out his shoe size.'

'Yes, guv.'

'The rest of you carry on with what you're doing, and I'll brief you on my return.'

She drove to Winchester Gardens and parked on the road beside the large, double-fronted stone cottage. A uniformed officer who she didn't recognise was standing outside. She went over and flashed her warrant card. 'DCI Walker. And you are?'

'PC Johnson.' The officer didn't look old enough to have left school yet.

Thoughts like that were a sure sign she must be getting old. Which terrified Whitney, in case she ended up like her mother. In a couple of years, she'd hit forty, and she'd been told that after then you spent your time looking backwards instead of forwards. That wasn't going to happen to her.

'Who was first officer attending?' Whitney asked.

'PC Brigstock and me. He left me out here,' she replied.

'Where's the crime scene log?' Whitney asked, noticing its absence.

The officer averted her gaze. 'We haven't got it yet.'

'Well, sort that out now. As I'm sure you were made aware during your training, it's imperative we have an accurate record of which individuals cross the barrier placed around the scene and when they leave.' She gave an exasperated sigh.

It was policing 101 and she shouldn't have had to bring it to the officer's attention.

'Yes, ma'am,' the girl said, going bright red.

'Where's PC Brigstock?'

'He's in the kitchen with the woman who found the body. She's a friend of the victim.'

'What's the friend's name?'

'I don't know.' The officer's voice was barely above a whisper.

'Where was the body found?' Whitney asked, deciding not to pursue the lack of a name. The young officer had already found herself in enough trouble.

'Upstairs in the bedroom.'

'Is the pathologist here yet?'

'Yes,' the officer replied.

'Is it Dr Dexter?' Whitney asked.

'I don't know.'

'A woman with short red hair?'

'Yes.'

'Good. That's Dr Dexter. Sort out the crime scene log

before anyone else gets here. I'm expecting Dr Cavendish. Send her upstairs once she arrives.'

Whitney walked into the house and headed straight for the dark wooden staircase. As she reached the top, she heard a noise coming from along the hall. She stopped outside the room with the open door. Claire was moving around with a camera in her hand. As usual, she was wearing white coveralls, but Whitney could still see a yellow and brown striped bow peeping out. She was also wearing a pair of red and black striped dangly earrings.

'Hello,' she said, stepping into the room.

'Stay where you are. I'm in the middle of something,' Claire bellowed.

'No problem. I won't move from this spot until allowed.' She gave a wry grin.

Claire continued snapping away at the body. The victim was wearing a pair of pale pink silk pyjamas and was gagged. Her hands and feet were bound together. A pink scarf was tied around her neck. Her heart sank. They'd definitely got a Lenchester Strangler copycat on their hands.

'Was a piece of hair taken?' Whitney asked.

'Yes,' Claire replied. 'You can come over now.'

The victim had short grey hair which hung just below her ears, and when Claire pulled back a section Whitney could see where some had been cut.

'The same bindings as last time?' She nodded to the cable ties holding the feet and hands.

'It appears that way. I'd planned to get in touch with you today regarding those used on the first victim. They're very old and you can no longer buy that type.'

'How old?' Whitney asked.

'Difficult to say. Could be thirty or more years. Most cable ties for sale nowadays can be reused, but these are

HellermannTyton and are single use only. Very traditional.'

'We need to get hold of the physical evidence from the old Lenchester Strangler cases to see if they are similar to the ones being used now,' Whitney said.

'You haven't got it yet?' Claire frowned.

'All we've got are the files. Frank's working on getting the rest.'

'Well, he needs to work harder.'

The sound of George coming into the room distracted her from replying. 'You've made it, then,' she said.

'I said I'd be here. I had to deal with a couple of things first.'

Whitney glanced at Claire who was staring in George's direction and frowning.

'Who got out of bed on the wrong side this morning?' Claire said.

'What do you mean?' George replied.

'Your tone of voice was abrupt, even for you,' Claire said, shrugging.

'Can we come over to the body yet?' Whitney asked.

'Yes. I've taken the photographs I need.' Claire ushered them over.

'Any signs of a struggle?' Whitney asked.

'You'll know that when I do my report, but at the moment it doesn't seem so.'

'Does that mean she knew her assailant or she was sedated?' Whitney said.

'Wait until I've gone through the evidence,' Claire said.

Whitney handed George a pair of disposable gloves. 'Let's look around.'

Everything in the bedroom was in perfect order, almost like they were in a show home. The cushions from the bed were piled on a chair. The en suite bathroom was bare, with nothing on show. Whitney opened the mirror fronted cabinet and inside was an electric toothbrush, toothpaste, and cleansing products. Under the sink in a drawer was make-up and other bathroom items.

'She was most likely single,' George said. 'There's nothing here belonging to anyone else and only one of everything.'

They headed back into the bedroom.

'Do we have a name for the victim?' Whitney asked Claire.

'Don't ask me. You're the detective.'

Whitney opened the handbag by the side of the bed. Inside was a blue leather wallet. She opened it and pulled out a driving license. 'Cassandra Billington, and she's fifty-eight years old. She's also got a wad of cash in her purse, so robbery wasn't the motive.'

'Who found the victim?' George asked.

'A friend who's waiting downstairs. I haven't inter-viewed her, yet. We'll go now and leave you to it, Claire. We'll wait for your report,' Whitney said.

'You will indeed,' the pathologist replied.

'Come on, then,' Whitney said to George.

They left the room and went downstairs.

'I'm not sure where the kitchen is. By the way, did you sign in when you arrived?' she asked, remembering the lack of a log.

'Of course. I always do. There was an officer on the door,' George replied.

Whitney was about to launch into an explanation about why she'd asked, then thought better of it.

'Good. Let's find the kitchen.' She pushed open one of the doors and looked in. It was the lounge. She then went across the hall and opened another door. In there was PC Brigstock and a woman in her fifties dressed elegantly in a pair of dark blue trousers, a pink and white striped shirt with a strand of pearls around her neck.

The woman was drained of all colour.

'Hello, I'm Detective Chief Inspector Walker and this is Dr Cavendish,' she said as they walked over to the large oak table situated in the middle of the room. 'Do you mind if we ask you a few questions?'

The woman sniffed and wiped her nose with the tissue she had in her hand. 'Yes, that's fine. My name is Erica Ridson.'

'You can leave us now,' Whitney said to PC Brigstock.

She sat on the chair next to Erica. George sat opposite.

'What time did you arrive this morning?' Whitney asked.

'Cassie asked me to pick her up at nine, as we'd planned to go into the city shopping.'

'Talk me through what happened when you arrived.'

'I was here at five minutes to nine and parked outside. I went to the door and rang the bell. I waited because Cassie can often take a while to answer. When she didn't come I rang again, and also knocked. She didn't appear, so I tried the door on the off-chance it was open. It was, so I walked in. I called her name, but still nothing. I came in here, but it was empty. I then went upstairs, wondering if she was getting ready. I walked into her bedroom and saw her. I-I…' Tears filled her eyes and she brushed them away with her tissue. 'I'm sorry. I can't get out of my head the picture of her lying there. It was awful.'

'Just take your time,' Whitney said gently. 'You've had a bad experience. You're doing really well. What did you do when you saw Cassie?'

'I went over and shook her. I wasn't sure whether she was still alive or not, but her body was stone cold, so I knew she wasn't. I pulled out my mobile and called emergency services and waited for the police to arrive.'

'Did you wait in the bedroom?'

'No, I couldn't stay there.'

'You've done very well. Is there anyone we can call to be with you?'

'No. I live on my own. Like Cassie. That's why we spend a lot of time together.'

'Did Cassie collect art?' George asked.

George got up and headed towards a painting on the wall.

'Not really,' Erica replied. 'We do go to art exhibitions occasionally, but I wouldn't say she was a collector.'

'What about this particular painting?' George asked.

'I don't recognise it. Who's it by?'

'I can't make out the signature,' George said.

'When was the last time you were here?' Whitney asked.

'We see each other every week. It could have been here the last time I was over, but I don't remember. Art isn't something I'm interested in, and not something we talked about. Is it important?'

'We're just trying to put together a picture of Cassie's life,' Whitney replied.

'I understand. Is there anything else you want to know?' Erica said.

'When you visited, did you notice anyone hanging around, looking suspicious? Or did Cassie comment on seeing someone out of place?' Whitney asked.

'No. She hadn't mentioned seeing anyone lurking. I didn't either. It's always quiet, that's why Cassie liked living here. She said she felt safe.'

'What else can you tell us about her? Was she married? Did she have any children?'

'Her husband died in tragic circumstances. They were on holiday in the Caribbean and he had a heart attack while swimming in the sea. He drowned.'

'How long ago was that?' Whitney asked.

'Six years.'

'Does she have any children?'

'No, she wasn't able to. She confided in me that she'd struggled with depression over it for a long time. But she tried not to show it and always kept herself busy.'

'Did she work?'

'Only voluntary work. She was very wealthy, thanks to her husband.'

'What business was he in?' Whitney asked.

'He was a venture capitalist. I don't know much about him, as he died before we became friends.'

'How did you meet her?'

'At the local soup kitchen where we were both volunteering.'

'Is there anything else you can think of that might help?'

'Not at the moment,' Erica said.

'Does she have any family we can contact?' Whitney asked.

'She has a sister, Iris, in Dublin, but I don't have her details.'

'Were they close?' Whitney asked.

'Once a year, Cassie would go to visit for a couple of weeks,' Erica said. 'What about her cleaner? Someone will need to let her know.'

'Do you know who she is?' Whitney asked.

'Her name's Vi, and she comes in once a week on a Thursday. You should find her number on the contact list on the fridge door.'

Whitney walked over to the fridge where there was a

list of names and phone numbers, including the sister and cleaner. She put it into an evidence bag and headed back to Erica and George.

'We'll contact them,' she said.

'Do you need me for anything else as I'd like to go home, now?' Erica said.

'You're free to go. Are you sure you're okay to drive?' Whitney asked.

'Yes, I'll be fine. I don't live too far away.'

Whitney pulled out a card from her pocket. 'If you think of anything else you'd like us to know give me a call.'

She escorted Erica out of the house and returned to George who was standing in the kitchen looking at the painting.

'Why did you ask about this particular picture?'

'Because both women were interested in abstract art. Not everyone is.'

'Is that what you call it? It looks like something a two-year-old could do.' Whitney tilted her head to one side, to see if she could work out what it was meant to be.

'To the untrained eye.'

'Don't tell me you're also an expert on art.' Whitney shook her head.

'No, but I know that abstract art isn't about being an accurate depiction, but instead the artist will use different shapes, colours, and form to represent something they've seen.'

'That's very interesting, but we now have murder number two and it's time for you to start earning your keep. I want a profile, asap We need to stop this offender before he strikes again.'

Chapter Twelve

George was glad she'd brought her own car to the murder scene because it gave her time to collect her thoughts on the way back to the station. Why had Whitney asked for the profile request? She knew as well as anyone it didn't work like that. Especially as there were only two victims.

Or was she overthinking because of the Tiffany situation? It wasn't as if she couldn't contribute anything to the investigation. Once Tiffany told Whitney of her plans then all the awkwardness would be over.

They arrived back at the station together and walked into the incident room and headed to the board.

'Listen up, everyone,' Whitney said. 'We've just come from the scene of the second murder, which is identical to the first. The victim is Cassandra Billington.' She wrote the name on the board beside Celia Churchill's. 'Let's start putting some of this together. What do we know about them?'

'They're both comfortably off,' George said.

'As in, rich. Except, theft wasn't a motive in either murder,' Whitney said.

'It could be someone who has a dislike of wealthy people,' Matt said.

'Okay,' Whitney said, writing 'rich' beside both names.

'They both have their names beginning with *C*,' Frank said.

Whitney glanced at George and arched an eyebrow. 'Well?'

'Nothing should be discounted,' George said.

'Okay.' Whitney wrote *C* on the board. 'Neither of them worked, apart from volunteering. We should check whether they volunteered at the same places.'

'The two of them employed a cleaner,' George said.

'Did they both live alone?' Doug asked.

'Yes. Which makes them easier targets,' Whitney said.

'They are similar ages,' George said.

'Do you think he's targeting a type?' Whitney asked.

'With only two victims it would be unwise to speculate,' George said. 'But we can deduce some things from the crimes and the victims.' She scanned the room and all eyes were on her.

'Which are?' Whitney said.

'Our offender is most likely well organised and methodical.'

'How do we know that?' Frank asked.

'The murders weren't opportunistic. He would have spent time observing his victims, to discover they lived alone and to know intricacies of their lives. The fact he spent time watching them would imply that he's able to blend in and be unobtrusive. More bodies will give more information.'

'But we don't *want* more,' Whitney said.

'I realise that, I was just saying in order to profile better that's what we need,' George said, a terse tone in her voice, which she immediately regretted.

'Okay, okay. We all know how you work. We've been together long enough.' Whitney laughed, but it sounded false.

George tried to relax her taut muscles and smile. 'Yes, we have.'

'Frank, I want another examination of the CCTV footage around Pennington Grove, which is very close to the second victim's house in Winchester Gardens. See if there are any cars hanging around both areas on both days, or people acting suspiciously.'

'Yes, guv,' Frank said, leaning forward in his chair and pulling his computer mouse towards him.

'We need to get in touch with the victim's sister, and also the cleaner. Ellie, I have phone numbers, please find out the address of the sister and ask the Dublin police to contact her? Also, contact Vi, the cleaner, and explain what has happened. We'd like her to come in for an interview.'

'You want me to tell her about the murder?' the officer said, uncertainty in her voice.

'It's good experience for you, but if you don't feel up to it don't worry, I'll ask someone else.'

'I'll do it,' Matt volunteered.

'Thank you,' Ellie said. 'If that's okay? She glanced at Whitney.

'That's fine. By the way, where are you on investigating Harold Skinner's finances?'

'I've tracked down twelve accounts in the UK and Europe. Some accounts are forty years old. Most are in his name, though I found two in his wife's.'

'How is that possible?'

'It's easy enough if a death isn't reported directly to the bank. Only one account has regular withdrawals, for payments to Featherstone Manor.'

'How much is he worth?' Whitney asked.

'I haven't completed all my research, but so far, I'd say twenty million pounds.'

'What?' Whitney's hand flew to her chest. 'Where did the money come from?'

'It's impossible to know as much of this money has been in the accounts for a long time. Before the Internet made tracing funds so much easier.'

'Good work. See what else you can find. Sue, I want you to check on eBay and other sites to see if it's possible to buy any HellermannTyton cable ties. According to Claire, they were used years ago and aren't now available in the shops. Doug, I want you to look into Cassandra Billington's background. Friends, social media, finances, any charity work she did. We need to get a full picture of her, as that will help in our understanding of why she was chosen as a victim. Sue can help once she's finished investigating the cable ties.'

Whitney finished giving out her orders. Not too dictatorial, but with enough guidance to keep them on track. They were loyal and hardworking in return, as they'd proved many times over. George admired her skill in navigating the managerial role.

'What did you find out about the Lenchester Strangler's victims?' she asked

'Frank. Here a moment,' Whitney called out.

'Yes, guv?' he said once he was standing with them.

'Tell George what you know about the Strangler's victims,' Whitney said.

'There were six of them. All women living in the Lenchester area.'

'Were they wealthy? Married or single? How old were they? Did they work? Did they live alone?' George asked.

'Hang on a minute.' He held up both hands, defensively. 'You can't expect me to know all that. There are loads of files to go through.'

He looked at Whitney, appearing to seek her support.

'You could find out more from an Internet search,' Whitney said, not giving it. 'I'll give someone else the CCTV footage to check. I want you to give one hundred per cent focus on the files from now on.'

'It's not going to be easy.' Frank gave a loud sigh.

'What about the physical evidence you requisitioned?'

'Still waiting.' He shrugged.

'Didn't you follow up on it?' Whitney asked.

'Once, but they still didn't have it. I was going to give them a bit longer, before contacting them again.'

'Frank, we have a central store. It shouldn't be an issue. Get in touch with them straight away.'

'Yes, guv.'

'What's the matter with you? You're not usually so slapdash.'

'Sorry, guv,' Frank said, hanging his head. 'I'm not thinking straight. We've trouble at home. Our daughter has left her husband and is living with us. With the children. It's playing havoc with my sleep, as they're up at all times of the day and night.'

That explained it. Frank needed coaxing and could sometimes be a bit lazy, but George had never seen him this slack before.

'I'm sorry to hear that. Chase the evidence, then go home and get some rest. I want you fit for work tomorrow, and no excuses. Leave the files by your desk, as George wants to go through them.'

'Will do, guv. And thanks, I appreciate it. We'll sort everything out at home. I promise.'

He turned and went back to his desk.

'Poor, Frank. His daughter's always been difficult. He

thought she'd settled down and was out of their hair. Thank goodness Tiffany's always been so easy. I'm really lucky with her,' Whitney said.

'Yes,' George agreed hurriedly. She needed to steer the conversation onto safer territory. 'Hopefully, Frank will be able to get the evidence soon.'

'Agreed.' Whitney's jaw tightened. 'Oh crap, what the hell does he want?'

George turned and saw Jamieson heading in their direction.

'Dr Cavendish,' he said, smiling broadly. 'I'm glad to see you here. Are you helping with the case?'

George glanced at Whitney whose lips were pressed together in a thin flat line.

'Yes, I am,' she said.

'Is there anything we can do for you, sir?' Whitney said.

'I've just heard about the second murder from the Chief Constable. She wants to be fully appraised of our progress.'

'How does she know about it? It's only just happened.'

'The victim was a personal friend of hers. This case must have top priority over everything. Report to me twice a day, so I know exactly where we are with it.'

'We'll give it *exactly* the same amount of attention as we do all cases of this nature,' Whitney said, coldly.

'You will give it even more. I want twenty-four-seven on this. Overtime no object. Do you understand?'

'Yes, sir,' she said.

'Are you able to continue working with us, Dr Cavendish?' Jamieson asked.

'I will be here whenever possible. I still have my work at university to consider.'

'Who do I speak to, for you to be seconded to us full-time while we're investigating this murder?' Jamieson asked.

'That's not possible,' she stated, categorically. 'I have other commitments. You will have my full attention those times I'm here. If you're unhappy with that, you could always find someone else, although I suspect no one with my level of expertise will commit themselves full-time.' She stared directly into his eyes and he looked away.

'No, we don't want to lose you,' he said. 'As much time as you can give will be appreciated. I'll leave you to get on with finding our killer. I expect to see you later today, Walker.' He turned and walked away.

'You go, girl,' Whitney said laughing, once he'd left the room. She patted George on the back.

'What do you mean?' she asked.

'Putting Jamieson in his place like that. His face was a classic once he realised he couldn't order you around. What I'd give to be able to do that with such ease and no comeback.'

'I'm not sure what you mean. I meant what I said. He could try to find someone as good as me, but it would be a wasted attempt.'

'Well, you might not realise what you did, but I certainly enjoyed it. Thank you for improving my day.'

'My pleasure.'

'I know you said we need more than two victims, but is there *anything* else you can tell me so far, profile-wise, about these murders?' Whitney asked.

'We know the killings are controlled, and although we don't know the motive behind them, I don't believe they were overtly sexual.'

'Meaning?'

'There was no sexual interference. Although that

doesn't mean the murderer didn't get sexual gratification from committing them.'

'You said they were controlled, in what way?'

'The way with the first victim there were no finger-prints, or any forensic evidence left behind. The kills involved a great deal of planning.'

'Anything else?'

'Yes. The killer could be viewed as cowardly in his selection of victims. They were single, older women asleep at the time of the murders. He ensured there was no partner or dog around, as they could potentially overthrow him. He might be a copycat, but something snapped, making him kill.'

'That makes sense.'

'Before I go, I'll take a look at the old files on Frank's desk. It will give me a fuller picture. And knowing the length of time between the previous murders, could help us predict the murderer's next move.'

'Are we to expect more?' Whitney asked.

'I can't be certain, but I would say it's probable. We know that previously there were six murders, so if this copycat is following the same pattern, then we have to expect it. Which isn't good. But as you know, the more we have the more likely it will be that we can catch the person committing them.'

Chapter Thirteen

The following day Whitney was pacing the room, staring at the board. They seemed no closer to solving the crimes. They'd been inundated with phone calls from the public, following the press conference, none of which were leading anywhere. On top of that, Frank had been informed earlier by the evidence store that all the physical evidence relating to the Lenchester Strangler was *unavailable*. In other words, it had been misplaced and no one was taking responsibility for it. All they had to work with was the paper files.

'Attention, everyone,' she called. 'We seem to be getting nowhere fast so let's go over what we do have. Matt, what happened with the first victim's gardener?'

'His name is Dave Driscoll and he has a small one-man gardening business called *Pimp your Garden*. He was there when I arrived. He has an alibi for the time in question which I'm just corroborating. He has size twelve feet.'

'*Pimp your Garden*. What sort of name is that?' Frank asked. 'It sounds like he's turning her garden into a brothel.'

'It's just a term that's used these days. Though at your age, I suppose it's passed you by,' Doug said, grinning at Frank.

'I'm not that old,' Frank said. 'I could beat you in a fight.'

'Thank you, *boys*,' Whitney said, staring fiercely. 'His feet are bigger than our print, so that also rules him out. Sue, any joy with the cable ties?'

'No, guv. I couldn't find them anywhere,' Sue said.

'I thought that might be the case. Frank, what have you ascertained from the files of the previous murders?'

'I'm still going through them. They're a mess and it's taking ages to sort everything out,' the officer replied.

'What can you tell me, so far?'

'Our six victims all lived in and around Lenchester,' he said.

'In posh areas, like our two victims?' she asked, refraining from mentioning that he'd already told her that the other day.

'No. They lived in a variety of places,' Frank replied.

Whitney returned to the board and put up two columns, one labelled *old* and the other *new*. Under *new* she wrote "upmarket locations" and under *old* she wrote "mixed locations".

'What else?' she asked.

'They were all alone on the night of their murder,' Frank said.

'Were they all single?' She had to restrain herself from letting out an exasperated sigh. It was like getting blood out of a stone. But if she had a go, he'd sulk and then she'd get nothing from him. He was a good member of her team. Loyal and trustworthy. And she'd miss him when he retired in a few years.

'Three of them were. Of the others, two were married,

but their husbands were away, and one lived with a friend who was also absent that night,' Frank said.

Now they were getting somewhere.

'So, these weren't random murders. The killer must have selected and stalked his victims to know when they were alone.'

'It looks that way.'

'What jobs did the husbands of the two married women have, and the friend of the other one?' Whitney asked.

'I'm not sure, guv. I'll check it out.'

'How old were the victims?'

'Between thirty-five and sixty-three,' Frank said.

Whitney wrote the ages in each column. 'In respect of the victims, there are differences, but maybe that's because we've only had two murders. I don't suppose by any chance their first names all began with the letter C?' Was she clutching at straws?

'No, guv,' Frank said.

'Anything else of relevance you can tell me? What about the length of time between murders?' she asked.

'Three weeks between the first and second murders, and they gradually got less until between the fifth and sixth there was only four days,' Frank said.

'Typical serial killer behaviour. The more he got a taste for it, the more he wanted that hit again. Ellie, have you got anything to add?'

'I've been continuing my research into Harold Skinner. I've discovered his son lives locally.'

'What about other members of his family?' Whitney asked.

'He only had one child,' Ellie said.

'We'll pay him a visit. What do we know about him?'

'I've been following his social media accounts. His

name is Craig Skinner. He's in his early fifties and is a free-lance photographer. He's married and lives above his studio.'

'Text me the address. Interesting that his name begins with a C. I wonder if that's relevant. I'm going to see if George can come with me to interview him. We'll take a chance on him being there as I don't want him forewarned.'

George had been away with Ross for the weekend and hadn't been into the station over the weekend. When Whitney had pushed her for more details the response had been vague, to say the least. Even more so than usual.

She pulled out her phone and called.

'Hello, Whitney.'

'Any chance you're free today? I'd like to visit the son of Harold Skinner,' Whitney said.

'What time?'

'Whenever you're available.'

'I've got a class in an hour, from eleven to twelve. I can get away after that but need to return by three as I have a tutorial.'

'No problem. We'll easily be back by then as he lives locally,' Whitney said, relieved that George was able to go with her. 'I'll wait for you here.'

'I'll meet you at his house,' George said.

'Whatever works for you,' Whitney said.

It was strange George didn't want to come to the station first, and they go together, or was she just imagining it. It was like the barrier between them had been put up again.

'Okay. I'll see you later,' George said.

'I'll text you his address and meet you at twelve-thirty,' Whitney said.

'Do we know he's definitely going to be there?' George asked.

'He lives above his studio, so he's likely to be. If not, we'll go back another time. Don't worry if you'd rather not risk a wasted journey, I know you're trying to balance work with helping us.'

'It's fine. I'll be there,' George said, ending the call without even saying goodbye.

Whitney stared at her phone. She'd definitely be having it out with George. They couldn't continue working like this. Whatever it was they needed to sort it out, or she'd drive herself crazy going over and over what was going on between them, instead of concentrating on the murders.

'George.'

She glanced up and saw Tiffany heading towards her.

'Hello.'

'Do you have a moment? I want to talk to you more about going away.'

'I've only got a couple of minutes as I'm going to meet your mother to work on the case.'

'I'm still not sure whether to commit to returning to the university or whether to drop out and wait until I come back before applying to return to the course.'

'Have you discussed it with someone in administration?'

'Not yet, because I wasn't sure.'

'You're not committing yourself to anything by speaking to them. You need to get onto that straight away.'

'What do you think I should do?' Tiffany asked.

'If you get agreement from the university to hold open a place, then you know you've definitely got it. If you wait on the off-chance there's one available, and the course is full, then you've lost out.'

'That does make sense,' Tiffany said.

'Have you spoken to your mother yet?'

'Nearly.' Tiffany averted her eyes.

'What does that mean?'

'She wanted us to have a chat the other day after I saw her at Granny's, but I said no because I was scared of what she would say.'

'You must tell her. And soon.'

She didn't let on that it was putting a strain on her relationship with Whitney. Once everything was out in the open, they could go back to normal because it wasn't an enjoyable situation to be in for either of them. Especially as Whitney had done nothing to deserve George's treatment of her.

'I will. Promise.'

'Make sure you do. Also, sort out your options with the university.'

'Thanks, George. You're the best.' Tiffany gave her a hug.

'I've got to go,' George said, pulling away, embarrassed at the display of affection from the girl. 'Next time we meet I expect this all to be sorted.'

'It will be.'

George arrived at the address and sat in her car until Whitney turned up.

The studio had a shopfront window, with a sign *Craig Skinner Photography* above it. As they opened the door, a bell rang. The shop area wasn't very large, and on the walls were blown up photos, mainly of weddings and a few of babies. There was no one behind the counter, but after a minute the door behind it opened and a man walked through. He was tall and slim, with a pockmarked face and thinning grey hair, cut short around his ears.

'Are you Craig Skinner?' Whitney asked.

'Yes.' He looked from Whitney to George. 'How can I help you?'

'I'm Detective Chief Inspector Walker and this is Dr Cavendish. We'd like to talk to you.' Whitney held out her warrant card.

'I was expecting you,' he said, a resigned look on his face.

'Why?'

'I watch the news. You think the Lenchester Strangler is back on the scene. My father was a prime suspect. I'm not stupid and can put two and two together.' His shoulders slumped.

'Is there somewhere we can sit down?' Whitney asked.

'I can't leave the shop. We can talk here,' he said, leaning forward and resting his elbows on the counter. He stared directly at them.

'Okay,' Whitney said. 'When did you last have any contact with your father?'

'Not since I was eighteen and he was arrested for killing my mother.' A shadow crossed his face. Remembering was clearly painful.

'Not even a letter?' Whitney asked.

'For the first couple of years, he wrote to me from prison, but I didn't reply. I wanted nothing to do with him,' he said.

'What did his letters say?'

'He asked for my forgiveness. Said it was an accident and he was truly sorry. Or some shit like that. I don't remember his exact words.'

'You didn't believe him?' Whitney asked.

'Would you have? Of course not,' he added not giving them time to answer. 'He's a cold-blooded murderer. My mother was just another of his targets.'

'So, you believed he was the Lenchester Strangler, even though nothing could be pinned on him?' Whitney asked.

'I was just a scrawny teenager at the time, but there was definitely something going on. I could tell by his manner. One time, after he'd been interrogated for hours, and he'd come home exhausted, I asked him about it. He didn't admit to being the strangler, but didn't deny it either. If he was innocent, wouldn't he have told me? It had to be true.'

'Did you report your suspicions to the police?' Whitney asked.

'No. He was my dad. I wouldn't do that. I wish I had, though. Then maybe my mum would still be alive.'

'How was your mum during the time he was being questioned? Did she talk to you about it?'

'Not directly. But she was angry.'

'With the police?' Whitney asked.

'No. With *him*. I heard them arguing about it one night when they thought I was asleep. I'd come downstairs for some water and they were fighting. She was convinced of his guilt and told him it was best for the rest of us if he admitted it.' Craig's eyes glazed over as if he was reliving the whole thing.

'Are you sure that's what you heard? Could you have been mistaken?' Whitney said.

'I'm sure. She accused him over and over. Said that she knew he crept out of the house at night, sometimes.'

'Why didn't she inform the police?'

'I don't know. Maybe she was scared of him. Or she felt some perverse sense of duty towards him as they were married. I wish I could tell you. It's something that's plagued me for years.'

'Why do you think he murdered her?' Whitney asked.

'I don't know. I was staying overnight with friends when it happened, or perhaps I could've stopped it. He said it was an accident. That she tripped and fell down the stairs. But the jury didn't believe him. The prosecution said he'd deliberately pushed her to cash in on the insurance policy he'd taken out. A plane ticket to Tenerife was found in his name only and that was used as evidence against him. I suppose it could have been the insurance policy but maybe he believed he couldn't trust her not to tell the police her suspicions about the other murders. We'll never know.'

'Were you interviewed at the time?' Whitney asked.

'Yes.'

'Did you tell the police about the argument between your parents?' Whitney asked.

'No.' He hung his head.

'Why not?'

'I was a kid and my mum had just died. I wasn't going to incriminate my father for those crimes, in case it wasn't true. I had no proof.'

He seemed to be contradicting himself, but that wasn't unusual for people in his situation. He'd clearly pushed everything to the back of his mind, and Whitney talking to him about it could have brought some memories back, and not others. George felt sorry for the man.

'What do you know about the recent murders?' Whitney asked.

'Only what I've read in the papers.'

'Do you believe your father could have had anything to do with it?'

'At his age?' He shook his head.

'Did you know he'd been released from prison?' Whitney asked.

'Yes. For some reason the prison wrote to inform me. I didn't even know they had my address,' Craig said.

'Have you been to see your father since his release?' Whitney asked.

'Are you trying to trip me up? I've already told you I haven't seen him since I was eighteen.' His face darkened.

'Do you know where he's living?' Whitney asked.

'No idea. Are we going to be much longer? I'm developing photos out the back.'

She doubted Whitney would get anything more from him. He was clearly losing his patience and hadn't given them any useful information.

'Would it surprise you to know he's still in the Lenchester area?' Whitney asked.

'I have no thoughts on the matter.'

'He's at Featherstone Manor, in Willington.'

'And?'

'*And* … it's an upmarket care home, costing a lot of money. Where does his money come from?'

'I don't know, and I don't care.'

'When you were growing up, what job did your father do?'

'He worked for himself.'

'Doing what?'

'Your guess is as good as mine. He referred to it as *wheeling and dealing*. All I remember is there were often dodgy characters in our kitchen. But whenever they were there, he sent me to my room.'

'And you did as you were told? You didn't hang around and try to listen to what was going on?'

'I was a kid and knew better than to get on his wrong side.'

'What were you doing between midnight and four last Monday morning and throughout the night last Thursday?' Whitney asked.

He stared at her, unblinking.

Was he about to lie?

'Why?' he asked.

Or was he stalling for time?

'Please answer the question,' Whitney said.

'I was here, at home. In bed.'

'Can anyone vouch for you?' Whitney asked.

'My wife.'

'Is she here?'

'No. She's at work.'

'Where does she work?'

'At the hospital. She's a health care assistant.'

'What time will she be home?'

'Around six this evening, as she's on a day shift.'

'When was she last on nights?' George asked.

'Last week. She...' He paused.

'Was she working nights on the dates of the murders?' Whitney asked, glancing at George and nodding.

'Yes.' He hung his head.

'So, you have no one to vouch for you,' Whitney said.

'I forgot that she wasn't here.'

'Are you sure you were at home for the duration of the time I asked about?' Whitney said.

'Yes. I rarely go out in the evenings, unless I have a photo shoot, or we go out for a meal. Which isn't often.'

'We'd like you to present yourself at the station so we can take a statement and take your fingerprints.'

'Why? I've already told you I was at home.'

'We'd like to eliminate you from our enquiries. If you're innocent, then you won't mind.'

'I can go in this afternoon after I shut the shop.'

'Good. Here's my card. Let me know when you're on your way.'

They left the shop and stood outside.

'Do you think he's got something to do with it?' George asked, interested to hear Whitney's take on the man.

'I was about to ask your thoughts,' Whitney said.

'He was definitely holding back. It was obvious by the way he didn't blink while concentrating on answering your questions and then blinking too fast after he'd finished. But that could just be because he wasn't used to talking about his father. He'd compartmentalised it because of the anxiety it causes him.'

'Or it could be because he's involved in these latest murders. I'll speak to his wife and when he comes in this afternoon, he'll be reinterviewed.'

Chapter Fourteen

Whitney walked in, holding the two pizzas she'd collected on the way home, as Tiffany had said she'd be in for dinner. She was glad to be home as it had been a frustrating day. Craig Skinner's wife had confirmed she'd been at work but had also told them she'd been using Craig's car for much of last week as hers was in for repair. When Whitney had spoken to Craig about it, he'd totally forgotten. They'd got his fingerprints, but as the scenes were clean, they weren't much use. Also, he had size thirteen feet, which was much larger than the footprint found at the first victim's house.

She was looking forward to a glass of wine with her dinner. Something to take her mind off everything. Including George's weird behaviour. Could Tiffany enlighten her? She knew they saw each other occasionally.

She entered the kitchen and saw her daughter's bag on one of the chairs.

'Tiffany,' she shouted. 'I'm home with dinner.'

Footsteps bounded down the stairs, and within a few seconds, her daughter was in the kitchen.

'Hey, Mum,' Tiffany said, giving her a kiss on the cheek.

'Get the plates, while I get the drinks. Would you like a wine?'

'Have we got any cider?' Tiffany took two plates from the cupboard and put them on the kitchen table beside the two open pizza boxes.

Whitney opened the fridge, took out a bottle, removed the top, and passed it to her. She drew the bottle to her lips and took a long drink.

'Steady on,' Whitney said.

'It's only cider. I was thirsty.'

They sat down and started eating. Tiffany seemed unusually quiet and wasn't wolfing down the pizza with her usual gusto.

'Tell me about your day,' Whitney said, wanting to break the silence.

'Pretty much the same as usual. Lectures. Tutorials. Hanging out with my friends.' She shrugged and averted her gaze.

Whitney stared at her daughter. 'Is everything okay?'

Tiffany glanced at her from under her eyelashes. 'Yes.'

Whitney gave an exasperated sigh. It was getting ridiculous. First George and now Tiffany. She banged her hand on the table in frustration.

'What did you do that for?' Tiffany said.

'Because something's going on, and I'm going to get to the bottom of it. George is acting totally weird. She's not talking to me. She's being distant and makes excuses not to be in the car with me. Every time I ask what's wrong, she denies there's anything. Now I come home, and I'm faced with you being quiet, evasive, and acting totally out of character, too. I want to know what's going on, and I want to know now.'

Tiffany flushed a deep shade of red. 'It's nothing,' she muttered.

'Pull the other one. You've gone bright red, which you don't normally do. I'm your mother, you can tell me anything.'

'Well, there is something,' Tiffany said.

'I knew it. What's going on and is George involved?'

'You can't blame George for this. She only knows because I spoke to her about it.'

Whitney tensed. Tiffany had confided in George? She'd never kept anything from her in the past. Hurt and panic pounded in her chest.

'I don't care about George's involvement. Tell me. There's nothing we can't handle together. You're not pregnant, are you?'

She could understand her daughter's reluctance to tell her if that was the case, because she'd known how Whitney's life had changed once she'd become pregnant. Not that she'd change anything. She hadn't regretted having Tiffany for one minute, and she could see herself being a grandmother.

'No, of course I'm not pregnant. I'd have told you if I was.'

Coldness washed over her. Was she sick?

'What's the matter? Whatever it is, we can deal with it. You can see the best doctors. Whatever it takes.'

'I'm not sick. It's nothing like that,' Tiffany said, biting down on her bottom lip.

'Then what the hell is it? Just tell me.' She stared directly at Tiffany, but her daughter wouldn't meet her eyes.

'Okay, I'll tell you, but don't get mad.' Tiffany sucked in a loud breath.

'Why would I do that?' Whitney said.

'I want to drop out of university to go travelling.'

Whitney's mouth fell open. She couldn't be serious.

'After all the hard work you've put in you suddenly want to give everything up. Why? Isn't it a waste?' She willed herself to remain calm. Going off on one wasn't going to get her anywhere.

'I want to go travelling with a friend to Australia.'

'Why don't you wait until you've finished your course? Surely that would be the sensible thing to do.'

'I don't want to. I'm fed up of being at uni.' She paused and stared at Whitney, defiance in her eyes. 'But that doesn't mean I won't go back. I'm looking into putting my course on hold for a couple of years.'

'Did George put you up to this?' she said, unable to hold back her frustration.

'No, she didn't. I went to her for advice.'

'And you didn't speak to me because I didn't go to university and wouldn't understand what you're talking about?' she said, immediately regretting how petty she sounded.

'No, it's not like that. You know I can tell you anything,' Tiffany said.

'Apart from this. Instead you went to George.'

'I spoke to George because she works at the university and could explain to me about dropping out. I wanted to know if it would be possible, and whether I could come back.'

'Are you telling me she thought it was fine for you to forget all the hard work you've put in and to go off travelling around the world?'

'That wasn't how it was. She didn't encourage me.'

'Did she discourage you?' Whitney challenged.

'No. She wanted me to speak to you about it,' Tiffany said.

'She should've told me herself, she's meant to be my friend,' Whitney said.

'I asked her not to. I wanted to sort it out for myself first,' Tiffany said.

'Did George think you should drop out?'

If she found out her so-called friend had encouraged Tiffany she'd have more than a few words to say about it.

'She didn't give me her opinion, she just told me to think about it before I made a firm decision. She said I needed to enquire if I could come back and, if so, whether I'd have to repeat the whole year.'

'What did they say?'

'I haven't sorted it out with them, yet. I'm only telling you now because you knew something was going on. I don't want you to take it out on George because it's not her fault.'

No. It was Whitney's fault for not being smart enough for her daughter to come to her first. The thought stung. It was followed by an even more painful thought. Tiffany was going to drop out of university and leave her.

'Are you mad?' Tiffany said.

'I can't stop you from doing whatever you want. But I'm disappointed you didn't speak to me about going. Are you going with a boy?'

'No, with Phoebe, a friend from uni. You've met her before. We want to work our way around Australia and maybe go to New Zealand.'

'What if the university won't let you go back to complete your studies?'

'If I can't do it here, I'm sure there'll be another place I could go to. I've got good grades.'

'But you like Lenchester. Why would you want to go somewhere else?'

'I'd rather return here if possible, and I'm sure they'll let me. I just have to sort it out.'

'What if they say no?' Whitney persisted.

'I'll let you know what they say before I make a final decision.'

Whitney wasn't convinced about that. She suspected the decision had already been made. Tiffany was very much like her. Stubborn.

'If you do go, when are you thinking of leaving?'

'In a month, before the flights get even more expensive.'

A month? The words echoed between them.

'That means you won't be here for Christmas. What about Granny and Uncle Rob?' Guilt flooded through her. Emotional blackmail hadn't been her intention, especially as a pained expression shot across Tiffany's face.

'We can have an early Christmas celebration before I go.'

'Why don't you wait until the New Year?' Whitney suggested.

'If we want to get work, now is the best time to go, as they're heading into summer and need people to work in bars and restaurants.'

'What about flights, and accommodation? You might not find a job straight away.'

'I've got some money saved and George is giving me some, as a twenty-first birthday present.'

What the…

'George is paying? I don't believe it,' she snapped.

'She was going to give me money for my birthday, anyway. Why does it matter?'

Whitney sucked in a breath. She didn't want to alienate Tiffany, and if she didn't stop, she'd end up doing so.

'If you've made your mind up, then you have my

support. I'll miss you, but we can keep in touch online. It's easy nowadays.'

'Thanks, Mum,' Tiffany said, as she ran around to where Whitney was sitting and flung her arms around her, giving a squeeze.

Tears formed in Whitney's eyes, but she blinked them away. She couldn't let Tiffany see she was upset. She'd miss her hugely. It was only going to be for a couple of years, but what if she met someone and decided to stay there permanently? Whitney forced those thoughts to the back of her mind, because she'd lose the plot if she allowed them to take over.

'I'll be happier once you've found out whether you can return to university when you get back.'

'I'll see about it tomorrow, promise,' Tiffany said.

They both sat in silence, engrossed in their thoughts.

'I'm going out with Phoebe tonight. You don't mind, do you?' Tiffany asked.

'No, of course not. You do what you want, I've lots to be getting on with,' Whitney said.

Tiffany left the house, and Whitney wasn't far behind. She wanted to see George. They had a lot to discuss.

Chapter Fifteen

George finished her meal, washed up, and spread her work out on the kitchen table. Ross had phoned earlier, and they'd agreed not to see each other until the weekend as he was busy working on a commission. She didn't mind, as she'd got plenty to do. A set of assignments from the new first years had just come in and she wanted to get started on marking.

A loud knock on the door made her start. She glanced at her watch. It was only seven-thirty. Perhaps Ross had decided to come over and surprise her. Except why would he? He'd never done so before.

She opened the door, to be greeted by Whitney standing on the doorstep, hands on hips, and eyes blazing.

'What are you doing here?'

'I think you already know that,' Whitney growled.

'It's about Tiffany, isn't it?' she said flatly, opening the door fully and ushering her in. She wasn't prepared to discuss it on the doorstep for her neighbours to see and hear.

'You bet your life it is.' Whitney scowled and stomped past her.

'Let's go into the kitchen and I'll get us a drink.'

George took out a bottle of wine from the fridge and poured them both a glass. She handed one to Whitney, who was standing only a couple of feet from her.

'Why didn't you tell me?' Whitney said, after taking a large swallow.

Her facial expression belied the aggression in her voice. She was hurting and George was more than partly responsible.

'Tiffany asked me not to. Let's sit down.'

Whitney pulled out a chair from the table and George sat opposite.

'I don't care. You should have told me,' Whitney said.

'Yes, but if someone confides in me, I don't spread it around. That's what keeping something confidential is all about.' It made sense to her, and she'd do the same again if the situation arose.

'Not when it's my daughter.'

'I understand that you're upset, but she came to me for advice and that's what I gave.'

'Call it advice when you persuaded her to drop out of university and go travelling? That's hardly responsible, is it?' Whitney said.

'She wanted advice on how to navigate university protocols, which can be confusing if you're not familiar with them.'

'What if she can't get back in? What if no university will take her? What if she goes to Australia and doesn't ever come back? What if…' She paused and leaned on the table, her head in her hands.

'You've got to let her live her own life,' George said,

gently. 'She'll always be there for you, and you for her, but you have to let her follow her own path.'

'Since when have you been so insightful when it comes to human emotions?' Whitney asked, sitting up and staring at George.

'I'm not being insightful, just saying it how it is. Be supportive of her.'

Unlike her parents, especially her father, who seemed to take great delight in belittling all of her accomplishments. But many years ago, she'd learnt not to let it affect her.

'Will the university let her back in, do you think?' Whitney asked.

'I don't see why not. She's an excellent student and has good grades. If she was in my department, I would certainly allow her to,' George said.

'I'm going to miss her,' Whitney said.

'So will I,' George admitted.

'I still don't like the fact she went to you before coming to me. I thought we had such a good relationship and that she could tell me anything.'

'It wasn't easy for me,' George said.

'How do you work that one out? You weren't the one being deceived,' Whitney said, frowning.

'No, but I was put in the difficult position of having to keep something from you. I disliked it intensely.'

Did Whitney understand? She wasn't sure.

'Is this why things have been strained between us recently?' Whitney asked.

'Yes. I thought it best to keep out of the way, in case I accidentally said something I shouldn't.'

'You do know the first rule of friendship is loyalty?' Whitney said.

'Tiffany's my friend, as well.'

'No, she's my daughter. Yes, you saved her life and we'll always be grateful for that. But that's even more reason why you should've let me know her plans.'

No. Whitney didn't get it.

'Well, that wasn't the decision I made, and we can't change that. I'm sorry. If you no longer wish me to work with you because of it then I understand.'

'Did I say we weren't going to continue working together?' Whitney asked.

'No, but I can tell how angry you are with me, and that's not going to help. If we're to return to having a good working relationship, I'd rather we stayed separate until we can get over this.'

'Of course I don't want you to stop working with us. But you must understand how it's affected me. The fact my daughter felt she couldn't confide in me and instead spoke to you is very hurtful.'

Did she understand? She tried to, but empathy wasn't her strong point.

'I hear what you're saying, but you have to be mindful of Tiffany's reasoning. It was because she's so close to you, and doesn't want to hurt you, that made her come to me first. If she didn't love you so much, she would've told you straightaway. It's a testament to her depth of feeling towards you that she chose to speak to me, as an objective outsider. She wanted to be completely sure of her decision before telling you, or it would've caused you unnecessary pain.'

Whitney stared at her, tears in her eyes. George took the box of tissues from the side and put them in front of her.

'Thanks,' Whitney said, sniffing.

'Lots of young people go travelling. She'll have a great time and come back a better person. She's your daughter and, like you, she's smart. She's going to do well in life.'

'What if she meets someone over there and doesn't want to come back?' Whitney said.

'Then you'll go over to visit. You could even relocate there yourself.'

'I can hardly do that, with Mum and Rob here,' Whitney said.

She could have kicked herself for being so insensitive. Whitney couldn't up sticks and follow Tiffany around the world, when she had all her other responsibilities. Not to mention her job.

'I'm sorry. I hadn't thought it through.'

'Tiffany told me that you were going to help fund her trip.' Whitney narrowed her eyes.

George stared at her. Had she done something else wrong? She'd offered because she thought it would be a good idea to know that Tiffany would have enough money when travelling.

'A birthday present.'

'You should have run that past me first,' Whitney said.

'Why? She's an adult. I think you're being unreasonable. Surely you'd rather she had enough money when she went and know that she won't be staying in any rough places.'

'Of course, but I would have liked to have been consulted. It's very kind of you to help and I'll be able to give her some money, too. Although I don't have much spare cash at the moment.'

'Between us, she'll be just fine,' George said. 'Plus, she's got some money saved. It won't take her long to find a job. She's extremely personable.'

'Some people would argue that if she wants to go travelling, she should fund it herself.'

'That was her original plan. She didn't intend to come to either of us for money. If we want to assist, then it's our prerogative,' George said.

'I suppose you're right,' Whitney said.

'All I want is what's best for Tiffany. She's very special to me,' George said.

'You are to us, too. I'm sorry for having a go at you, but you have to understand these past few days have been weird. I've not known what's been going on with you. I thought it was something I'd done. Then I find out about Tiffany not confiding in me. It all mounted up.'

'At least now it's out in the open, we can move on. Especially as we have more important things to focus on. The murders,' George said.

'Nothing is as important as Tiffany, but I understand what you mean,' Whitney said.

'I thought you were getting somewhere with Harold Skinner's son.'

'So did I, but it didn't work out.'

'Damn,' George said.

'We've got nothing to connect the new murders with the original murders, other than the method. There's no connection between victims,' Whitney said.

'I know I always say this, but we need more bodies. As that will give us the most chance of linking the murders,' George said.

'Not an ideal way to operate,' Whitney said.

'Agreed.'

'Are you coming in tomorrow?' Whitney asked.

'I've got meetings and lectures, and I doubt I'll be able to get away. Keep me up-to-date with what's going on.'

'I'd better be going,' Whitney said, as she finished her glass of wine.

'Would you like another drink?' George offered.

'No thanks. I've already had one with my dinner, any more will put me over the limit.'

George stood on the doorstep and watched Whitney drive away. Although they'd discussed their problems, she could still sense the tension between them. Hopefully that would improve as time went on. The fact Whitney didn't want to exclude her from the investigation was a wise decision, because together they made a formidable pair, and that was what the current murders needed.

Chapter Sixteen

Whitney pulled up outside the large, red-brick Edwardian house, and slammed on the brakes. A third victim, Pamela Whitehouse, had been found in Woodford, a village on the outskirts of the city. She'd driven there with Matt immediately after getting the news. They walked up the circular drive to the front door where there stood a uniformed officer, and signed the log.

'Where's the body?'

'In the bedroom,' the officer replied.

'Who found her?'

'The son. He's inside with PC Timms.'

'Matt, go and find the son, and speak to him. I'm going upstairs to the crime scene. I'll be down shortly.'

Whitney reached the top of the stairs and was greeted by Claire pulling on her white coveralls. She smiled to herself as she caught a glimpse of the pathologist's bright purple trousers and turquoise shirt. One day she'd ask her where she shopped.

'Good morning, Claire.'

'I haven't got in there yet, so you'll have to stay here. I'll call you when you can come in.'

'No problem. I'm assuming it's the same scenario as the others?' she said.

'We don't assume anything,' Claire said.

'Okay, let's say it's most likely, based on what we've been told.'

'Where's your other half?'

'Matt's downstairs with the victim's son.'

'I meant George.'

Whitney frowned. 'She's not here. Why do you ask? We're not always together.'

'Is there something going on between you?'

'Why?' What the heck was going on? Claire rarely spoke about anything personal.

'It was obvious by the tension between the two of you when you came to the morgue the other day.'

'We have some issues that we're trying to sort out. We're getting there.'

'What issues?' Claire stared at her, hands on her hips.

'Tiffany wants to drop out of university, to go travelling. She said she'll go back to studying later on, but who knows. She went to see George instead of me to discuss it.'

'Why wouldn't she speak to George, as she works at the university? She's the perfect person to ask.'

Whitney pursed her lips. 'Don't you start. *I'm* the perfect person to ask as I'm her *mother*. No one else. We've never had secrets in the past.'

'But you can't be objective in the same way as George,' Claire said.

'It doesn't need objectivity.'

'Now you're being ridiculous.' Claire rolled her eyes.

'I don't wish to discuss this further. Everyone is ganging

up on me. Tiffany's my daughter and she should have spoken to me first, and then we could have approached George together. End of story.'

'How old are you?' Claire said, shaking her head. '"*Everyone's ganging up on me*". You sound like a teenager. Pull yourself together. You're a grown woman, with a responsible job, so I suggest you act like it.'

Whitney's fists clenched by her side. She could swing for Claire. What the hell did she know? She didn't have children. Then again…

She dragged in a long, calming, breath.

Was Claire speaking the truth? Did she sound childish?

'Maybe you're right. It's just as far as Tiffany's concerned, it's hard for me to be objective,' she admitted.

'Glad you see it my way. Anyway, I can't stand here talking all day. I've got a job to do.'

She gave a wry grin at the way Claire ended their conversation.

'Can I come in yet?' she called after five minutes. All she'd been able to see from the doorway was the body on the bed.

'Yes, but keep away from where I'm taking photographs.'

The room was large and rectangular, decorated very luxuriously in grey and gold, with a huge glass droplet chandelier hanging from the middle of the ceiling. There was a long grey sofa situated at the bottom of the bed complete with grey and gold striped cushions. Modern artwork adorned the walls, some of it abstract.

'It would be nice to afford something so fancy,' she said.

'It's a bit too blingy for me,' Claire said.

Whitney stared at her open-mouthed. How could

Claire, with all her outlandish clothes and jewellery, think that?

'Each to their own. What's your bedroom like?'

'Brown and cream. Very plain,' Claire said.

'From what you've seen so far, is it the same as the previous two deaths?'

Whitney stepped closer to the bed and scrutinised the gagged victim who looked to be in her fifties. She was wearing a green silk nightshirt and matching shorts, her hands and feet bound. Her long dark curly hair was splayed across the pillows. A pink scarf tied around her neck.

'It certainly appears that way,' Claire said.

'Any signs of a struggle?'

'I'll let you know later. There is a rip in her top, but I need to investigate further.'

'I'm going to speak to the son. I'll be in touch later for your preliminary findings.'

Whitney left the room and pulled out her mobile to call George.

'We have a third victim,' she said when George answered. 'I'm at the scene now. We would like your insight, can you come over?' Whitney was surprised at how formal her voice sounded. She clearly hadn't got over their problems.

'Not until this afternoon,' George replied.

'I'm going to interview the son who found her, and then I've got to go back to the station. I'll come back later and meet you here. Once SOCO have left, we can have a look around together. I'll text you the address.'

She ended the call and went downstairs to the kitchen where she found Matt with a man in his twenties, with short blond spiked hair, sitting at the table.

'I'm Detective Chief Inspector Walker,' she said, walking over to them.

'This is Sean Whitehouse, Pamela's son,' Matt said.

'I'm very sorry for your loss. Are you up to answering some questions?' she asked.

The guy sat there, his hands tightly wrapped around the mug in front of him. His face was ashen. He stared at her with his piercing blue eyes.

'I think so,' he said, softly.

'Matt, please could you check everything is under control outside?'

'Yes, guv.'

'I'd like to go through everything that happened when you found your mother this morning,' she said to Sean after Matt had left.

'I called in to see her on my way to work, because she was going to sort out some old photographs for me. It was for a montage I'm doing at work.'

'What do you do?' Whitney asked.

'I'm a graphic designer. I was putting together a proposal for an advertising campaign for a client.'

'How did you get into the house?'

'I have a key.'

'Was the door locked when you arrived?' she asked.

'Yes.'

'What did you do once you were inside?'

'I called out, but there was no answer. I came to see if she was in here, but she wasn't. Then I went into the living room and saw the patio door was open.' He paused.

'Then?'

'I thought maybe she'd gone into the garden, so I went to check, but she wasn't there either.'

Damn. If the offender had entered the house through those doors, Sean had probably compromised the evidence. They'd need to take his fingerprints and footprints.

'Where did you go then?' she asked, prompting him.

'I wondered if she was still in bed, even though it was unlikely because she always got up early, no matter what day of the week, unless she was unwell. I went upstairs. Her bedroom door was open, and I walked in. I found her lying there. She…' His voice cracked. 'Sorry.'

'Please don't apologise, you've had an awful shock. What did you do then?' she asked, gently.

'I phoned the emergency services.'

'Did you touch your mother's body?'

'No. The man who answered my call told me not to.'

'Do you have any other family?'

'My father died eighteen months ago, and since then it's just been the two of us. I'm an only child. They adopted me because they couldn't have their own children.'

'Is there anyone we can contact to be with you?'

'My partner's at work. We work together. He's expecting me, but I can't face going in.'

'Would you like us to call him for you?' Whitney asked.

'I'll text him, and then drive home,' Sean said. 'Do you need me to stay here?'

'We'll need to take your fingerprints and footprints, especially as you went through the door the intruder may have used. When was the last time you saw your mother?'

'Monday, we met for lunch.'

'Did she mention seeing any unfamiliar people hanging around, or had anything strange happened to her recently?'

'No. She'd only just been getting back into socialising. After my father died, she didn't do anything for nine months. She'd started taking part in different clubs and activities.'

'Which clubs?'

'She enjoyed gardening and was part of a local gardening club which met once a week. She also played bridge twice a week and had started going to art appreciation classes with a friend. She'd begun collecting art, too.'

Art? This was becoming a recurring theme. She glanced at the walls of the kitchen but there wasn't anything apart from a calendar.

'How recently?'

'In the last three or four months,'

'Do you know where these paintings are?'

'I'm not sure. Maybe in the lounge.'

'How many paintings had she bought recently?'

'Quite a few. I'm not sure exactly, maybe ten.'

'Did she show them all to you?'

'Some of them,' he said.

'Do you know where she bought them from?'

'Sorry, no. She visited so many galleries, and I've no idea which ones she bought from.'

She'd take a look later.

'Can you think of anyone who would want to harm your mother?'

'Absolutely not. Everyone liked her.'

'Did she have any help in the house? A cleaner, or gardener?'

'She has a cleaner who comes in three times a week.'

'Three times? That's a lot for someone living on their own,' Whitney said.

'She's more like a housekeeper. She also helps Mother in the garden and does her food shopping.'

'Do you have her details?'

'Yes, I have a phone number. Her name is Lynne and she comes in Tuesday, Thursday, and Saturday.'

Whitney pulled out her notebook. 'Please could you write down her number?' She passed the notebook to him.

The door opened and Colin and Jenny from SOCO walked in. Whitney introduced them to Sean and left them to take their samples. She went outside and found Matt with the uniformed officer.

'We need to go to the station. George is meeting me here this afternoon and I'll have another look around then to see if there's anything that might help us.'

'Okay, guv,' Matt said.

Once they'd returned to the incident room, she called everyone to attention.

'We have a third victim. Pamela Whitehouse.' She wrote the name on the board. 'She's also wealthy, or seems to be, as she lived alone in a large house. She's in her fifties. Her name doesn't begin with a C, so we can rule that one out.' She crossed that off the board. 'Our main connections between the three victims are: they lived on their own, were wealthy enough to have staff, and they collected art. Someone is picking off rich women. George should have a better profile for us later. In the meantime, I want CCTV footage checked around the latest area over the last twenty-four hours. Matt, I'd like you to contact the cleaner. Find out what she knows and if there was anything suspicious going on. Take Sue with you.'

'Yes, guv,' he said.

'We know this latest victim played bridge, went to art appreciation classes, and gardening club. Ellie, look into the other victims and see if there's any connection. Maybe they'd attended the same clubs. It's unlikely the victims were chosen randomly. A great deal of planning is involved in these attacks. Also, check if there's any link between the cleaners who worked at each house. Our first two victims did volunteer work. See if Pamela Whitehouse did, and, if so, whether they all volunteered at the same places.'

'Yes, guv,' Ellie said.

'The rest of you, I want background checks on the victim. Friends, family, finances. You know the drill. Once Dr Cavendish is here, we'll know more. She's always said we needed more than two bodies to give us a better picture of what's going on. Well, now she's got it.'

Chapter Seventeen

George pulled up outside the house of the latest victim. She'd arrived a little early and there was no sign of anyone. If it wasn't for the cordon across the gate, no one would have known it was a crime scene. She hoped the Tiffany issue was over and her relationship with Whitney was on its way back to normal. Maybe she should have gone to collect Whitney from the station.

After a few minutes, Whitney pulled up in her old Ford. They both got out of their cars, smiled, and said hello, but it seemed a little stilted.

'Let's go in. It looks like no one else is here,' Whitney said. They ducked under the tape and walked up to the front door. 'Another lovely house. Our murderer's certainly going after the rich and more mature woman.'

'Yes, he does seem to be seeking them out.'

'I've got Ellie looking into any links between the three, other than the money and being on their own. They might have all belonged to a particular club. Somewhere he can target them. Collecting art seems to be a common thread.'

'Is this victim also a collector?' George said, her curiosity piqued.

'According to her son, she'd recently started. He wasn't sure where her new pieces were. We'll see what we can find when we're looking through.'

'Interesting.' George nodded.

'I believe the intruder came in through the patio doors in the lounge. Let's start in there,' Whitney said.

They walked into the large square room, with high ceilings, ornate ceiling roses, and coving. The furniture was very traditional; brown leather sofas with rolled arms, and three, high-backed armchairs. A large fireplace with a black surround was in the centre of the far wall. On the walls were a number of paintings, mainly country scenes. George took a look.

'Judging by the fine layer of dust on these frames, these aren't new acquisitions.'

'She has a cleaner,' Whitney said.

'Not all cleaners are made equal,' George quipped.

'I wouldn't know.'

Deciding to ignore Whitney's barbed comment, George wandered over to take a look at the built-in mahogany bookcases which lined one of the walls. 'An eclectic mix of books. I wonder if anyone read them or whether they were just for show?'

'This room is very different from the bedroom,' Whitney said.

'In what way?'

'The bedroom is luxurious and modern, whereas this is very traditional.'

They walked over to the patio doors which still showed signs of powder from where SOCO had been dusting for prints. The doors were closed but Whitney opened them and they stepped outside into the garden.

'A typical country-style garden,' George said.

'Do you like it?' Whitney asked.

'Yes, much more than the one belonging to Celia Churchill, which was too manicured. This is in keeping with the house.'

'Let's go upstairs to her bedroom, the actual crime scene,' Whitney suggested.

Once they'd reached the top of the stairs, George followed Whitney into the bedroom. She glanced around. 'I see what you mean, it's totally different from the rest of the house. It looks newly decorated,' George said.

'Maybe she was going to decorate the whole house and started here,' Whitney said.

'Or wanted something totally different in the bedroom after her husband died.' She scanned the room and noticed the large abstract painting on the wall. She walked over to it. 'That's interesting.'

'What is?' Whitney said, walking over and standing beside her.

'This painting is very similar in style to one in Cassandra Billington's house.' She leaned in and took a look at the small signature in the bottom right corner. 'The signature is the same. Is it okay if I take it off the wall, to look at the back?'

'Go for it,' Whitney said.

George lifted the painting so the wire didn't get caught on the picture hook. It was large and heavy. She rested it on the floor and turned it around. On the back was a label. 'It came from Pictura Art Gallery and is called *Cows in a Field*. There's a short biography of the artist. Drury Wilde. He painted it in 2018. I know the gallery, it's in Lenchester. I think we should go back to Celia Churchill's house and check who painted her abstract paintings.'

'It doesn't look like cows in a field to me,' Whitney said, getting up close and frowning.

'That's what abstract art is all about. We're looking at the artist's interpretation of what he's seen.'

'We should also go back to the Billington house, to take another look at Cassandra's painting.'

While Whitney was on the phone making arrangements for them to be let into Celia Churchill's house, George leaned the picture against the wall and continued looking around the room. There was another modern painting, but not by the same artist. She took it down to check, but it came from a different gallery, so she put it back.

'Right, let's go,' Whitney said as she finished on the phone. 'Ellie's going to contact Sandy, as she's got a key, and arrange for her to meet us. Shall we leave my car at the station and go in yours, as we'll be going right past?'

'Yes, that's a good idea,' George agreed.

'Do you have to get back to work, or can you stay with me for the rest of the day?' Whitney asked.

'I'm free all afternoon,' she said.

They left the house and drove to the station. Whitney dropped off her car and George waited for her.

'I've just heard from Ellie. Sandy's there now. She's also arranged for an officer to meet us at the Billington house with a key. We'll go there second.'

'What did Claire tell you about the latest victim?' George asked as they were on their way.

'Not a lot. You know Claire, she wouldn't commit to anything but it was obviously the same murderer. She'll let us have her report soon. She did surprise me by getting personal about you and me.'

'What did she say?' George asked.

'She wondered what was going on between us. She'd noticed the strain in our relationship.'

George's heart sank. She didn't want to dredge everything up again so soon, especially as they'd been getting along fairly well.

'Oh, I see.'

'Don't you want to know what she said?' Whitney asked. 'No, of course you don't,' she added before George had time to answer.

'I don't envisage anything Claire said would be beneficial. We've discussed everything and overcome our differences.'

'Actually, what she said did make sense. At least, to me. She made me realise that perhaps I did get a little carried away by everything, and for that I'm sorry. I know you were put in a difficult position, and I respect your decision to keep Tiffany's confidence.'

George glanced quickly at Whitney who was staring directly in front of her, out of the window. Was she expected to apologise in return? She was sorry Whitney had been upset, but not for what she'd done. If the situation arose again, she'd do exactly the same.

'I'm glad it's all over,' she said.

'Please don't tell Tiffany I had a go at you, because she'd be really upset if she knew.'

'I won't say a word. The main thing is she's working it all out, and that you're on board,' George said.

'You're right. I don't want to fall out with her, and I don't want to fall out with you, either. I'm going to behave myself from now on.'

George turned to look at Whitney who was grinning. 'I'll believe that when I see it.'

Once they'd arrived at Celia Churchill's house they

drove up the long drive and parked outside. Whitney rang the bell and Sandy answered.

'Thanks for meeting us here,' Whitney said.

'No problem. I'd already planned to be here to get things ready for Natasha, who'll be arriving tomorrow. She wants to spend some time going through her mother's belongings.'

'We'd like to take another look at the paintings in the drawing room. Has anything been changed?' Whitney asked.

'Nothing's been touched.'

Once they were in the drawing room, George made a beeline for the painting she'd seen before. It was a mass of dark colours, with shades of grey randomly scattered. She looked at the signature.

'Yes, this is by the same artist as the last one. I'll take it off the wall and see what's on the back.' On the back was a Pictura Art Gallery label. 'It came from the same place. This one is called *Night Terrors*. Now we know two of the victims went to the same gallery and bought paintings by Drury Wilde.'

'Coincidence?' Whitney asked.

'You know my view on coincidences. There's no such thing. But that doesn't make the link conclusive. They were both affluent women, and it's hardly surprising they would've shopped at the gallery, as their art is expensive,' George said.

'Do you know this place?' Whitney asked.

'I've been once to an exhibition, about eighteen months ago. I haven't ever bought anything from there,' George said.

'Right, let's go to Cassandra's house and see if her painting also came from the gallery. If it did, then I'd say we're definitely on to something.'

When they arrived at the Billington residence, an officer was waiting outside with the key. They let themselves in and headed for the kitchen. George looked at the signature on the painting and saw it was the same. She removed it from the wall.

'Yes, this is by Wilde and is from Pictura. It's called *Spring Fling*.'

'Don't tell me, that's because of all the colour,' Whitney said.

'If that's your interpretation.'

'At least now we're getting somewhere. Let's go to the gallery now,' Whitney said.

George looked at her watch. It was gone four. 'We'd better check the opening hours, as I suspect they might be closed.' She googled the gallery and found that on Wednesdays it shut at three. 'It's closed until tomorrow morning at ten.'

'Blast,' Whitney said. 'How are you fixed? Can you come with me in the morning? I could do with your art knowledge.'

'Yes, I can. Would you like me to pick you up from the station or shall I meet you there?' she asked.

'Up to you. We don't have to decide this minute, as I do have to get back to the station to collect my car. Or were you planning on leaving me here?' Whitney said.

'I know that. I was just asking the question,' George said, frowning.

'I was joking. Why don't you meet me at the station at ten? It will give the gallery time to open up.'

'Okay. It also gives me the chance to go into work first and be seen.'

'You're not having more trouble are you? I thought that was all done and dusted,' Whitney said.

'No, it's fine. But being seen will stop people from complaining about me.'

'It's ridiculous,' Whitney said. 'They want your research, which is based on what you do with us, and you're doing a good job. I can't believe you're still having issues.'

'Just as I think it's sorted someone else comes along and makes a comment,' George admitted.

'Since when have you been bothered by that?' Whitney frowned.

'Normally I wouldn't be. But the trouble is, we're dealing with all these high-profile cases, and people I work with assume I'm spending all my time with you. I seem to be the centre of attention, now. I wasn't before.'

'If you ask me, they're jealous,' Whitney said.

'I don't want to talk about it. Usually I put it to the back of my mind and get on with my job.'

'Do you have much to do with the guy who took the job you went for and didn't get?' Whitney asked.

'Why bring him up?' George asked.

'Just curious. You never mention him. I wondered how you got on together.'

'I have very little to do with him. In my opinion, his research output is minimal and nothing he's produced is groundbreaking. As I've just said, I don't wish to discuss him.'

'Has he ever asked you about working with me?' Whitney asked.

'Are you deliberately being obtuse?' George let out a frustrated sigh. 'When he first arrived he was interested, and read my papers, but since then he hasn't said anything so I don't think he's bothered. And that really is the last thing I'm going to say on the matter. Understand?' She locked eyes with Whitney.

'Got it. Do we know anything about this painter?'

'According to the label on the back of the paintings, he originates from Hampshire. The rest we can look up. Do we need to take the paintings in as evidence?' George asked.

'Yes, so SOCO can dust for fingerprints. We'll need the other two. Do you have time to collect them from the other houses?'

'Yes,' George said.

After collecting them, they returned to the incident room.

'Listen up, everyone,' Whitney said. 'We've found ourselves a link between the three victims. They all have paintings by Drury Wilde which were bought from Pictura Art Gallery. Ellie, I'd like you to research into the painter and the gallery. Frank, I want you to check out CCTV footage near Pamela Whitehouse's residence, and the rest of you continue with background checks on her. George and I will go to the gallery first thing in the morning to interview the owner. Doug, can you arrange to put these paintings in the evidence room and get SOCO to dust for prints, in case they didn't before?'

'Yes, guv,' he said.

She headed over to the board and George followed. On there she wrote the name of the artist and the gallery.

'Finally, we're getting somewhere,' Whitney said.

'They might have all been to an exhibition at the gallery and the murderer was also there. He checked them out and made his move,' George suggested.

'Do we know whether there's been an exhibition of Wilde's work recently?'

'I've no idea, I don't follow this gallery's exhibitions,' George said.

'But I thought you said you went to an exhibition there,' Whitney said.

'I've only been to one.'

'Okay, never mind,' Whitney said. 'We'll just wait till tomorrow and then we'll find out.'

Chapter Eighteen

'I thought it was meant to open at ten,' Whitney said as she saw the closed sign on the gallery door. All they needed was for it not to be open today.

'That's what it said on their web page,' George said.

Whitney peered through the window and saw a woman at the back staring at a painting on the wall. She knocked hard on the door and the woman visibly started. She made some sort of gesture, implying they weren't open. Whitney took out her warrant card and held it against the glass for her to see. The woman came closer and looked at the warrant card, her brow furrowed.

She was dressed elegantly in a sky-blue chiffon top and a pair of wide-legged, dark brown, crepe trousers. She had on a gold necklace and some pearl drop earrings.

They waited while she unlocked the door, then walked in closing it behind them.

'Good morning. I'm Detective Chief Inspector Walker and this is Dr Cavendish.'

'I'm Serena Hastings. I own this gallery.'

'We'd like to speak to you about the painter Drury Wilde,' Whitney said.

'What's happened? Is he okay?' she exclaimed.

'How well do you know him?'

'Quite well, I suppose. We had an exhibition for him not long ago, and we still have some of his art for sale.'

'We believe several of his paintings might be connected to a series of murders which took place in the area,' Whitney said.

Serena Hasting's eyes widened. 'Murders? What murders?'

'You may have seen them on the news recently,' Whitney said.

'I try not to watch the news or read the paper as I don't like to hear about anything negative. It's too depressing.'

Whitney glanced at George trying to read what she was thinking. Was Serena Hastings being genuine, or deliberately vague?

'Do you know Celia Churchill, Cassandra Billington, and Pamela Whitehouse?'

'Yes, of course. I know them. They're clients of mine.' Colour drained from the woman's face. 'Oh my God.' She took hold of the back of a chair situated near the door. 'Have they been murdered?'

'Is there anywhere we can go to sit down?' Whitney said.

'Yes, I have space out the back.'

Serena locked the front door and then they followed her behind the glass counter and through a door leading to an office. They sat on some low chairs situated around a coffee table.

'Would you like some water?' Whitney asked Serena, who was still pale, and her eyes glassy.

'No, thank you. It was such a shock. I'll be okay. How can I help?'

'All three women had bought Drury Wilde paintings. We'd like to know when.'

'I'll check my records.' Serena went over to a wooden filing cabinet, opened the top drawer, and looked through the files. She then pulled a folder out and opened it. 'Celia bought hers at the exhibition, as did Cassandra. Pamela was at the exhibition but didn't buy hers for another week.'

'When was the exhibition?' Whitney asked.

'Tuesday, the twenty-second of October.'

'Do you have a list of everyone who attended?'

'I have a visitor book. I can get that for you if you like?' Serena said.

'Yes, please.'

She left them to go back into the shop. After a short while she returned, holding a large green leather book. She opened it and passed it to Whitney.

'These are the people who were here. We asked everyone to sign it on their arrival.'

Whitney glanced at the lists of names, there were a couple of pages. Perhaps sixty people in total.

'Did some people not sign in?' Whitney asked.

'That's possible, though I'm sure most did. I always have someone on the door to greet people as they arrive.'

'What can you tell us about Cassandra, Pamela, and Celia?' Whitney asked.

'I've known Celia and Cassandra for quite some time. They're good clients of mine. Pamela's only been coming here recently, so I don't know her so well.'

'Do you have a list of everything they've bought?' Whitney asked.

Serena went back to the filing cabinet and brought over three manila folders. She pulled out a sheet of paper from each. 'These are lists of everything they've bought. I keep separate lists for every client so we can refer back to them. When we have an exhibition we think they'll be interested in, we send them an invitation.'

Whitney took the sheets of paper from her and glanced down at the first one belonging to Celia Churchill.

'Celia was a very good client of yours,' she said, trying to hide her disbelief that someone would spend so much on pieces of art. It was enough to put Tiffany through university for four whole years.

'Yes, she did like her art,' Serena said, a little too smugly for Whitney's liking.

'Why don't you keep your records on computer?' George asked.

'I keep both. Several years ago I lost everything on my computer as it hadn't backed up.'

'May we take these with us?' Whitney asked, holding up the sheets of paper.

'Yes,' Serena said, nodding. 'I can print them again.'

'We believe the link between the murders could be these paintings, or your gallery. What company do you use to deliver them?'

'I have my own delivery driver,' Serena said.

'Full time? Do you have enough work to keep him occupied?' Whitney asked.

'It's a busy gallery. He works for me three days a week. He delivers and hangs the paintings.'

Whitney looked at George and nodded. How easy would it be for the driver to get a good look at the victims' houses?

'So your driver knows exactly who's bought the paintings and is invited into their homes?' Whitney said.

'Yes.'

Her senses went on high alert. Could he be the one?

'What can you tell me about your driver?'

'He's been working for me for three years, and he's totally trustworthy,' Serena said.

'How do you know?' Whitney asked.

'If he wasn't, I'd have found out by now. Someone would have told me if anything had gone missing or if he'd done anything inappropriate. He's always been loyal and hardworking. I can't think that this would be anything to do with him.'

'What's his name?' Whitney asked.

'Rod Kerr.'

'I'd like his details,' she said.

Serena picked up her phone from the desk. 'This is his number,' she said after writing it down on a piece of paper. 'He lives at 26 Rosamund Street.'

'Is today one of his work days?'

'No. He works Monday, Wednesday, and Friday, plus the occasional weekend if someone can't arrange to be there to take delivery during the week.'

'Does he have another job?'

'I think he makes deliveries for somebody else, but I'm not sure. You'll have to ask him.'

'When people buy the paintings, do they ever take them away with them?' George asked.

'Rarely,' Serena said. 'Our service includes delivery and hanging.'

'What dates did you deliver the three paintings in question?' Whitney asked.

'It will be on the records you have. The last column on the right for each piece has a date.'

'What about other deliveries Rod has made?'

Serena went to her computer which was in the centre of the antique desk, situated in the corner of the office.

She printed off some sheets of paper and handed them to Whitney.

'Here are Rod's time sheets for the last two months.'

'If you could think back to the night of the exhibition and the people who were here, did you know all of them?' Whitney asked.

Serena was silent for a few seconds. 'I think so, yes. Most of them. They were all invited. It was a closed exhibition because it was in the evening.'

'Did they show their invites when they came in?' Whitney asked.

'They didn't have to. We had a list of names of people we were expecting.' She paused a moment. 'Having said that, some people did bring partners or friends. So, actually I didn't know everyone.'

'Who was on the door when the guests arrived?'

'One of my staff members. A young girl called Francesca. She was here for the entire evening, and asked everyone to sign the visitor book, as I explained. She also gave them the catalogue of the art on display.'

'Was there anyone you can think of who stood out as acting strange?' Whitney asked.

'No, definitely not.'

'Was the artist here during the exhibition?' George asked.

'Yes, he was. He became a little angry at one point because people kept asking him questions. But you know what artists are like.'

'I don't. Tell me,' Whitney said.

'Some of them can be a bit precious and think they're on a higher plane than the rest of us.'

'Was there an altercation?' George asked.

'No, not at all. It's just I had to intervene and ask people to leave him alone.'

'How many people do you think came to the exhibition?' Whitney asked.

'It was on for three hours from six until nine. People drifted in and out. Maybe we had up to one hundred in total.'

'There are only two pages filled out in the visitor book,' Whitney said, opening it up and showing Serena. 'There aren't a hundred names here.'

'It's possible not everyone signed in. I'll have to speak to Francesca and make sure that doesn't happen again. It was a busy night and I had to keep on top of things. Talking to people, taking sales. I couldn't keep an eye on her all the time,' Serena said, a defensive tone in her voice.

'How many paintings were sold that night?' Whitney asked.

'Six, and we've sold four more since.'

'Would you class the exhibition as successful?' Whitney asked.

'Definitely. He's a popular painter. We were very happy with the turnout, and sales. So was Drury.'

'Thank you very much for your help. If you can think of anything else that might help, please let me know. Here's my card.' Whitney handed over her card and they then left.

'Very illuminating,' George said, once they were back in the car.

'Yes. The art gallery is our link, and the delivery driver a likely suspect.'

'Is there anything of note regarding when our victims took delivery of their paintings?' George asked.

Whitney opened the file and took a look at the sheets relating to the three women and compared them with the driver's time sheet. 'Both Cassandra and Celia took delivery of theirs two days after the exhibition. Pamela's was delivered one day after she bought hers.'

'So that doesn't really tell us much.'

'No. But we do know the driver has been inside all three houses, which would enable him to check out the best place to break in. We need to speak to him. Now.'

Chapter Nineteen

Once they'd returned to the incident room, Whitney went directly to Ellie's desk. She needed her officer to get to work straight away.

'I want you to research into Rod Kerr. He's the delivery driver for Pictura Art Gallery, and he's been in the homes of all three murdered women. He lives on Rosamund Street.'

'Yes, guv.'

Whitney headed over to the board and wrote the name Rod Kerr at the top, with arrows pointing to all three women. 'Are you still free, because we need to go out and interview Kerr,' she asked George, who'd followed her over there.

'I've already told you I'm available for the rest of the day.'

'Right, we'll go now. Frank,' she called out to the older officer who was sitting at his desk. 'Check the CCTV footage for Tuesday, twenty-second October around the art gallery. It's on Favell Street. Look for anything which rings alarm bells. See if there are any cars that were also seen close to the murdered women's houses.'

'Yes, guv,' Frank said.

They left the station and drove to Rosamund Street. In front of the small terraced house was a white van with *Pictura Art Gallery* in signwriting on its sides in black and gold.

'It looks like we're in luck,' Whitney said. 'He's in.'

The door was answered by a man in his forties, of medium height, slim build, and with light brown hair which was thinning on top.

'Rod Kerr?' Whitney asked.

He stared at her. 'Yes. Who are you?'

She held out her warrant card. 'Detective Chief Inspector Walker and Dr Cavendish. We'd like to speak to you.'

'What about?'

'We'd rather talk inside.'

'Has something happened? Is it the wife?'

'No, it's regarding another matter,' Whitney said, not wanting to alarm him in case he decided to do a runner.

He stepped to the side and they walked into the narrow hallway. 'We'll go in the lounge.'

He opened the first door on the right, and they went into a small room which had a sofa and an easy chair focussed around a large television that had been placed on the wall. Everything was neat and tidy, although worn.

Whitney and George sat on the sofa and Kerr on the chair.

'We'd like to ask you about your work for Pictura Art Gallery,' Whitney said.

'All I do is deliver paintings for Mrs Hastings. I don't work in the gallery itself.' He avoided eye contact. What was he hiding? George would soon tell her.

'You recently delivered to Celia Churchill, Cassandra Billington, and Pamela Whitehouse. Do you remember those deliveries?'

He was silent for a moment. 'Yes, I think so. Pennington Grove, Winchester Gardens, and Rochester Avenue.'

'Had you delivered to these houses before?' Whitney asked.

He paled slightly. 'I'd delivered to Mrs Churchill and Mrs Billington, but not the other one.'

'These women are now dead. They've been murdered,' Whitney said.

'I know,' he muttered.

'About all of them?' Whitney asked. Surely he couldn't trip himself up so easily. Details of Pamela's murder had yet to be released.

'No. Just the first two. The wife said you'd be round here accusing me. But I said you wouldn't because I didn't do anything.'

'Your wife was right,' Whitney said.

'You think I did it?' A bead of sweat glistened on his forehead.

'Didn't you think it strange that two people whose houses you'd recently been to were now dead?' Whitney asked.

He looked away again. 'I thought it was a coincidence. I swear I had nothing to do with it.' He shifted in his seat. He couldn't look guiltier if he tried.

'Don't you read the papers, or listen to the news? We asked for people who knew anything to come forward,' Whitney said.

'I don't know anything about their deaths. I delivered paintings to their houses a while ago and not around the time of the murders. I didn't want to get involved. In case you thought I had something to do with it.'

'Yet, here we are. You should've listened to your wife and saved a lot of time by contacting us first,' Whitney said.

'So you could fit me up? I know what happens.' He folded his arms across his chest.

'How did you feel when you found out about the deaths?' Whitney asked, taking a different approach. Upsetting him wouldn't get them very far as he'd only clam up.

'I was shocked. But I didn't know them well, all I'd done was hang pictures for them.'

'How much time did you spend at their houses?'

'Not long.'

'What were you doing on the eleventh, fifteenth, and twentieth of November between the hours of midnight and four in the morning?' Whitney asked.

'On the eleventh I was here. On the fifteenth we were away visiting the wife's sister in Bournemouth.'

'Can anyone vouch for you?' Whitney asked.

'Yes, I was with my wife the whole time.'

'Where is your wife at the moment?' Whitney asked.

'She's at work,' he replied.

'What time will she be back?'

'She's usually home by six.'

'Where does she work?'

'Fresh Ways supermarket in town.' He strummed his fingers on his knees.

What was he hiding?

'We'll need to speak to her later, to confirm your alibi,' Whitney said.

'That's fine. Because it's true,' he replied.

'I'd like to look in the back of your van,' Whitney said.

'Why?' He tightened his hands into fists and released them several times in succession.

'Are you refusing?' Whitney asked.

'Can I?' He glanced at George and then returned his gaze to Whitney.

'It's your prerogative, but if you do, I'll arrange for a search warrant and things will get a lot worse. We'll have to take you in for questioning.' Whitney wanted to push him into agreeing.

'I suppose I've got no choice, then. I'll get the key.' Within a few seconds, he returned to the lounge. 'Come on,' he said gruffly.

They followed him out onto the street. He unlocked the van, and Whitney pulled on a pair of disposable gloves and opened the driver's door. It was very clean and tidy. No food wrappers or clothes, unlike in her car. She looked in the glove compartment and there was nothing in there other than the logbook. They walked around to the back of the van and she opened the doors. It was empty, other than a large, red, plastic box, which she pulled towards her. Inside there were a number of different sized screwdrivers, three hammers, and a selection of other tools which she couldn't identify. There was also an open packet of long cable ties.

'What do you use these for?' she asked, holding one up.

'I've got them just in case,' he replied.

'In case of what?'

'Just in case,' he said. 'That's my toolbox and I have lots of different things in there. They often come in handy.'

'For hanging pictures?'

'I just have them, that's all,' he said, shifting from one foot to the other.

'I'm taking them with me.' She picked up the packet and dropped it into an evidence bag. She'd have to check with Claire whether they were the same make as the others.

'Are you allowed to do that?' he asked.

'With your permission, which I'm assuming you're giving because, as you told us, you had nothing to do with the murders and so have nothing to hide.'

'Okay,' he muttered.

Whitney closed the van door and they went back into the house.

'We'd like to have a look around,' she said. 'With your permission.'

He shrugged. 'Do what you like, but I'm not letting you out of my sight. I'm not having you planting any evidence.'

'You've been watching too many TV programmes. We're not in the business of planting evidence. I want to have a look around, and you've agreed.'

She went into the kitchen, but there was nothing out of the ordinary there. Upstairs were two bedrooms, one of which had a bed, an empty wardrobe and chest of drawers, and nothing else. The main bedroom was clearly used for Rod and his wife. Whitney opened the drawers, then looked in the wardrobe and under the bed. She could see nothing connected with the murders.

'Thank you for your cooperation,' she said, once they'd returned downstairs.

'It's not me you should be investigating,' Kerr said. 'You should see the artist. The guy who painted the pictures I delivered to those women's houses.'

'Why do you say that?' Whitney asked.

'Because he's weird.'

'When did you meet him?'

'He was at the gallery when I collected the paintings to deliver to Mrs Churchill and Mrs Billington. He gave me instructions on transporting and hanging them. I told him

I'd been doing this work for a long time and no one had ever complained. But he still went on about his art and how precious it was. Have you seen his paintings? I wouldn't want one, even if it was given to me for free. No thank you.'

'There's nothing wrong with him being protective of his paintings,' George said.

'Check him out. I'm telling you, he's weird. He could have done those murders. Not me.'

Whitney glanced at George. She knew where they were heading next. But first they'd go back to the gallery for Wilde's details. She'd rather see Serena in person than phone her, so she couldn't fob them off. For all they knew, Serena and Wilde were in cahoots, so it was best not to alarm them.

'Thank you for your time and your cooperation. We'll be in touch to speak to your wife.'

They left his house and went straight back to the gallery. Serena Hastings was on the phone when they arrived. After she'd finished, Whitney approached her.

'You've come back.'

'We'd like Drury Wilde's address and phone number.'

'Why?' Serena asked.

'Because the dead women all bought his paintings. I take it you have his address?'

'Yes. He lives in the country on a remote farm. I haven't been there myself. I just know from what he's told me.'

'What else can you tell us about him?' Whitney asked.

'Well, like all creatives, he has his idiosyncrasies.'

'What do you mean by that?' Whitney asked.

'Sometimes, he's elated, bubbly, and full of himself, and other times you can barely get a grunt out of him. But, like

I said, creatives can be like that. It's his art my customers love. And if he's a bit strange, then so be it.'

Whitney took his details from her and they left the gallery.

'Now we're getting somewhere,' she said.

'I'm not sure I agree with her view that all creatives are idiosyncratic,' George said. 'Because Ross isn't. He's perfectly normal.'

Whitney smiled to herself. George didn't usually volunteer information about her relationship with Ross. Serena's comment must have got to her.

Chapter Twenty

George and Whitney drove out to the countryside where Drury Wilde lived. They sat in companionable silence for much of the time and George was happy they now seemed to be back on an even keel. There hadn't been any signs of the strain they'd been through recently.

'It's nice out here. Especially on a day like today,' Whitney said.

'Yes. We're lucky with the weather, considering how late it is in the year. Usually it's much greyer and miserable than this. It makes all the difference when the sun is shining.' Even George realised that discussing the weather was unusual for them. But she didn't want to broach the subject of Tiffany unless Whitney mentioned it first, in case she got all uptight again. The weather was a safe topic of conversation.

They drove out of town for about fifteen miles until coming to Blue Bell Farm where there was a small rusty sign saying *Artist in Residence*.

'Let's drive down this track, it looks like the right place,' Whitney suggested.

George was glad they were in her car because the track was bumpy and in need of repair. They drove between the fields, which didn't appear to have been farmed at all recently, and after a mile came to a large dilapidated farm-house. The roof was in dire need of replacing and the garden was overgrown. Did anyone live there? It looked deserted.

'Are you sure this is the place?' George asked.

'It's the address Serena gave me.'

'It hardly looks lived in,' George said.

'I'm sure he must be in there somewhere. Pull up and we'll investigate.'

George knocked on the wooden front door of the farmhouse which at one time she suspected was a racing green colour, but now was dirty and cracked. Paint was peeling from the window frames.

'I don't think he's in,' Whitney said after a few minutes. 'Let's see what else is out here.'

Around the back of the farmhouse was a barn with the door open. As they got close, a man came out wearing a white shirt covered in paint. He had long grey hair tied back and he was tall and skinny. The archetypal starving artist.

'Can I help you?' he said.

Whitney took out her warrant card. 'Detective Chief Inspector Walker. And this is Dr Cavendish. Are you Drury Wilde?'

'I am. What do you want?'

'Serena Hastings gave us your address. We'd like to speak to you about some of your paintings,' Whitney said.

'Why?'

'Is there somewhere we can go and talk rather than standing outside?' Whitney asked.

'Come into my studio.'

They followed him into the large, open-plan barn. In one corner was a small kitchen area, with a wooden table and four old, mismatched, wooden chairs.

'We can sit here,' he said. 'What do you want to know?'

'We're investigating the murder of three women, all of whom bought paintings from the exhibition you had at Pictura Art Gallery,' Whitney said.

'What's that to do with me?'

He had no trace of an accent. Definitely privately educated. Possibly Eton. George had been around enough men who'd been there to recognise the telltale enunciation.

'It's to do with you, because they all bought your paintings,' Whitney said.

'They bought them from the gallery, not me. Take it up with them.'

'Do you just sell your paintings at the gallery or is your work elsewhere?' Whitney asked, clearly ignoring his response.

'I used to sell through a gallery in Rugby, but decided to move and have an exhibition at Pictura.'

'Why was that?' Whitney asked.

'I know Serena's brother, Ralph. We went to school together. He told me about the gallery and mentioned it hadn't been doing very well. To help him out, and be a good friend, I decided to exhibit with her.'

Interesting that Serena implied business was very good. She'd made no mention of it being because of Wilde.

'Has it been successful?' Whitney asked.

'I've certainly been selling more paintings than previously. Possibly because Lenchester's a bigger area than Rugby,' Wilde said, nodding.

'How long have you been with Serena?' Whitney asked.

'Nine months, maybe a little longer. I'm not sure.'

'Do people come here to buy? You have a sign outside,' Whitney said.

Wilde looked at her, an incredulous expression on his face. 'I don't want people here. That sign belonged to the previous tenant. I just haven't bothered to take it down yet.'

'Do you own this house?' Whitney asked.

'I rent it.'

'Through an agency?'

'No. It belongs to the parents of a friend. They moved into a retirement village several years ago, but still kept the farm. They rent out the grazing land separately from the farmhouse.'

George frowned. 'The fields we've just driven through had no animals on them, nor were they being used for crops.'

'Not my issue. I rent the house. Take it up with the owners if you're not happy with how their land is taken care of,' he said.

'Do you own any property yourself?' Whitney said.

'I don't wish to be shackled with a mortgage. I'm quite happy renting.'

'Where did you live before here?' Whitney asked.

'Why is that relevant? I don't see the point in this conversation.' He folded his arms across his chest and scowled at them.

'We're trying to get an idea of your life as an artist. Why don't you tell us a bit more about your work?' Whitney said.

'There's nothing to say. It speaks for itself. You can have a look at the paintings I have here,' he said gruffly. 'But I'm not sure how that's going to help you. In fact, I'm not sure why you came to visit. So what if three of my paintings were owned by people who've been murdered? That doesn't mean I'm involved.'

He hardly seemed bothered by the deaths of the women. What sort of man was he? Rhetorical question. From even the short time she'd been observing him, he was clearly a narcissist.

'Could someone be targeting you, do you think?' Whitney suggested.

'Why? I've got nothing anybody wants.' He shook his head.

'Have you upset anyone recently?' Whitney asked.

He gave a hollow laugh. 'I've upset plenty of people over the years, but not enough to cause them to murder people who've bought my paintings. It's ludicrous. What would they gain by it?'

'Ruin your reputation,' Whitney said.

'Would it? If anything, it might make my work more desirable.' He paused. 'And before you say anything that isn't a motive for me to commit the murders. I'm selling plenty at the moment.'

It could be a motive for the gallery owner, though. Something she'd bring up with Whitney once they'd left.

'We've got to look into every possibility. Did you know any of the victims? Celia Churchill, Cassandra Billington, or Pamela Woodhouse?' Whitney asked.

'No.'

'Did you speak to them at the recent exhibition?'

'I don't know. Lots of people wanted to speak to me. I told Serena it wasn't a good idea for me to be there, but she insisted. She said having the artist on hand makes it even more profitable and I'd sell more paintings.'

'Was that the case?' Whitney asked.

'I sold quite a few on the evening. But it's not something

I wish to repeat. All of those people trying to impose their view on why I painted with this stroke or that stroke, or how much paint I had on my brush to obtain the effects I did. It's all a load of bollocks. I paint how I paint because I like it, and it doesn't have to be analysed to the nth degree.'

Rather a strong reaction from someone who must be used to having his work dissected. Anyone in the art world knew it came with the territory.

'Back to the night in question. I understand from Serena that she had to intervene at one point because you were being rude to guests,' Whitney said.

'I wouldn't call it rude. I might have been a little short with people who asked too many pointed questions.' He shrugged.

'Was it men or women who annoyed you?'

'I can't remember. You'll have to ask Serena.'

'It's not that long ago, how come you can't remember?' Whitney pushed.

'It might not seem a long time to you, but to me it is. Four paintings ago. I judge all time in line with my paintings.'

George would ask Ross if his concept of time was in direct correlation with his sculptures. Although she suspected not, as it was rather pretentious. Something Ross wasn't. Wilde, on the other hand was pretention personified.

'What were you doing in the early hours of the eleventh, fifteenth, and twentieth of November?' Whitney asked.

'I have no idea of exact dates but most likely I was here working,' he said.

'Can anyone vouch for you?' Whitney asked.

'No, I live on my own. Surely, you're not accusing me of having something to do with these murders.'

'We have to investigate all possibilities. That includes you, as all three victims recently purchased your work,' Whitney said.

'I don't know the women and I have no alibis, other than always being here,' he stated.

'Do you recall the Lenchester Strangler from the eighties?' George asked.

'I don't. Why do you ask?'

'Because these murders are copycats of his work. Haven't you seen it on the news or read about it in the papers recently?'

'I don't have a television and don't read the newspapers.'

'How do you find out the news? Internet?' Whitney asked.

'No. I have no desire to know what is going on in the world. I spend most of my time alone. And that's how I like it. Is that an issue?'

'That's your prerogative,' Whitney said. 'The Lenchester Strangler was notorious for strangling women with a pink chiffon scarf.'

'Oh, yes, I do vaguely remember that. I was in my late teens. But, to be honest, it didn't really register as I was too busy enjoying myself at art college.'

'Where did you go?' George asked.

'The Royal College of Art.'

'What have you been doing since then? Have you always painted? Might I have come across your work in the past?' George asked.

He narrowed his eyes. Had she insulted him?

'I lived in Canada for thirty years and only came back a few years ago.'

'What made you return?' George asked.

He averted his gaze. What was he hiding?

'I fell out of love with the country,' he said, dismissively.

'What work did you do over there?' Whitney asked.

'I was a graphic designer for an advertising agency.'

'And you decided to chuck it all in and come back home to paint full time?' Whitney said.

'Something like that,' he muttered.

'Are you married?' Whitney asked.

'Not now.'

'Is your ex-wife in Lenchester?'

'She's in Canada with my daughter and son. Why all these questions? I fail to see how they can be relevant. It's an invasion of my privacy. All you need to know is I'm here now. I painted the paintings the murdered women bought and I've no idea why they were targeted. If you've finished, I've got to get on. Serena is planning another exhibition of my work in a few months and I have to produce a lot more pieces.'

'That will be it for now. We may return to have another word with you,' Whitney said.

'As you wish. See yourselves out.'

He walked back into the main studio area and they left the barn and headed to the car.

'There's certainly a lot going on there, and obviously something happened in Canada that he didn't wish to talk about. I doubt it's anything to do with the murders, though. Odd that he hardly showed any interest at all in the deaths,' Whitney said.

'Agreed. But it did lead me to think that he wasn't involved in them. He genuinely didn't care. Often, guilty people will overdo their concern and their shock. Whereas he blatantly didn't give a damn,' George said.

'We need to go back to the gallery, and Serena Hastings. I want to know more about this brother of hers,' Whitney said.

'My thoughts, exactly,' George said. 'The murders might not help Wilde, because he's selling more than he can actually paint. For Serena, if she can get more people into her gallery buying paintings, and not just his, that's got to be a plus. She might be doing well now, but that wasn't always the case.'

When they reached the gallery, there was a sign on the door saying it was closed for two days and would open again on Saturday.

'I wonder why she's not opening tomorrow? According to her opening hours, she should be. I don't have her mobile number. We'll go back to the station and see what Ellie can find.'

Once they arrived back, Whitney stopped at the young officer's desk. 'Find Serena Hastings' number and contact her. I want her at the station asap.'

'Yes, guv,' Ellie said. 'By the way, the Super's been looking for you. He said for you to see him immediately after you arrived back.'

'Okay, thanks. I'll go now.'

'Do you need me for anything else? George said.

'No, you can go. Are you in tomorrow?' Whitney asked.

'Sorry, not possible, but I can be here on Saturday.'

'First thing Saturday it is. Once we get hold of Serena Hasting's brother, we should have more to work on.'

Chapter Twenty-One

Whitney left the incident room and made her way to Jamieson's office. What did he want? As she got closer, she heard him on the phone. As usual. She waited a few minutes until he'd finished and then knocked on the door and walked in.

'You wanted to see me, sir?' she said.

'Sit down, Walker. Where are we on the case? We've now had three murders, and the Chief Constable is breathing down my neck.'

'We're making progress. The pathologist has confirmed the death is identical to the other two, and that a piece of hair was taken as a trophy. We've also established all three women bought paintings from a gallery in town, by an artist named Drury Wilde. He's a friend of the gallery owner's brother. That's where we're directing our lines of enquiry.'

'Things aren't moving forward fast enough, so step it up. I also wanted to speak to you about the press conference for the third murder. I'll arrange it for tomorrow, because I'm not available for the rest of today and my presence is needed. I don't want you handling it on your own.'

'Of course not, sir,' she said, well aware the only reason he wanted to be seen was to aid his promotion prospects.

'It's much better if we provide a united front. Especially after the field day the media have been having regarding it being a Lenchester Strangler copycat. We need to give them something. Do you have anything else to report?'

'No, sir. You know everything,' she said.

'Right, off you go.' He rested his hand over the mouse and clicked. A clear sign she was being dismissed.

She left his office and returned to the incident room. 'Attention, everyone. We're having a press conference tomorrow which will hopefully bring us more information, and quell the speculation on behalf of the media. We still need to speak to Serena Hastings about her brother, Ralph. Ellie, an update?'

'I've been calling her mobile, but there's no answer.'

'Keep trying. Do you have her address?'

'Yes.'

'Send a uniformed officer around to her house and bring her in. I want to speak to her today.'

'Yes, guv,' Ellie said.

'The rest of you, finish up what you're doing and go home. I want you here bright and early in the morning, when we'll reconvene and go over progress.'

The following afternoon, Whitney left the team working and made her way to the room where the press conference was being held. She was running late. Jamieson wouldn't be pleased. As she approached, she saw Melissa from PR talking with him.

'Sorry I'm late. I got held up on a call,' she said.

Her usual go-to response. He'd never questioned it.

'Okay, let's get started,' he said.

They walked into the packed room, with reporters sitting on chairs, and cameras at the back, their long mics hovering over the crowd. They sat behind a long table.

Melissa pulled the microphone towards her. 'Hello, everyone.' She paused while the room became quiet. 'Detective Superintendent Jamieson is going to give you an update on the recent murders.'

She slid the mic over to him.

'Thank you,' he said. 'Regretfully, we have to report that we now have a third murder victim. We are seeking as much information as we can from the public. We—'

'The Lenchester Strangler, again?' one of the reporters called out, interrupting him.

'I'll hand over to Detective Chief Inspector Walker and she will fill you in on the details,' Jamieson said.

Talk about déjà vu. This happened every time they were in a press conference. Anything tricky he passed on to her, terrified it might blow up in his face at a later date. He'd no doubt disagree, but that was how she saw it.

'We're waiting for the report from the pathologist, but it's likely that the perpetrator is the same as in the other two cases,' she said.

'What is the victim's name?' a voice from the crowd of reporters called out.

'Her name is Pamela Whitehouse, and she lived in Lenchester,' Whitney said.

'Was it the same MO as the others? Was she strangled with a pink chiffon scarf?' the reporter continued.

'Yes, she was. We can confirm we are looking for a

Lenchester Strangler copycat, and would like anyone who has been in and around the Pennington Grove, Winchester Gardens, and Rochester Avenue areas, or who thinks they know anything that might help, to contact us immediately. All information will be treated in confidence,' Whitney said.

'Have you got any leads or lines of inquiry?' someone called out from the back.

'I'm not at liberty to discuss an ongoing investigation, but I can tell you that we are making progress.'

'The previous strangler was never caught. Do you think he has anything to do with this?' the same reporter said.

'We're not excluding anyone from our enquiries.' She wasn't prepared to go down that track. It wasn't public knowledge about Harold Skinner. 'Thank you all for coming in.'

They ended the conference and left the room.

'I don't think that went very well,' Jamieson said as they walked down the corridor together.

'There's not a lot I can tell them at this stage. All we want to know is if anyone has seen anything suspicious. We're not going to tell them about the trophies, and that they were never informed about them in the past. This will do for now.'

They reached the end of the corridor and parted ways. She glanced at her watch. She was going to leave early that evening as she wanted to visit her mother and take her brother Rob.

'I want the phones manned at all times, as we've just had the press conference. The rest of you, I'll see you first thing in the morning,' she said once she arrived back at the incident room.

She left the station and went to collect Rob from the care home he lived in. He was unable to support himself because of his learning difficulties which resulted from being beaten up as a teenager, leaving him with brain damage.

When she walked in to see him, his eyes lit up.

'Hello, Whitney.'

'We're going to visit Mum,' she said.

'But I haven't had my tea.' He stuck out his bottom lip.

'Don't worry about that. We'll get something for you on the way home.'

'A burger?' he asked, his face lighting up.

'If that's what you want,' she said, smiling. 'Go and get your coat and we'll leave.'

After a few minutes, he came back and they drove to their mother's care home. She hoped today was going to be one of her mum's better days, as Rob found it difficult when it wasn't.

'Is Mum in the day room, Angela?' she asked the carer who she'd come to know well, and who was always very patient with the residents.

'Yes. They've just finished their dinner.'

They hurried to find her; Rob two paces in front.

'Hello, Mum,' Rob said, running over and giving their mum a huge hug.

Whitney swallowed a lump in the back of her throat. She loved seeing the two of them together and hated that they had to live separately. But they had no choice. She couldn't provide the care they needed at home.

'Hi, Mum,' Whitney said.

'This is lovely, my two children here to see me. Sit down.' Her mum patted the two empty seats either side of her. 'Tell me what you've been doing today.'

Whitney breathed a sigh of relief. Today was a good day.

'You know what it's like. The usual. Nothing changes,' Whitney said.

'Are you in the middle of another murder case?' her mum asked.

'How did you know that?' She didn't think her mum read the papers. Maybe she'd seen it on the TV news.

'Because that's what you're always involved in. It's what you do.'

'Yes, we do have a case on at the moment.'

'Tell me about it.' Her mum's eyes were alert.

Tears stung Whitney's eyes. Having her mum like this was just like it used to be. How long would it last? She glanced at Rob, not sure whether it was appropriate for him to hear this, despite him being older than her.

'It involves a case from the eighties. Do you remember the Lenchester Strangler?'

Her mother looked thoughtful for a moment. 'Yes, I do. He murdered women with a pink chiffon scarf.'

'Has he come back?' Rob asked.

'Not exactly. He's being copied. Anyway, I don't want to talk about work while I'm here. I want to know how you're getting on.'

She sat back and listened to her mum and brother. Hearing her mum talking so lucidly and seeing her brother enjoying himself wasn't something that happened often. It had been a while since they'd all been able to sit down and have a normal conversation.

'Are there any new residents?' she asked.

'Yes, but some of them are a bit batty,' her mum said.

Whitney laughed. 'What do you mean by "batty"?'

'A bit different from the rest of us. See that lady over there.' Her mum pointed to an elderly woman sitting in the corner.

'Yes,' Whitney said, nodding.

'She'll often wear her dressing gown and nightie during the day, and then I've seen her getting dressed in her day clothes when it's time to go to bed. It's very strange.'

'As long as she's happy, that's all that matters,' Whitney said.

'How's Tiffany getting on?' her mum asked.

Whitney hesitated for a moment. Should she tell her what Tiffany was planning? She supposed she ought to as she was going to find out sooner or later.

'I've been having an issue with her.'

'What do you mean?' Her mum asked, wringing her hands together in her lap. 'She seemed fine the other day when she came to visit.'

'She's told me she wants to leave university.'

'Oh, that. I'd hardly call it an issue.' Her mum shrugged, like it was no big deal.

'She told you about wanting to go travelling?'

'She did mention it. Australia, isn't it?'

'Yes, and there's nothing I can do to stop her.'

'You shouldn't even try, love. It's Tiffany's life.'

'As her mother I should point out to her the reasons why she should stay and finish her studies.'

'If she's not happy, there's no point in trying to force her to stay. Let her go travelling.'

'She did say she might return to university when she gets back,' Whitney said.

'If she wants to come back to finish her course, then that's up to her. You know, you can't live your life through her.'

'I'm not.'

'Maybe not intentionally. You always wanted to do more studying, but you didn't because you had Tiffany and your life changed. Now Tiffany's at university, maybe a part of you is enjoying it because it's what you wanted to do. But this is Tiffany's life. Let her lead it and be there if she needs you.'

Since when had her mum got so philosophical? Had George been hanging around here?

'You're probably right, but I still can't help worrying. She worked so hard to get onto this course. It seems ridiculous to drop out when she's already halfway through. Especially as we don't even know if they'll accept her back when she returns.'

'She might decide not to,' her mum said.

That wasn't something she wanted to contemplate.

'She said she probably would, though.'

'Are you sure she's not saying it to keep you happy?'

Was she? No. She wouldn't.

'I don't think so. Our relationship is different from that. I think she genuinely means it because she doesn't know whether she's going to enjoy travelling. She wants to keep her options open.'

Did she believe that, or was her mum right?

'It sounds very sensible, and the best thing you can do is support her in whatever she wants to do. Like we did with you.'

'What do you mean?' Whitney asked, frowning.

'It wasn't easy when you came home and told us you were pregnant. But we stood by you and helped all we could. And look how well you've done in your career.'

'Is Tiffany going on holiday?' Rob asked.

'She wants to go to Australia,' Whitney replied.

'May I go with her? I'd love to go over there. I want to buy a boomerang and see kangaroos.'

'Unfortunately, you can't, Rob. She's going with a friend. You have to stay here because Mum and I need you.'

'Oh, yes. I forgot,' he replied.

'We're a family and we stick together, and although Tiffany's going away, it doesn't mean she won't come back,' Whitney said.

'I'll miss her when she does go,' he said, biting down on his lip.

'We all will. But we can keep in contact. She'll phone us all the time and send photos.'

'It's not like years ago when we didn't have things like the Internet,' her mum said. 'When people went abroad, you couldn't speak to them, you just had to wait until their letters arrived or when they came back.'

'You're right. I need to let her find her feet and do what she wants. It's her life, not mine.'

'Exactly. Now, what about dinner?' her mum asked.

'I thought you'd had your dinner.'

'Have I? Maybe it's time for breakfast. You know, I can't remember. What are we doing? Are we going out somewhere?'

Whitney's heart sank. Her mum was drifting off and there was nothing she could do about it.

'No we can't go out as it's too late. Rob and I have to go now. We'll see you next week.'

Her brother said goodbye, but her mother didn't seem to register. At least they'd had a good conversation and she now accepted Tiffany's decision.

Chapter Twenty-Two

After both Ellie and the uniformed officer had been unsuccessful in contacting Serena Hastings to get her into the station, on Saturday morning Whitney decided she'd go with George to the gallery. There were two people in there looking at paintings and Serena was standing behind the counter. When she looked up and saw them a shadow crossed her face, and then almost immediately she smiled and headed over.

'DCI Walker and Dr Cavendish, you're here again. How can I help?'

'We'd like to ask you some further questions,' Whitney said. 'We've been trying to contact you, but couldn't get through on your phone nor were you at home.'

'I went to London for a couple of nights and didn't have my mobile with me. I'd … mislaid it. I found it this morning when I arrived at work. It had been hidden under some packing material.' She glanced over at the customers. 'Can it wait? I'm rather busy and it's not something I wish to discuss in the shop,' she said quietly.

'No, it can't, but we'll wait until they've left,' Whitney said.

They headed to the rear of the gallery where there was a selection of Drury Wilde's paintings running along the wall.

'Do you believe her story about the missing phone?'

'She didn't appear to be lying?' George said.

'If she found it so easily once she'd got back to work, how come she couldn't find it before she went away.'

'I don't know.'

'Maybe it's nothing. I just can't imagine what I'd do without my phone for two days.' She glanced at Drury's art, on the wall. 'What do you think of his work?'

'As with a lot of abstract work, he has a fresh perspective on ordinary things, but it's not my cup of tea.'

'I don't really get it.'

'You don't have to. People look for meanings, but it might not have one. As Jackson Pollock once said "Abstract painting is abstract. It confronts you."'

'If you say so.' She leaned in and saw the price. Fifteen thousand pounds. 'Bloody hell, people pay that much for a painting? He'd only need to sell ten a year to make one hundred and fifty thousand pounds.'

'He wouldn't receive all of that because the gallery would take a commission,' George said.

'How much?'

'I'm not sure, but probably in the region of thirty to thirty-five per cent.'

'That would still leave him with plenty of money,' she said.

After a further ten minutes the people in the gallery left and Serena came over to them.

'I can spare you a few minutes, now,' she said.

'We've been to see Drury Wilde and he said he exhibits

with you because he's a friend of your brother, Ralph. Is that correct?' Whitney asked.

'Yes. I've known him for years,' Serena said.

'Is your brother a part of your business?'

'He's not directly involved, but he does take an interest in the gallery,' Serena replied.

'Do you see him often?'

'Not really.'

'Does he live locally?'

'He's in Bletchley.'

'Where is he at the moment?'

'I've no idea.'

'We'd like to speak to him. Do you have his contact number?'

Serena pulled out her phone and called out the number while Whitney wrote it down in her notebook.

'I'm not sure how he'll be able to help you,' she said.

'You mentioned when we were here before that you'd sold ten of Wilde's paintings in total?'

'Yes.'

'I'd like details of the other seven buyers,' Whitney said.

'Is it absolutely necessary? My client list is confidential,' Serena said.

'Three people who bought his paintings have been murdered, the other seven could be at risk.' Whitney gave an exasperated sigh. Surely the woman must have realised.

'I hadn't thought of it like that. I'll get you their details.'

She left them alone in the gallery while she went to her office, returning a few minutes later with a sheet of paper in her hand, which she handed to Whitney. 'Names and contact numbers. I've also included the name of the painting they bought.'

'Thank you,' Whitney said, putting the list in her pocket.

There was a ring as the door to the shop opened and a couple walked in.

'I really have to go,' Serena said, nodding in the direction of the customers. 'Are there any other questions?'

'Not at the moment, but we'll be in touch with Ralph. What's his last name?' Whitney asked.

'It's Lloyd.'

They left the shop and went back to the car.

'Where to now?' George asked.

'The station.'

Once they'd arrived, Whitney went over to Ellie's desk. 'Here are seven more people who bought paintings by Drury Wilde from the art gallery. I want to know if any of them are single, live on their own, whether male or female, where they're based. As much detail as you can find. I also want you to get in touch with Ralph Lloyd, Serena Hastings' brother, and ask him to come to the station. Here's his number.' She held out her notebook.

'Yes, guv,' Ellie said, as she copied it down.

Whitney went to the board with George and wrote the brother's name and also 'seven further paintings sold'.

After ten minutes, Ellie called out. 'Guv, I've spoken to Ralph Lloyd. Is it possible for you to go to him? He's seeing clients all day, but he can fit you in for half an hour at three-thirty.'

'Clients on a Saturday. What does he do?' Whitney said.

'I don't know.'

'Okay. Tell him we'll be there.' She turned to George. 'Is that okay with you?'

'Yes. You've got me all day. But I can't be late because I'm going out with Ross this evening.'

'Anywhere nice?' Whitney asked.

'I don't know. He's surprising me.'

'Sounds fun. Even if you don't like surprises,' Whitney said.

'I'm getting used to them.'

The address Ralph Lloyd had given them was in an upmarket residential area. The man who answered the door was clearly related to Serena, as they shared many of the same features, in particular the eyes, nose, and chin.

'I'm Detective Chief Inspector Walker, and this is Dr Cavendish, we've come to speak to you as arranged by my officer.'

'Yes, come on in,' he said, in a soft voice with an accent which reminded Whitney of George.

He took them to a large study, furnished with modern furniture. 'Please take a seat.' He gestured to the easy chairs situated beside the window. 'How can I help?'

'What do you do that means you have to work on a Saturday?' Whitney asked.

'I'm a financial adviser. I see clients at the weekend, as very often they're busy during the week.'

'We'd like to ask you about the painter Drury Wilde. You know him well?' Whitney asked.

'Yes, I do. We went to school together.'

'You recommended he exhibit at Serena's gallery. Is that correct?'

'I mentioned the gallery one time when we bumped into each other and he said he was looking for somewhere new to exhibit.'

Not exactly how Wilde explained it to them.

'I thought he was exhibiting in Rugby prior to going with Serena,' Whitney said.

'He did have a few paintings, there, but I believe he fell out with the owner. If you've met him, you'll understand why.'

Whitney refrained from answering; she didn't need to go down that path.

'You thought he'd be a good fit for Serena. Why?' she asked.

'Because she was still getting her gallery off the ground. Her reputation was growing slowly and, for all his eccentricities, Wilde's a very good artist. It's turned out successful for both of them.'

'Did you keep in touch with him when he was living overseas?'

'No, I didn't. I had no idea he'd returned until bumping into him at the theatre. After which, we resumed contact.'

'He sells his paintings for a lot of money, considering he's not well-known,' Whitney said.

'That's where you're wrong. He used to be recognised when he was at art school. He won a prestigious prize for his art and had his career set. But then, out of the blue, he moved overseas.'

'Do you know why?'

They needed to look further into it.

'No idea. If I had to guess, I'd say there was likely to be a woman involved. He had a series of inappropriate relationships in his youth.'

'Inappropriate?' Whitney said.

'With married women. But don't quote me on that.'

'So, now he's picking up on his past success,' Whitney said.

'Why do you want to know?'

'We're investigating the murder of three women who bought Wilde's paintings from your sister's gallery.'

His eyes widened. 'You surely can't believe that he, or my sister, had anything to do with them.'

'We're investigating all possibilities.' Whitney trotted out her usual response.

'It makes no sense. It would stop people from buying his paintings if he was linked to murders.'

'Wilde has sold ten paintings since exhibiting there. And, as I've said, three of the people who bought them are now dead.'

He shook his head. 'This is crazy. I don't understand how it could happen. Why do you want to speak to me about it? I don't go to the gallery. I haven't been there since the exhibition.'

He'd attended. She didn't know that.

'We hadn't realised you were there. During the evening, did you notice anyone suspicious hanging around?'

He was quiet for a moment. 'No, I can't say as I did. Guests were coming and going all evening looking at the paintings. We didn't stay too long, as my wife is uncomfortable in crowds. We only went to show our support for Serena and Wilde. I don't remember seeing anybody looking out of place there.'

'If you do remember anything, please get in touch,' Whitney said, handing him her card.

'Certainly. But I don't think I will,' he said.

He showed them to the door.

'Before we go, please could you tell me what you were doing between the hours of midnight and four am on the eleventh of this month, and the early hours of the fifteenth and twentieth?'

'Am I a suspect?'

'We just want to eliminate you from our enquiries.'

'I was here.'

'Can anyone vouch for you?' Whitney asked.

'Yes, my wife. She was sleeping next to me all night on each of those dates.'

They left the house and went back to the car.

'Something that's puzzling me is how did the murderer know who had bought the paintings? It's not obvious. People look around and might speak to Serena, but we know that during the exhibition payment isn't taken,' Whitney said.

'She would put a red dot on any painting that's been sold. But that doesn't mean someone would know who'd bought it.'

Were they looking at an inside job? And, if so, who else worked at the gallery or had access to the information?

Chapter Twenty-Three

George was deep in thought, despite being the one driving, when Whitney's phone rang.

'Walker.' She nodded. 'Okay. Text me the details.'

'What was that about?' George asked as the call ended.

'Out of the seven names on the list, there are two women who live on their own. Ellie's texting me the addresses. I think we should speak to them straight away. Do you have time to come with me now?'

George glanced at the car's clock. She wasn't due to see Ross for a while and it was important to warn them of the danger they could be in. 'Where do they live?'

'In the Lenchester area. I promise you won't be late for your date with Ross, if that's what you're concerned about.'

'I'm not worried. I can text him if we're going to be late. It's best we see these women.'

Whitney's phone pinged. 'First stop Greta Cook, who lives in Briddlebury, and then we'll go to see Megan Faulkner who lives closer to the station. You'll be back in time to see Ross. I wonder where he's taking you. If it's a surprise, maybe it's paintballing or something like that.'

'Paintballing? Why on earth would he want to do that?' She frowned.

'I don't know, it could be fun. Or perhaps he wants to take you to one of those escape rooms when you have to work out all the clues. That would suit you better.'

'I've never even heard of an escape room.' When Ross had mentioned a surprise, she hadn't envisaged anything strange, maybe a restaurant they hadn't visited before.

'I haven't been, but I understand they're fun. You get locked in a room for an hour and can't leave until you've worked out all the clues.'

'I suppose it would be quite fun to do, but I doubt that's what he's got planned for us tonight. It's most likely a meal out and nothing out of the ordinary.'

Now she was left wondering what to wear. If it was paintballing, maybe she should be casual. Then again, what were the chances it would be that? It was just Whitney getting carried away.

They drove into Briddlebury, a small village north of Lenchester, and parked on the high street where Greta Cook lived. It was a three-storey stone cottage with a thatched roof.

'Another rich client,' Whitney said, narrowing her eyes.

'You've no idea whether she's rich or not,' George said.

'Anyone who can afford to spend fifteen thousand pounds on a painting has got to be rich, in my book.'

'You do know that fifteen thousand pounds isn't much for a piece of art. Just recently, a painting that had been hanging in a woman's kitchen in France for decades was sold for twenty-four million euros. It was found during a house clearance. It was an early Renaissance masterpiece.'

'Wow. Well, in that case, I stand corrected. It's only a

lot to me. I could no more afford to pay fifteen thousand for a painting than I could book myself a flight on the next space shuttle.'

They walked through the tiny garden up to the front door. George rang the bell, but there was no answer.

'Come on, let's go,' Whitney said.

As they walked down the short path, a woman with short dark hair jogged along the street towards them.

'Hello,' the woman called out. 'Can I help you?'

'I'm Detective Chief Inspector Walker and this is Dr Cavendish. We're looking for Greta Cook,' Whitney said.

'That's me. I've just been visiting a neighbour. Has something happened to my daughter, Evie?' She ran a jerky hand through her hair.

'No. Everyone's fine as far as we know. May we talk inside?' Whitney said.

'Yes, of course.' She pulled out a key from her jacket pocket and unlocked the door. They followed her into a lovely light and airy hallway, with high ceilings.

'We can go in here,' Greta said as she ushered them into the sitting room.

Immediately, George's eyes were drawn to the Drury Wilde painting hanging above the fireplace.

'We've come to see you about the painting you recently bought from Pictura Gallery,' Whitney said.

'The one over there, by Drury Wilde?' the woman replied nodding at the painting on the wall. 'I fell in love with it as soon as I saw it. I also met the artist at his exhibition, which made it even more special.'

'He's known to be grumpy. Was he like that with you?' Whitney asked.

'Yes. But that's part of his charm. Have you ever met an artist who's not like that? It's as if they exist on another planet.'

'While you were at the exhibition, did you notice anybody acting strange? Or did you notice anyone outside hanging around looking suspicious?' Whitney asked.

'No, I can't say as I did. Everything seemed perfectly normal. It was a lovely evening. There were a lot of people there, but I can't think of anything odd happening. Why?'

'Three women have recently been murdered and they'd all bought a painting by Drury Wilde from Pictura.'

Greta's hand flew up to her mouth. 'Oh, my goodness. That's dreadful.'

'Another similarity between the victims is they all lived alone. Is it right that you're here on your own?'

The colour drained from Greta Cook's face. 'Y-yes. Am I at risk?'

'We don't know. Is there anyone you can stay with, or who could stay here with you?' Whitney asked.

'For how long?' Greta asked, frowning.

'Until we've solved these murders.'

'Are these the Lenchester Strangler murders? I heard about them on the radio.'

'Yes. Now you know why we can't leave you alone.'

'I could stay with a friend for a couple of nights, but not indefinitely. I've got my business to think about.'

'What do you do?' Whitney asked.

'I'm an accountant and run my business from home.'

'Is there anywhere else you can go to do your work?'

'Not really. I have all my files here. Some of my clients still insist on sending me paper copies of everything,' Greta said, shaking her head.

'Can you find someone to stay with you?' Whitney suggested.

'I could ask my cousin. If I explain the situation, she should be able to come over.'

'Please do. It's important,' Whitney said.

'Yes, I understand. Is there anybody else in the same situation as me?'

'There's one other person who we're going to visit now. The main thing is you're vigilant and keep the doors and windows locked. You can contact us at any time if you see anything suspicious.'

'I will do,' Greta replied, nodding.

'We'll make sure there's a patrol car going past your house at regular intervals from now on,' Whitney said.

'Knowing someone will be checking makes me feel a lot better, but it's still scary to think someone might try to harm me.' She wrapped her arms tightly around her middle.

'Try not to worry. Just be on your guard and leave everything to us,' Whitney said.

'Thank you,' she said as she opened the door and showed them out of the house.

'Do you think having a patrol car going past regularly is enough?' George asked, once they were away from the house. 'Mind you, if the killer keeps an eye on her, he'd realise someone was staying and hopefully that should be enough.'

'Unless he waits until the other person isn't there, especially as Greta works from home. He could change his pattern and murder during the day instead of the night.'

'It's possible, but the planning and execution is so meticulous, I'd be surprised if he changed it,' George said.

'I'll speak to Jamieson about placing an officer outside the house twenty-four-seven. He might resist, though, as it would be a huge chunk from our already stretched overtime budget.'

'Considering he was the one who wanted the murders clearing up as soon as possible, because of the Chief

Constable, he may agree,' George said. 'Also, didn't he say overtime was no object?'

'True.'

They drove to Megan Faulkner's house, a large modern, detached property in Parkvale.

'What is it with all these women living on their own in big houses?' Whitney said. 'Why don't they just get a flat? They don't need anything larger.'

'We don't know their situation or background. This could be small compared with what they were used to,' George said.

Whitney looked at her. 'You're kidding, right?'

'No. All I'm saying is we have no idea. Stop making snap judgments.'

They walked up the long drive and Whitney knocked on the door using the brass knocker. Within a few minutes, a woman dressed in running gear answered.

'Are you Megan Faulkner?' Whitney asked.

'Yes.'

'I'm Detective Chief Inspector Walker from Lenchester CID and this is Dr Cavendish. We'd like to speak to you for a moment about a painting you recently bought.'

'I'm just on my way out to meet a friend. We're going for a run.'

'This won't take long,' Whitney said.

'Okay. Come on in.' She led them into the kitchen, and they sat around the large oak table.

'I understand you recently purchased a painting by Drury Wilde, from Pictura Art Gallery.'

'Yes, that's right. Why?' The woman frowned.

'We're investigating several murders in the area and have discovered that all of the victims recently bought his paintings from the same gallery.'

'What?' Megan said, her eyes wide. 'Is someone coming after me?'

'We're not certain, but until we've caught the offender, we'd rather you weren't on your own,' Whitney said. 'We don't want to take any unnecessary risks. All the victims were women living on their own.'

'But why would buying one of his paintings make me a target?' Megan asked.

'We're unsure, but we're erring on the side of caution as this appears to be the only connection. Is there anyone who can stay with you in the meantime?'

'My daughter's away at university, but she might be able to take a few days off. How long is this for?'

'We can't speculate. If you could ask her to come home and stay with you that would help.'

'I'll get in touch with her straightaway.'

'Thank you. We think that's for the best. We'll make sure to keep a police presence around here. But be extra vigilant. Keep doors and windows locked, and don't let anybody into the house who you don't know or trust.'

Chapter Twenty-Four

The police are no nearer catching me than they were before. I knew that would happen because they're totally incompetent. I don't know why they're paid so much because they couldn't catch a criminal if they were face-to-face in a locked room with them.

I'll admit now, before the first murder I was plagued with doubt.
Should I do it?

What if I couldn't bring myself to follow through?

What if I got caught?

Did they deserve to die?

My questions were endless….Now the fourth is in my sight, just try to stop me.

I understand the meaning behind the term 'exquisite pleasure'.

And if that wasn't enough, even added to my enjoyment is that I'm showing up the police for who they really are.

A bunch of ineffectual arseholes.

Forgive me for the repetition. I can't help myself.

I can tell you things about them they'd never want publicised in a million years.

Maybe I will divulge my secrets.

Maybe I won't.

I don't know.

It doesn't matter. Completing my task takes priority. That and the impending increase in my bank balance. Because that's why I'm doing it. For the money.

What? You thought I'd become a copycat killer because I suddenly felt like it?

No. That's not me at all.

The opportunity presented itself and I took it.

I needed the money and I wanted revenge.

So, who will be my number four? I'm going to stake out the two possibilities and then decide.

This is such fun.

Chapter Twenty-Five

'Hello.' George had just arrived at the station and was standing outside the rear entrance. She hadn't recognised the number on her screen when she answered.

'Is that Dr Cavendish?' a familiar sounding male voice with a London accent asked, but his name escaped her.

'Yes.'

'This is Detective Inspector Terry Gardner. We met on the Carriage Killer case. My sergeant and I came to Lenchester to help with the investigation.'

That's who it was. What on earth did he want?

'Yes, I remember you.'

'How are you?' he said.

'Very well, thank you.'

'Do you remember we discussed the forensic psychologists we'd used in the past?'

Of course she did. They didn't have a regular person, just took whoever they could get. Which screamed second-rate to her. And then they'd tried to defend their decision.

'I do.'

'I wondered if you'd be free to assist us on a difficult case we have?'

She hadn't been expecting that.

'I'm sorry, my time is tied up with DCI Walker and her team.'

'Before you turn me down, let me tell you about the case,' he said.

There was no harm in listening, but she wouldn't be getting involved. She hardly had enough time to juggle all her responsibilities as it was. Lenchester CID took precedence over any other force.

'If you wish,' she said coolly.

'Babies are going missing across the country and we're making little progress on the operation.'

Babies? That was awful.

'How many are we talking about? And why haven't I heard of this?' Surely it would have been front page news.

'From our investigation, we believe that many of the stolen babies belonged to women who were illegally in the country, so they didn't report it.'

Her stomach churned. That was bad on so many levels.

'I'm assuming some of them reported it, or you wouldn't know,' she said.

'Yes, you're right. Also, there have been babies taken from parents who legitimately live here,' Terry said.

'Living here as immigrants?' George confirmed.

'Some are, and some are British. But mainly the former.'

'Do you know where the babies go?'

'Possibly overseas. We're not a hundred per cent sure.'

'Why do you need my help? I thought you had several forensic psychologists you could call on?'

'We did try several, but they were stumped. I remembered how much you contributed to the Carriage Killer case and that's why I'm calling. We want the best. Can you help?'

Babies were at stake. How could she refuse? But she didn't have the time, not without jeopardising the current case, and she couldn't do that to Whitney.

'We're in the middle of an important case. Until that's solved all I can offer is a day of my time, as a consultant.'

'If that's all there is, I'll take it. How soon can you get here?' Terry asked.

'Wednesday. I'll speak to my head of department at the university, as the invoice for a day's consultancy will come from him. I'm not sure what the charge will be.'

'Don't worry about that. Shall I email our files, so you can get up to speed in advance of your visit?' Terry said.

'Yes, please.'

She ended the call and made her way to the incident room. As she opened the door she was, as usual, hit by the almost deafening sound of chatter. She was glad she'd cancelled her meeting that morning and instead decided to come into the station, as she now had a lot to think about, not least whether she was going to tell Whitney about the Regional Force's request.

She walked over to where Whitney was talking to Ellie.

'Morning,' she said.

'What are you doing here? You said you couldn't come in this morning.'

'Change of plan. I wanted to get away from the uni and decided to come in here to help.'

'Is everything okay?'

'Yes.' She nodded. 'Where are we on the investigation?'

'I've just got off the phone to Don Mason, my old boss. He was on the original investigation. I'm going to visit him with Matt. But if you'd like to come instead, I'll leave him here.'

'Sounds good. We can go in my car, before you ask.'

'I wasn't going to say anything,' Whitney said.

'Where does he live?'

'He's moved to Mearsford.'

'I've never heard of it,' George said.

'I forget that you're not from around here. It's about a thirty-minute drive. Probably less with you at the wheel,' Whitney said grinning.

∿

'Tell me a bit about Don,' George said, while they were driving.

'He was great, and really looked out for me. You couldn't wish for a better boss. He was kind and considerate, but still tough. It was thanks to him I progressed in my career. He retired just before I made inspector. I miss him, even now. There are times when I'd like to go to him to discuss a case, but obviously I can't. You'd like him. He's straight talking.'

'Sounds like a good man,' George said.

'Yes, he definitely is. And now we've got that out of the way. You're going to tell me what's wrong.'

'What do you mean?'

'I know we've had our issues recently and things have been a little difficult between us, but I'm sensing there's something else. You're distracted. Is it Ross? What was this surprise date?'

'He had tickets for a lecture on the Terracotta Army which I'd wanted to attend.'

'The what?'

'It's a collection of sculptures from China, going back

thousands of years. They were discovered in the 1970s by some peasants working in the fields.'

'So, if Ross isn't what you're distracted by, what is it?'

'I don't wish to discuss it,' George said.

'Okay. It's up to you. I'm not going to push,' Whitney replied.

George breathed a sigh of relief. It was unusual for Whitney to let something go so easily. Whether she'd start up again, was anyone's guess. Luckily, though, they'd arrived at Mearsford. She pulled up outside a quaint little cottage. The sky was blue, but there was a nip in the air and George pulled her coat tightly around her.

'This is lovely,' Whitney said. 'I haven't been here before. Once he'd retired, they sold their house in Lenchester and moved here. Just Don and his wife.'

'Is he expecting us?' George asked.

'Yes. He's just arrived back from holiday, which is why we haven't been able to speak to him sooner. I phoned earlier to arrange it. He seemed more than happy to see us.'

They walked up the path and before they'd even reached the door, it opened and a tall man, who looked to be in his seventies, was standing there with a broad smile on his face.

'Whitney,' he said. 'Come on in.'

She gave him a big hug. 'This is Dr Cavendish. George. She's a forensic psychologist and has been helping us on our cases.'

He shook her hand. 'Good to meet you, George. I'm glad to see Whitney's using someone with your specialist skills.'

'What's that supposed to mean?' Whitney said, frowning.

'I know how you like to do everything yourself,' he said. 'You always have done.'

Whitney shrugged. 'Guilty.'

'Come on in and let me take your coats. Katie's looking forward to seeing you again,' Don said.

He hung their coats on pegs by the door and they followed him into the house, through to the kitchen where a small well-rounded woman stood by the sink. The delicious smell of baking permeated the air.

'Hello, Whitney,' she said coming over and giving her a hug. 'How about a hot drink? I know how much you love your coffee.'

Whitney looked at George and grinned. 'Thank you, that would be lovely.'

'We'll go and sit down,' Don said.

The small lounge was cosy, with a floral sofa and matching chairs. Logs were stacked either side of the fireplace, and a fire was blazing. The flames swirled as the wood crackled. On every conceivable surface there were photos.

'Sit down, we don't want you standing on ceremony,' he said.

'As I mentioned on the phone, we'd like talk to you about the Lenchester Strangler case, which I know you were on in the eighties,' Whitney said.

Mason sat back in his chair looking thoughtful. 'I remember it very well, even though it was over thirty years ago. I was a detective sergeant at the time and the SIO was Inspector Gibbs. It caused us a lot of aggravation.'

'Can you tell me more about that?' Whitney asked.

'We thought we had the person responsible, but—'

'You mean Harold Skinner?' George said interrupting.

'Yes. But we couldn't pin it on him. He was way too cunning.'

'Is there anything you can tell us about the case itself?' Whitney asked. 'How did you identify him as a suspect?'

'Back then, we didn't have the forensic capability you do now. We had to do it by hard graft. We had a break-through in the case quite by accident when he'd been seen hanging around one of the victim's places. We put a tail on him and then he was spotted near another victim's house. Unfortunately, we didn't catch him at a time when he was attacking and even though we searched his house, we couldn't find anything. It was totally clean. We assumed he had a lock-up somewhere but were never able to trace it. And then, as you know, he murdered his wife and was sent to prison. So, even though we didn't have him for the Strangler murders, we knew he was off the street. The murders ceased once he'd been sent down, which was further evidence it was him.'

'You didn't think of charging him with the other murders?' George asked.

'We did, but we had an issue with somebody working on the case who made it difficult for us to do so.'

'Who?' Whitney asked.

'A DC called Larry Cane. He falsified evidence so he could incriminate Skinner.'

'What evidence?' Whitney asked.

'He stole one of Skinner's boots and left a print beside the window of one of the victim's houses. He almost got away with it.'

'How did you find out?' Whitney asked.

'Before and after photos. The forensic team had photographed the exact spot prior to Cane finding the footprint. Cane had managed to *mislay* the photographs. What he hadn't realised was copies had been made for training purposes.'

'What a dumb mistake to make,' Whitney said.

'We're talking thirty years ago. Nothing was digital. I wouldn't call him dumb. Devious, is more appropriate.'

'What happened once it was discovered?'

'He was reprimanded. But that was all, because we had our man locked up.'

'What happened to Larry Cane?'

'He was moved on to another force. Rugby, I think. I don't know from there.'

The door opened and Katie came in holding a tray.

'I made some of your favourite cake this morning, Whitney.'

That's what George had been able to smell.

'You're too kind,' she said. 'I still miss the cake you'd send in with Don. Tell me now, how are you both getting on here?'

'We love the village. There are lots of activities going on and we've made some good friends,' Don said.

'You both look very well, so it's clearly doing you good. It's been lovely seeing you and I'm so happy to see you settled.'

'What's it like being a DCI?' Don asked.

'It has its moments. Currently I'm having issues with my Detective Superintendent, Tom Jamieson.'

'That's a surprise,' Don said, laughing.

'What's so funny?' Whitney asked.

'Because some things never change. Don't tell me, he doesn't do things the way you like them to be done.'

'A lucky guess. It doesn't help that he came in on the fast track scheme and he doesn't know much about proper policing.'

'One day, Whitney, you're going to learn that you have to deal with these people. I seem to remember many years ago explaining to you that just because people don't do things as you wish, doesn't mean you have to fall out with them. Very often they're the people who are your superiors and control your life. If you want to get on, you'll have to learn to do as they say, whether you like it or not.'

'Well, I don't wish to go any higher. DCI is enough for me. I enjoy the role and it keeps me out in the field.'

Don looked at George. 'And how do you get on working with Whitney?'

'We get on very well, thank you,' George said.

'And that's about all you're going to get out of her. George is very different from me. She brings the logic and the brains.'

'You have brains as well,' Don said.

'Not like George. There's nothing she doesn't know.'

'A slight exaggeration. There's plenty I don't know,' George said.

'I've been following your career and the cases you've had to deal with just recently. Kudos to you,' Don said.

'I couldn't have done it without George's help.' Whitney smiled at her.

It seemed she'd forgotten everything that had happened with Tiffany. Which was good. She had enough on her plate without that hanging over her.

After Don and Katie regaled them with stories of their recent holiday, George and Whitney got up to leave.

'It's been wonderful seeing you,' Whitney said, giving them both a big hug.

'You must come over again,' Katie said. 'You don't have to wait until you need to discuss something to do with the police. We'd enjoy seeing Tiffany, too.'

'I will. Promise.'

As they drove out of the village Whitney turned to George.

'Right. Let's go back to the station and continue with the investigation. Did you find anything Don said useful?'

'I'd like to look more into Larry Cane and what he actually did.'

'Agreed. And now perhaps you can tell me what's on your mind.'

Blast. She thought Whitney had forgotten.

'Why?'

'You're even more reserved than usual. You've been holding back. Is it about Tiffany? Is there something else you're keeping from me?' Whitney asked.

'No. We've sorted that out,' George said.

'What, then? Is it Ross?' George looked away. 'It is. It's Ross, isn't it? Have you two had a falling out?'

'No. It's nothing to do with him. Our relationship's going well. We enjoy each other's company. Even the wedding, which was a bit of a disaster because of my parents being so rude to him, he took in his stride.'

'So, what is it?' Whitney asked

'Do you remember DI Terry Gardner?'

'From the Regional Force, yes. What's he got to do with it?'

'He contacted me earlier today. He'd like me to go and work with them on a case to do with missing babies.'

'I hope you told him where he could go,' Whitney said.

'No. I didn't.'

'W-what?' Whitney spluttered. 'You surely didn't agree to help them, did you?'

'Not exactly.'

'Then what "*exactly*"? I bet Dickhead Douglas put him up to it, to get back at me.'

'He didn't mention Detective Superintendent Douglas at all. When they were here, we all parted on good terms and that's why he felt able to contact me.'

'So, are you going to work with them or not?'

'I've offered a one-day consultancy, but that's all.'

'Won't your head of department kick off, seeing as you're getting it in the neck for working with me?'

'I don't think so. A single day consulting is perfectly acceptable,' George said.

'Whereas working with me isn't?'

'Stop being so defensive. It's not like that at all. I knew I should've kept this to myself.'

'Well, you're certainly good at that,' Whitney sniped.

George sucked in a breath. Was it going to be like this from now on? Every time she did something Whitney didn't like she'd make reference to the Tiffany incident. She couldn't work that way.

Chapter Twenty-Six

Whitney sucked in a deep breath. Ahead of her, George's back was stiff as they walked into the incident room. She shouldn't have snapped at the psychologist. She'd sort it out with her later, but at the moment she needed to focus on the case.

They headed over to Ellie's desk.

'I want you to investigate a police officer, Larry Cane. I'm not sure of his rank. Last known he was a DC, but he could have been promoted. He may be working at Rugby. See what you can find out.'

'Yes, guv,' Ellie said.

Whitney went up to the board. 'Listen up, everyone. We've just been to visit Don Mason, my old boss. He worked on the original Lenchester Strangler case when he was a DS. They interviewed Harold Skinner, but even though he was seen close to two of the crime scenes, they couldn't prosecute. They searched his place, but found nothing, so it was all circumstantial. Mason mentioned a DC who was on the case, a Larry Cane, who falsified evidence against Skinner, in an attempt to nail him. He was disciplined by his superiors and moved to a different force. We're going to find him. George and I have also been to see the two single women on the art gallery list. They've been alerted. Matt, I'd like you to confirm with uniform that they're making regular patrols past their houses.'

'Yes, guv,' Matt said.

'Guv,' Ellie interrupted. 'I've found out that Larry Cane was at Fielding Station in Rugby, but he was recently sacked.'

'For what?' Whitney said.

'I can't access the record, it's above my pay grade.'

'When exactly was he dismissed?' George asked.

'October.'

'That's interesting. Not long before the murders started. That would give him a motive. Retaliation,' George said.

'It makes sense. He would know everything about the investigation, including the hair being taken as a trophy,' Whitney said. 'Get me his address, Ellie. I'm going to see Jamieson. We need to access his records to find out exactly what happened and why he was let go.'

'Yes, guv.'

When Whitney arrived at Jamieson's room, she could hear him on the phone. She waited for him to finish, knocked on the door and walked in.

'If you've got a minute, sir,' she said.

'What is it, Walker?'

'We have a suspect for the copycat Lenchester Strangler murders.'

'Excellent. Well done.'

'It's not that simple. We think it might be a police officer who's recently been sacked from his position at Rugby.'

'Better tell me all about it,' he said, gesturing with his hand for her to sit.

'I went to see Don Mason, my old boss. He was on the original case and so was this officer, Larry Cane. Cane falsified evidence which made it difficult to prosecute Skinner, their main suspect. But as the murders stopped once Skinner murdered his wife, they didn't continue with the investigation.'

'Get to the point, Walker,' he said, looking at his watch. 'I have a meeting shortly.'

She tensed but forced herself not to react.

'We've researched into Cane and found he's recently been dismissed from the force. We can't access the records and I'd like to know more before interviewing him. I need you to get the information for us.'

'Leave it with me,' Jamieson said.

'I want to interview him now. Any chance you can hurry that along?' she asked impatiently.

He gave an exasperated sigh. 'Okay. Give me a minute.' He picked up the phone. 'This is Detective Superintendent Jamieson. I'd like you to send me the file on Larry Cane who was recently let go.' He paused. 'Yes. Okay. Thank you.'

'What did they say?' Whitney said as soon as he'd hung up.

'They're emailing me the file now, but I don't know whether it can be shared until I've looked at it.'

'Has it arrived yet?'

He looked in his email. 'Yes, it's here. Give me a second.' He stared at his computer for what seemed an age.

'Well?' she said.

'A sexual harassment complaint was made against him by a female officer. He was suspended pending an investigation. He was later dismissed after the complaint was upheld.'

'I assume he would have lost his police pension.' Whitney said.

'It would certainly seem that way,' Jamieson said.

'Which means he's got a grudge against the police.'

'Maybe.'

'Okay, thanks for that. I'm going to bring him in for questioning. In the meantime, can you see about getting a search warrant for where he lives?'

'I doubt we'll be granted a warrant on the grounds of a police officer being dismissed. He may have a grudge against his department, and know about a case from thirty years ago, but that's hardly sufficient.'

That was debatable, and he could at least try, but she didn't have time to discuss it.

'We'll bring him in for questioning anyway and we can see what he's got to say for himself.'

'Keep me informed,' Jamieson said.

'Will do,' she said as she left his office and went back down to the incident room.

She called everyone to attention. 'It seems that Larry Cane was sacked for sexual harassment. I'm going to send uniform around to bring him in for questioning. Hopefully we can get hold of him straight away. Matt, you can interview him with me, and George listen outside. Let's see what we can get from him.'

Chapter Twenty-Seven

George stared at Larry Cane. A thin, grey haired man, his lips set in a thin line. Whitney and Matt sat opposite him.

'Interview between Detective Chief Inspector Walker and Detective Sergeant Price with Mr Larry Cane on Monday, November the twenty-fifth. Larry, thank you for coming in to speak to us.'

'I didn't have much choice. I was ordered in,' Cane said.

'We're investigating three murders which were a copy of those carried out by the Lenchester Strangler.'

'What's that got to do with me?' He stared unblinking at Whitney; his gaze cold.

The textbooks could've been written using him as an example. It was classic lying behaviour manifested in a fashion designed to intimidate and control.

'He definitely knows something about it,' George said, into the earpiece.

Whitney gave an almost imperceptible nod. 'You worked on the case originally, with Don Mason. Is that correct?'

'You know it is.'

'And during the case, you were subject to an investigation because of falsifying evidence?'

He glared at Whitney.

'He doesn't like what you're saying,' George said. 'Keep going.'

'Tell me more about this incident,' Whitney said.

'Things were different in those days. We did what it took to get a prosecution. We knew Harold Skinner was guilty and all I wanted to do was make sure we had him nailed. What's wrong with that?'

'Everything. For a start, your evidence wouldn't have stood up in court, not to mention what you did was against regulations,' Whitney said.

'What do you know? This was way before your time. You think what you do is so much better? Everything by the book. Well, the fucking book doesn't catch criminals. Something you'd know if you actually engaged in proper policing. You're just playing at it.'

'He's trying to wind you up. Don't let him,' George said.

'Your assessment of my ability doesn't bother me in the slightest. You were moved on to Rugby after the case, is that correct?'

'You know it is,' he sneered.

'And you were recently dismissed from there because of sexual harassment allegations.'

His eyes narrowed. 'It was all a misunderstanding.'

'How many times have we heard that one?' Whitney said.

'Think what you like. I know the truth. The stupid bitch came on to me when we were out one night having a drink. I know the signs. Then she got all silly about it. I did nothing wrong.'

'Except guilt is written all over his face. Look at the way he's avoiding your eyes, by staring down and to the side. His eyebrows are arched outwards, too. Classic,' George said.

'The investigation found otherwise. What were you doing in the early hours of the eleventh, fifteenth, and twentieth of November?'

'What? You're now accusing me of being the Lenchester Strangler?' He let out a hollow laugh. 'I'm not saying anything.'

'I repeat. What were your movements on those dates?'

'I don't remember.' He shrugged.

'Do you live on your own or is there someone at home who can vouch for you during these times?' Whitney asked.

'I live alone, now. The wife left me a few months ago.'

'Let's take one day at a time, that might jog your memory. The early hours of the fifteenth?'

'I might have been at home. The Lenchester Strangler worked during those hours, so let's assume I was in bed, alone.'

'Ask him about the art gallery.' George said.

'Do you like art?' Whitney said.

'Art? Why?' He frowned.

'Just answer the question.'

'I have no opinion.'

'Do you know of an artist called Drury Wilde?' Whitney asked.

'Never heard of him.'

'He's lying. His blink rate went up as soon as he'd answered the question,' George said.

'Are you sure about that? He used to exhibit in Rugby,' Whitney said.

He shifted in his seat. 'I might have heard of him, but I don't collect his art.'

'What about Pictura Art Gallery? Have you ever been there?'

'No. But I know they're in Lenchester,' Cane said.

'They had an exhibition of Drury Wilde's work recently. If we were to check the visitor book, would we find that you went?'

'Maybe ... I don't remember. I might have done,' he said.

'How can you not remember? Are you suffering from some sort of memory loss?' Whitney asked.

'You know what? I'm not speaking to you anymore. Despite you forcing me to come here, I'd been fully prepared to assist. Not now. If you want to interview me, you can do it with my solicitor present. You're just fishing for something to pin on me. If you were capable of doing your job properly, you wouldn't be wasting your time interviewing me.'

'All right, you may go,' Whitney said. 'But we will be wanting to speak to you again.'

'Only through my solicitor,' Larry said.

'That's fine. Matt, see Mr Cane out.'

Once they'd left, Whitney came in to see George. 'Definitely suspicious?'

'He's hiding something. He lied at times, but about what, I don't know. It could just be related to the sexual assault allegation that caused him to lose his job.'

'Or it could be he's our murderer. He has all the information at his fingertips and he has a grudge against the police,' Whitney said.

'But where does the gallery fit into it?' George asked.

'I don't know. We need to find out if he was actually at the exhibition. The visitor book will tell us,' Whitney said.

'That's if he signed in under his own name. Or signed

in at all. We know they were pretty relaxed about that on the night.'

'I'll get Frank to check the CCTV footage near the gallery and cross-reference it with what he's already checked from around the victims' houses. Plus, use ANPR to double check whether his car was in the area.'

'Good idea.'

'I'll ask Ellie to track his credit card records, too. In case he went by train and used it to buy the tickets.'

'What about searching his place?' George asked.

'According to Jamieson it's unlikely we'll get a search warrant, but I'll try him again. In the meantime, we'll put a tail on him. He doesn't have alibis for the murders.'

'I'm going back into work for a short time, if you don't need me?' George said.

'Okay, I'll see you soon,' Whitney said.

After leaving the station, George went to the university. As she got out of her car, she heard her name being called. She turned and saw Tiffany jogging towards her.

'Hi. How's it going?' George said.

'I'm getting there. I was hoping to see you because I know you and Mum fell out over me.'

'Don't worry about it. We're over our differences.'

'I hate to think I'd caused a rift between you. It's not what I intended. I confided in you because I knew you'd be able to give me an objective point of view.'

'I think your mum's coming around to you going,' George said.

'Is she?'

'She seems to be. And we're certainly back on speaking terms. She understands why you did what you did.'

'I hope you're right, because I've definitely decided to leave. I've been in touch with the admissions department, and it looks like they'll allow me to come back. I won't be able to join midway through the term, as you said. I'll have to take the whole year again.'

'That's probably for the best. If you're starting with a new cohort of students and new tutors, it will enable you to get to know them and what's expected of you,' George said. 'What's going to happen now?'

'I'll let all my tutors know. I've handed in some of the work for this term, but I guess there's no point doing the rest of my assignments now.'

'Agreed.'

'I need to apply for my visas. They can take a while to come through,' Tiffany said.

'Do you know exactly where you're travelling to?'

'We're going straight to Brisbane because Phoebe knows some people out there already. We'll do some sightseeing and then try to get jobs on either the Sunshine Coast or the Gold Coast. It's a good time for hospitality work. After that, who knows.' Tiffany grinned. 'I can't wait.'

'Any nerves?' George asked.

'Some, but we're going to have a great time. It's even better now I know I can return to my course, *if* I decide to.'

'If?' George asked.

'Who knows what's going to happen? But don't say anything to Mum.' Her hand flew up to her mouth. 'Oh, I'm sorry. I shouldn't have said that. I don't want to cause any more problems between you.'

'I'm sure your mother realises there's a chance you might not want to come back. The main thing is you've left the door open in case you do.'

'Thanks, George. You're the best.' Tiffany flung her arms around her and squeezed.

'I'm always here. Anytime you want to talk, you know that. I'd better go, as I've got work to do. I'll see you soon. We'll have a drink before you leave.'

'I'd love that. Thank you,' Tiffany said.

Chapter Twenty-Eight

Whitney was sitting behind her desk, wishing she could magic away the admin work that was piling up, when there was a knock on the door and Matt came rushing in.

'You're never going to believe this, guv,' he said.

'What's happened?' she asked.

'We've had a message from Harold Skinner. He's asked for you to visit him.'

'What about?' she asked, frowning.

'I've no idea. That's the only message I got. One of the care assistants phoned and passed it on.'

'What did you say?'

'That someone will be out there as soon as possible. The care assistant said he specifically asked to see you and Dr Cavendish.'

'I'm not sure whether George is available. Leave it with me. Are they expecting us to confirm or go when we can?'

'I think you can just turn up. It's not like he's going anywhere. I'd probably avoid meal times but, apart from that, I don't think it matters.'

'Okay, great. Thanks, Matt.'

He left the room and she called George.

'Whitney,' George answered.

'What are you doing at the moment?'

'I'm driving.'

Why was she sounding cagey?

'Where to?'

'I'm out for the day.'

'Are you with Ross?'

It seemed most strange. George had never gone away for the day without telling her, especially when they were in the middle of a case.

'No,' George said.

'I don't have time for guessing games. Where are you?' Whitney said, unable to hide the impatient tone in her voice.

'I'm on my way to the Regional Force station to meet with Terry,' she said.

'You're what?'

'I told you about the consultancy,' George said.

'Yes, but you didn't say it would be so soon. You do know we're in the middle of a murder investigation?'

'Of course I do. It's only for one day. Has there been another murder?'

'No.'

'What's so important it can't wait a day?'

'Harold Skinner's been in touch. He wants to talk to both of us.'

'Really? That's interesting. I wonder what that's about. Did you actually speak to him?'

'No. One of the care assistants phoned and spoke to Matt.'

'You can go on your own, you don't need me.'

'He's asked for both of us,' she said belligerently.

'Can it wait until tomorrow?'

Could it? Or should she take Matt?

'What time can you be here?' If Skinner wanted both of them, there was more chance of getting something from him if they did as he requested.

'Whatever time suits you.'

'Be here at ten,' Whitney said.

'I'll have to be back at the university by two.'

'No problem. Let's hope he's got something useful to tell us. Though, I'm not sure, with his dementia.'

'I'm fairly certain a good part of it is put on.'

'Have a good day with the Regional Force. I'll see you tomorrow.'

Chapter Twenty-Nine

At ten on the dot, George entered the incident room to collect Whitney, who was waiting beside the door. She'd prepared herself for her friend's onslaught, as she knew it would come at some stage during the day. She wasn't prepared to take any nonsense from her, though.

'Ready?' she said.

'Yes. How did it go with Terry yesterday?' Whitney asked as they headed towards the car. 'I was going to call last night but thought you wouldn't want disturbing.'

That was a first. Maybe things weren't yet right between them.

'There wasn't much I could do. They would have liked your help, too, but I explained about this case. I did mention the baby smuggling ring from that case you had years ago and said I'd ask if you had any information for them. Do you?'

'We didn't pursue it. All I can tell them is what Becky from Radio Lenchester told me. She'd researched into a company called Lullaby Nannies, in London.'

'Who were they?' George said.

'An upmarket nanny agency for the rich. I've no idea if they're still in existence. It was owned by someone called Salma Abaza, if I remember correctly. Their clients came mainly from the Middle East and Asia. One of Becky's friends was persuaded not to have an abortion, but instead have the baby and sell it to them.'

'Was this part of the nanny agency?'

'Becky's friend was approached by someone who worked for Lullaby. Becky thought the agency was a cover so they had legitimate access to wealthy people here and overseas.'

'And they paid women for their babies? That's nothing like what's going on in Terry's case.'

'She also thought they stole babies to order. I didn't get involved, but I know it was almost impossible to prove because they dealt with people from overseas.'

'Terry is dealing with babies being stolen from Moldovan illegal immigrants.'

'I'll put him in touch with Becky. She might be able to help. We certainly don't have the time.'

'Good idea,' George said.

When they arrived at the care home, they parked and went inside.

'We're here to see Harold Skinner,' Whitney said to the care assistant who was sitting at the desk. 'He's asked to see us. Detective Chief Inspector Walker and Dr Cavendish.'

'I'll find out where he is.'

'Thanks.'

The woman left and headed down the long corridor, returning after a few minutes.

'He's in the day room, but wants to speak to you in his room. Someone is bringing him along and you can go there together.'

They waited by the desk until Harold Skinner was

wheeled along a few minutes later. When he saw them, he just nodded and didn't say a word. They followed him to his room and once inside, the care assistant closed the door and left them.

He was able to walk the last time they saw him. Why was he in a wheelchair? Was it an act to make himself seem older and more frail?

'You wanted to speak to us?' Whitney said, as she sat on one of the easy chairs.

He remained in the chair and stared at them both, but still didn't speak.

'Harold, you asked for us to come out to talk to you. So, talk. Now,' Whitney said, before exchanging a glance with George and rolling her eyes.

He continued staring.

'If you're not going to say anything, we're leaving. As you know, we have the copycat Lenchester Strangler murders to solve, and you're just wasting our time.'

'Lenchester Strangler copycat,' he said slowly.

George scrutinised his face, still convinced there was more to him than he was making out, simply because of the alertness in his eyes. To the untrained eye, he might be able to act as if he didn't understand, but he couldn't fool her.

'Yes, the Lenchester Strangler,' George said, sitting on the other easy chair and locking eyes with him. 'Now, what is it you would like to tell us?'

'It's not me,' he said.

'We know it's not you because you're not physically capable. Are you admitting to it being you previously?' Whitney asked.

'I want immunity for all the other murders, and then I'll tell you what I know.'

'I don't have the power to do that.'

'I suppose it doesn't matter.' He shrugged. 'I'm an eighty-year-old man diagnosed with dementia. I'll never repeat what I'm about to tell you, so I'm safe.'

'What we want to do is catch the person who copied you and is currently murdering women. Tell us what you know,' Whitney said.

'I *was* the Lenchester Strangler,' he said, his voice stronger and more fluent than before.

'What about the trophies you took?' Whitney asked.

'I cut some hair from every victim. Just a little piece. Enough for me to remember them by.'

'And where are these locks of hair?' Whitney asked.

'I'm not sure where they are now,' he said, glancing away.

George stared at him. She didn't believe that for one moment. She wasn't going to pursue it now because, more importantly, they needed to catch the current offender.

'Okay, so that's confirmed what we thought. And you were lucky it wasn't proved,' Whitney said. 'Now, what is this information you have for us?'

'This person is definitely a copycat and knows exactly what I did.'

'Is that because it's someone you know?' Whitney asked.

'When I was in prison, I shared a cell with a man called Jeremy Jacobs. We were there for several years and I might have told him.'

'Might? Or did?' Whitney asked.

'Okay. I did tell him what I'd done. When you're with someone twenty-four-seven, you do tend to get close and share a lot of secrets.'

His eloquence was proof to George that all this time he'd been pretending to be less than lucid. But why? What was in it for him? Unless it was simply so he wasn't prosecuted for being the original Lenchester Strangler. But that seemed too obvious.

'How long did you share with Jacobs?' Whitney asked.

'Six years.'

'What was he in prison for?'

'Mortgage fraud.'

'What else can you tell me about him?' Whitney asked.

'He came from money and spoke like he'd got a stick up his arse.'

Judging by Whitney's glance in her direction she was no doubt thinking he was one of George's sort. Some things never changed, no matter how well they got to know each other.

'Anything else?'

'He was let out two years before me and knows all about the Lenchester Strangler murders. What else do you need to know? It's obvious he's the one. Go and arrest him.'

None of this was sitting right.

'Did you tell anyone else about the murders? You were in there a long time before Jacobs turned up,' Whitney said.

'No, I didn't. I was in a maximum security prison and didn't share a cell with anyone. I met Jacobs when I was moved and we were put together.'

'Why did you commit the murders?' George asked.

He shrugged. 'I enjoyed it.'

'When you say you *enjoyed it*. Which part of it did you enjoy?' she pushed.

'The whole thing. Seeing the fear in their eyes. Tying the scarf around their necks and pulling it tight. Watching the final breath leave their body. Nothing can prepare you for the adrenaline rush you get from that.' His eyes were bright.

'Did you feel any guilt?' Whitney asked.

He looked at her. 'I'm not saying anything else. You've had everything there is from me.' He closed his eyes.

'Let's go,' Whitney said to George.

'Okay,' George said.

'Well?' Whitney said once they'd left his room.

'I think it's incredible he's suddenly decided to spill the beans after all this time. It's all falling into our laps too easily. There's got to be a reason behind it.'

'Remember, he's got dementia,' Whitney said.

'So he wants everyone to believe. You only had to witness the alertness in his eyes, and his understanding about immunity to realise he uses it to his own ends. There's something going on here, and we need to bear that in mind. Including how he can afford the fees to live there. But, obviously, first we need to track down Jeremy Jacobs, because if Skinner is telling the truth, he could be our murderer.'

'Ellie, I want everything you can find on Jeremy Jacobs. He was in prison for fraud and spent time with Harold Skinner. He left two years before Skinner,' Whitney said.

'Yes, guv.'

She returned to her office as she needed to contact Jamieson and give her update so he could report to the Chief Constable.

'Sir,' she said once he'd answered his phone. 'I wanted to let you know we've got a new lead in the case, which you can report back.'

'Good work, Walker. Tell me more,' Jamieson said.

'Harold Skinner admitted to being the Lenchester

Strangler. He was in prison with a Jeremy Jacobs, who he confided in about all the murders.'

'Are you going to contact the CPS regarding prosecuting Skinner?'

'No point. He's been diagnosed with dementia. We can't prove he doesn't have it. He'll never repeat what he's told us. It's more important for us to catch the current offender.'

'You should have discussed it with me first.'

'There was nothing to discuss, plus I wasn't prepared to risk any delay, in case Skinner changed his mind about giving us the information.' The last thing they needed was for Jamieson to start interfering with witnesses.

'We'll discuss this later. Keep me informed and I'll let the Chief Constable know.'

She ended the call and the phone immediately rang.

'Walker.'

'Guv, I've got something for you,' Ellie said.

'Okay, I'm coming through.' She went back to the incident room, to the officer's desk. 'What is it?'

'Jeremy Jacobs went to Eton and then on to Cambridge. He was a property developer until he got involved in a mortgage fraud. After being released from prison, he went off the radar.'

'Well, that's no good,' Whitney said. 'If he's disappeared, how are we going to find him?'

'He can't escape me, guv,' Ellie said, smirking. 'I discovered he'd actually changed his name to Alastair Hepworth and is living at the same address as Serena Hastings.'

'What? He's Serena Hastings' boyfriend?' The tension in her chest eased. Finally they were getting somewhere.

'I'm not sure yet, guv. But we've certainly found ourselves a link. He also owns another property in town which I'll look into. He may be renting it out.'

'Excellent work, Ellie.' She turned away from the desk. 'Listen up, everyone,' she called to the team. 'We've discovered that Serena Hasting's boyfriend, or partner, or friend, is Alastair Hepworth, aka Jeremy Jacobs, and he used to be in prison with Harold Skinner, who's admitted to being the Lenchester Strangler. He also admitted to confiding in Hepworth about the murders. Ellie, I want you to continue with your research into him. Matt, you and I are going out to the gallery to see Serena and find out where Hepworth is. Frank, use the photo Ellie has and examine the CCTV footage. See if you can find evidence of him being close to the victims. Also, see if he was at the exhibition. Matt, you ready?'

'Yes, guv.'

'Come on. Let's go. This could be it.'

Chapter Thirty

Whitney pushed open the door to the Pictura Art Gallery and walked in, with Matt beside her. Serena was alone, covering a painting in bubble wrap. Good. They didn't have time to pussyfoot around her customers.

'Hello, Serena,' Whitney said.

'DCI Walker,' Serena said, smiling at them. 'What can I do to help?'

'Alastair Hepworth. How is he connected to you?' Whitney asked.

'He's my boyfriend.' Serena frowned. 'Why?'

'Does he live with you?' Whitney asked.

'Yes.'

'Where is he?'

'I'm not sure? What's this about?'

'Didn't you see him this morning?' She wasn't prepared to tell her about their suspicions.

'No. He could be at his flat.'

Was this the property Ellie mentioned, or an additional one?

'He lives with you and also has a flat. Why?'

Serena flushed. 'It's complicated. He likes his own space. Most of the time we're together. But sometimes he spends time at his own place.'

Now they were getting somewhere. Was he *alone* on the nights of the murders?

'Did he stay with you last night?'

'No, which is why I didn't see him this morning. I expect to see him this evening, we've arranged to have dinner together.'

'What's the address?' She'd check if it was the same flat Ellie had identified.

'Why are you asking?' Serena said.

'We want to speak to him regarding our investigation.'

'The murders? I don't understand. Surely you don't think he's involved?' Her hand clutched at her chest.

Whitney wasn't prepared to elaborate. For all she knew, Serena was involved, and she didn't want her to warn him. 'Just give me his address. I'm going to ask a uniformed officer to stay with you.'

'Am I under arrest?' Serena asked.

'No. But if you don't cooperate I will apply for a search warrant, which will not only close your gallery while it's being executed, but could very easily make the headlines. That wouldn't be good for business.'

'Do what you have to,' Serena said, a resigned sigh escaping her lips.

Whitney took out her radio and called for an officer. Once he'd arrived, she strode out, Matt not far behind.

After discovering Hepworth wasn't at his flat, they went straight to Serena's house, in case he'd gone back there.

'Alastair Hepworth?' Whitney said to the good-looking, dark-haired man who answered the door. He looked to be in his forties and was of medium height. His open-necked, pale-blue shirt showed off his suntan and accentuated his toned body.

'Yes. Who are you?'

'I'm Detective Chief Inspector Walker, and this is Detective Sergeant Price.' She held out her warrant card 'We'd like you to come with us to the police station to answer some questions.'

'What's this about?' he asked, his eyes darting from Whitney to Matt.

'We can discuss it at the station.'

'I'm not going anywhere, without knowing more about it.' His lips were pressed together into a thin line.

She wasn't prepared to spend any more time discussing it.

'Alastair Hepworth. I'm arresting you on suspicion of the murders of Celia Churchill, Cassandra Billington, and Pamela Whitehouse. You do not have to say anything, but it may harm your defence if you do not mention something which you later rely on in court. Anything you do say may be given in evidence. Do you understand?'

'M-murder? Me? You've got the wrong person,' he spluttered.

'We'll discuss this at the station. Do you understand the caution?'

'Yes,' he nodded his head vigorously.

Matt handcuffed him and they put him in the back of the car before heading back to the station. Once they'd logged him into the system, Whitney got on the phone to George.

'Can you come over? I want you to watch an interview with Alastair Hepworth the boyfriend of Serena Hastings. We're waiting for his solicitor. He's been arrested for the murders.'

'Give me half an hour, and I'll be there,' George said.

'That's great. I'm sending SOCO around to his flat. He's agreed and given us his key.'

∼

George and Whitney were in the incident room waiting for Hepworth's solicitor to arrive when a call came through.

'Walker.' She paused for a moment. 'That's fantastic. Thank you.' She ended the call and punched the air.

'What is it?' George asked.

'That was Jenny from SOCO. They've been to Hepworth's flat, and hidden at the back of a cupboard they found a small tin containing locks of hair. It's the trophies. We've got him.'

'Did they find anything else?' George asked.

'Not that I know of. They're bringing in the hair which will be DNA tested. But that's it. I can't believe it was so simple. We've done it. I won't let Jamieson know until we've interviewed Hepworth and got his full confession.'

'It seems a little too easy, though, don't you think?' George sensed something wasn't right.

'Sometimes it takes us a while. Sometimes it doesn't. You should know that by now. The main thing is, we've got the evidence.'

'Okay,' George said, unable to keep the doubt from her voice. The whole set up, first with Skinner and then with Hepworth, was too smooth.

'Guv,' Matt, called out. 'Hepworth's solicitor is here.'

Whitney handed George a mic and earpiece, and they left.

George went into the observation room and looked at the man and woman sitting there. His body was tense and his arms folded. His solicitor, an attractive woman with straight blonde hair, appeared calm and relaxed.

Whitney pressed the recording equipment.

'Interview on Thursday, twenty-eighth November with Detective Chief Inspector Walker, Detective Sergeant Price and…' She nodded at the other two. 'Please state your names for the recording.'

'Alastair Hepworth.'

'Phillipa Gordon, solicitor for Mr Hepworth.'

'I'd like to remind you that you're still under caution. Do you understand?' Whitney said.

'All I understand is you're accusing me of something I haven't done,' Alastair's upper-class voice rang out.

'Well, Mr Hepworth, maybe you'll change your mind on your denial when I tell you our forensics team have been to your flat and found a tin containing locks of hair, which we believe are from our three victims.'

His eyes widened. 'What are you talking about? There's nothing at my flat. Not unless … unless I've been framed. You have to believe me, I had nothing to do with those murders.'

'We understand you knew exactly how the original Lenchester Strangler operated and the way he went about his business,' Whitney said.

'I don't know the Lenchester Strangler.'

'You were in a prison cell with Harold Skinner, is that correct?'

Despite not being in the room, George could sense the ominous tension hanging in the air.

'Yes, I was.'

'And is it not correct that while he was in there, he confided in you that he was the original Lenchester strangler?'

'No. I had no idea that's who he was.'

'He would disagree. He's quite certain he told you, in great detail, everything he did, including taking locks of hair as trophies from all of the victims. That fact was never released to the public. So it could only have been known by either the murderer or someone who'd been told about it.'

'This is absolute nonsense. He said he was in prison for murdering his wife.'

'Why would he tell us you knew all about it and that you were committing the crimes as a copycat?'

He paled and remained silent.

'He's debating whether to tell you something,' George said. 'Give him some space. If you speak too soon, he might refrain.'

'He's doing it to get back at me,' Hepworth finally said.

'Why?' Whitney asked.

'Because I stole his money.'

That made sense. Whitney might have been convinced he was their murderer, but she hadn't been sure. Was Hepworth being set up? It could very easily be the case. Skinner was crafty enough to do it, and with his *dementia* could get away with it.

'What money?'

'When we were in prison, he told me about some money he had hidden.'

'Why would he tell you?' Whitney asked.

'Because we had an agreement that I'd retrieve it and, in exchange, get to keep a percentage.'

'Why did he want it at that particular time? Why couldn't he wait until he was released? It wasn't going anywhere,' Whitney said.

'He was worried somebody else might find it, because where it was buried had been turned into a building plot.'

'And you agreed to get it for him?'

'Yes.'

'How much money are we talking about?'

'One and a half million pounds.'

'No wonder Skinner wanted it back,' George said.

'But instead of returning it, you kept it.'

'Yes.' He lowered his gaze.

'Why?'

'He couldn't prove anything and had begun to get dementia. His memory was going, so I figured by the time he got out, he wouldn't need it. I was wrong.'

'What happened when he was released? Did he contact you?'

'I changed my name, on the off-chance he remembered and tried to find me.'

'Did you know he was out of prison?'

'Yes. I read about it online. I also employed a private investigator who told me he was living at Featherstone Manor.'

'Why didn't you leave the area altogether once you knew he was around? Why are you still here?'

'Because I'd met Serena and thought he'd never find me. I didn't think anyone would. I was banking on his dementia stopping him from remembering our arrangement.'

'Clearly, you were wrong. How do we know what you're saying is the truth? Where's the money?'

'I invested some in shares and bought my flat. The remainder is in the bank, and I'm using it for everyday expenses.'

'Don't you work?'

'I don't need to. Serena's doing well, and I've got the money.'

'You didn't think of returning any to Skinner?' Whitney said.

'He doesn't need it. He's in a luxury private care home,

he must have enough money to pay, or he wouldn't be there.'

'If what you're saying about him framing you is true, it means he knows your new name, and where you live. How? It doesn't make sense. It doesn't tie up,' Whitney said.

'That's for you to find out. You're the police and have the resources. I'm just telling you, I'm not to blame for any of the murders.' His solicitor rested a hand on his arm and whispered something to him. 'You've got to believe me,' he said, pleading.

'All we have is your word for it. We'll investigate your claims. In the meantime, what were you doing during the early hours of the eleventh, fifteenth, and twentieth of November?'

'I'm not sure without my diary which is on my laptop. I'm usually at the flat or with Serena.'

'You'll be kept in custody until such time as we have more to go on,' Whitney said.

'You don't have long. Either charge him or let him go,' Phillipa Gordon said.

'I'm well aware of the legalities,' Whitney said. 'If you expect us to believe this story, then we need to follow it up. In the meantime, you'll return to your cell and wait. Interview suspended. DS Price will take you back.'

'I'm inclined to believe him,' George said when Whitney came into the room. 'His mannerisms, the expression on his face, his breathing. They all indicated he was telling the truth. When you told him about the trophies being found, he appeared genuinely shocked. He didn't believe it. I think we've got to take what he said and investigate it, especially as we know Skinner can't be trusted. If Hepworth had taken his money, he would want to exact revenge.'

'I agree with you, and if that's the case, then somebody else is working with Harold Skinner to commit the murders, as he isn't capable of doing them himself. We need to find out who that *somebody* is.'

Chapter Thirty-One

'Right,' Whitney said, staring at the board. 'Let's think of all the people we know who could be working with Skinner.'

'The one person who sticks in my mind is Larry Cane,' George said. 'With his training, he'd have been able to stalk the victims without being observed. We know from Don Mason that he was devious, and that trait would be invaluable in this situation. He also knows everything about the case.'

'And let's not forget he's recently been fired by the police. He's the person who links this whole thing together.'

'Did you get anything from the tail you put on him?'

'He hasn't done anything to alert us, but it's early days. I'll contact Jake and Fiona, the officers tailing him, and find out.' Whitney pulled out her radio 'Update on where you are with Larry Cane?'

'He spends most of his time at home. Although he has just left and we're following him now. He's heading south on Landcross Road.'

'Landcross Road, that's towards Willington and Feath-erstone Manor where Harold Skinner lives,' Whitney said. 'Let me know as soon as possible whether that's his destination.'

'Yes, guv.'

'I think you could be right,' she said to George. 'If Cane is visiting Skinner, it points to Hepworth telling the truth about being framed.'

'Well, it does make sense,' George said.

Several minutes later, Whitney's radio crackled. 'Target has driven into Featherstone Manor. He's parked and heading towards the entrance.'

'Stay there and keep an eye on him. We're coming over,' Whitney said. 'Come on, George, let's go.'

'What are we going to do? Follow Cane or speak to Skinner?' George asked.

'We'll confront them together,' Whitney said.

They drove to Featherstone Manor and just as they arrived saw Cane heading back to his car.

'Keep tailing him,' Whitney told the officers. 'I'm going to visit Harold Skinner. Let me know where Cane goes.'

They strode into the home and up to the desk. 'Where's Harold Skinner?' Whitney asked.

'I believe he's in his room,' the care assistant on recep-tion said.

'Okay, thanks.'

They hurried there and walked in without knocking.

'What are you doing here?' Skinner said.

'We've come to speak to you about Larry Cane.'

'Who?' he said.

'Don't play dumb with me. We know he's just been to visit,' Whitney said. 'We've also been talking to Alastair Hepworth and he said you set him up and planted evidence because he stole money from you.'

'Don't be fooled by that scheming bastard. He'll say anything to stop you from arresting him for what he's done. It's nothing to do with me. I can hardly walk. I'm here all the time and lots of people will vouch for me.'

'Why did Larry Cane visit?' Whitney asked.

He stared at them. His eyes alert. 'I don't know what you're talking about. You'll have to go. I'm not feeling well.' His whole demeanour changed, and suddenly he looked like an incapacitated elderly man.

'Cut the theatrics, Harold. Is it true that Alastair Hepworth, aka Jeremy Jacobs, stole your money?'

'What money?' he said, shrugging.

Whitney glared at him. 'You know exactly what I'm talking about. The million and a half you had buried. You're trying to frame him.'

'I don't know what you're talking about.'

'Cooperate or we will take you in for questioning,' Whitney threatened.

'How's that going to look?' he said. 'An old man with dementia. You've got no chance of making anything stick.'

Her fists clenched. He was right. They had little hope of pinning anything on him.

'Don't go anywhere,' she said. 'Because we'll be back.'

'Suit yourself. It'll be a total waste of time if you do.' He grinned.

Before leaving the home, Whitney arranged for a staff member to be with Skinner at all times, ensuring he didn't use his phone. She couldn't risk him warning Cane.

Once outside, she radioed the officers tailing him.

'Where is he now?' she said.

'I'm sorry, guv. We've lost him.'

They had to be kidding. She emitted a loud groan. 'What do you mean you've lost him?'

'We got stuck at some lights and he disappeared in the Royston area.'

'That's nowhere near his home. What was he doing around there?'

'We don't know.'

'Has he been out that way before?' she asked.

'No.'

'I suggest you keep looking and if you can't find him go back to his house in case he's daft enough to go back.'

Whitney turned to George. 'I can't believe they lost him.'

'What shall we do now?' George said.

'Go back to the incident room.'

When they arrived, Whitney went over to Frank, who was sitting at his desk, with his legs outstretched and his hands linked behind his head.

'Frank, get hold of the CCTV footage close to Feather-stone Manor, where Harold Skinner lives. I want to look at roads leading into the city, in particular the Royston area as that's where we lost Cane. He's driving a red Toyota Corolla.'

'Yes, guv,' he said.

'We need to track down where he went.'

She tapped her foot impatiently on the floor while he loaded up the footage.

'There's his car,' Frank said, pointing at Cane heading down the road from the care home.

'And there's Jake tailing him,' she added.

They watched while Cane went over the traffic lights, where her officers had lost him, and saw him turn right into Tanner Street and then go left into Napier Road.

'Where's he heading?' Whitney said.

'We've gone as far as the cameras pick up,' Frank said.

'What's down there?' Whitney asked, pointing at the screen.

'Not a lot. There used to be some industrial units which are now empty. I believe there's an old storage depot.'

'Storage, as in lock-ups?' George said. 'Do you remember when we were talking to Don Mason? He mentioned they thought Harold Skinner had one somewhere, but they couldn't find it. It could be there?'

Whitney flashed a smile at George. 'Good call. Give me the address of this storage place. George and I will go out there. I need a photo of Larry Cane to take with us.'

When they arrived, they went into the office. A young man was sitting behind the counter. He looked up when they entered, a bored expression on his face.

'Detective Chief Inspector Walker from Lenchester CID,' she said, holding out her warrant card. 'We're looking for this man.' She took her phone from her pocket and pulled up the photo of Larry Cane. She slid it over to him. 'Do you recognise him?'

'I'm not sure,' he said.

'Not good enough. We think he visited here a short time ago. Do you have any CCTV footage we can look at?' Whitney asked.

'I'm not allowed to show people.' He stared at her belligerently.

'I'm not *"people"*. I'm the police and investigating a series of murders. So, either you show us or I get a search warrant. And if that happens I will tear this place apart.'

'Okay. Okay. Keep your hair on.' He pulled up the CCTV footage on his screen, and they could see Larry get out of his car and go over to one of the storage units.

'How old is this place?' Whitney asked.

'It's been going for about forty years.'

'How many storage units do you have?'

'It's small. Only fifty.'

'I want to look in the unit this man went into.'

'I don't know if I can do that,' he replied.

'Do I have to go through all that again?' Whitney said. 'Show me the unit.'

'They all have their own individual codes to their keypad.'

'Are you telling me you can't get in? Because, if so, I'll get that search warrant I mentioned earlier, and we'll break down all the doors,' she threatened.

'No, I'm not saying that. I can override it,' the young man said.

'Good. Take us now.'

'Okay.' He sighed and got out of his chair. 'Come this way.'

When they got to the unit, he keyed in a number and rolled up the door.

'You can leave us,' Whitney said.

'I better not get in trouble for this,' he said, as he turned to walk away.

'I can assure you you'd have got in more trouble for not showing us.'

They entered the storage unit, which was virtually bare, apart from six plastic containers on the floor. Whitney handed George a pair of disposable gloves and they started looking through. The first box Whitney opened was full of men's clothing, but there was nothing in there of note. Then she went to a second box and opened a white plastic carrier bag that had been folded up in the corner.

She gasped.

It was full of pink chiffon scarves.

'We've got him, George. We've got him,' she shouted,

unable to hide her excitement. 'I've found a bag of scarves. Why else would Cane come here if it wasn't to get what he needed for the next kill? Let's see what else we can find.'

They carried on searching.

'Look.' George held out a small plastic container. 'Locks of hair. I'm assuming these were from the original victims. There appear to be six different hair samples in here.'

'And I've just found a load of cable ties,' Whitney said. 'We've got a slam-dunk.'

'A what?' George said, frowning.

'It's a basketball metaphor.'

'I didn't know you followed basketball.'

'I don't … it's an everyday phrase.'

'It can't be common parlance, if I haven't heard of it,' George said.

'Because you always use everyday language in your *common parlance?*' Whitney said laughing.

'One day you'll cease with the mockery.' George let out an exasperated sigh.

'You know it's only meant in fun. Anyway, back to what's important. This is now a crime scene. I'm going to call in SOCO. We need to establish that Cane has actually been in here and touched these items.'

'Unless he used gloves,' George said.

'He may have. Actually, as an ex-copper he should have. But as he has no idea anyone knows about this place, he might not. Or he might intend on destroying all of the evidence when he's finished carrying out the murders.'

'All good points,' George said.

Whitney pulled out her radio. 'This is DCI Walker. I want SOCO at the storage units on Napier Road. Also, send two uniformed officers as soon as possible.'

They went back into the office where the manager had returned to his desk.

'The storage unit is now a crime scene and I'm waiting for my officers to arrive,' Whitney said. 'You're to close the facility. I don't want anyone coming in or out until you have my permission. Scenes of crime officers will be here shortly to do their forensic testing.'

'Does that mean I can't go home?' he asked.

'When does your shift end?' Whitney asked.

'Not for another five hours.'

'You can stay until then. One of my officers will take a statement from you. Did the man who went into the unit earlier come into the office?'

'No, he didn't. He went straight there.'

'But you kept your eye on him?' Whitney said.

'It's very quiet here and he was the only visitor, so yes, I did watch him on the CCTV.'

'Have you seen him here before?' Whitney asked.

'Once. But that doesn't mean he didn't visit more often. Unit holders can get in when we're closed. They're given a code for the keypad on the front gate.'

'Can you tell who's been in? Does each lock-up owner have a different code?' Whitney asked.

'No. They all have the same.'

'How long has this particular unit being rented?'

He looked at his records on the computer screen. 'This one's been held by the same person for the past thirty-five years. It's in the name of Beatrice West.'

Whitney didn't recognise the name.

'How do they pay?'

'This one is different. Thirty-five years ago, someone paid for forty years, upfront.'

'Have other holders done the same?'

'No. But this was when they first opened. The owners might have needed the money.'

'Or whoever paid was investing into the business. Who owns the facility?' George asked.

'It's a company called Long Haul. I don't have anything to do with them.'

'How long have you worked here?'

'Two years. I have a manager who visits on a regular basis. The owners have a lot of similar businesses, I believe.'

'I'll need their details,' Whitney said.

He wrote them down on a piece of paper and handed it to her.

'Thanks.'

Whitney turned as she saw a police car driving in. She walked over to the car.

'I want a cordon put up around unit fifteen,' she said to one of the officers.

'Yes, guv.'

'SOCO will be here shortly. Take a statement from the man in the office. We think this is the storage facility used by the Lenchester Strangler, and his copycat. We're going back to the station.'

Chapter Thirty-Two

'Attention, everyone,' Whitney called out to her team as she entered the incident room. 'We've found the lock-up belonging to the previous Lenchester Strangler, who we know is Harold Skinner. We believe he's paying Larry Cane to frame Alastair Hepworth, who stole a large sum of money from him. After visiting Skinner earlier today, Cane went to the lock-up, most likely to take the equipment needed for the next murder. He's now gone missing. We visited Harold Skinner after Cane's visit, but he wouldn't admit to anything.'

'Wasn't that a mistake, guv?' Frank said.

Whitney looked at him, amazed he'd actually thought it through. 'Why?'

'Because if Harold Skinner gets in touch with Cane, he's going to know we're onto him.'

'Good point, Frank. But I made sure Skinner wasn't left on his own, so there's no chance of that happening. Right now, we need to capture Cane before he can murder again.'

'But we've no idea which of the two women are going to be next,' George said.

'We need to alert Greta Cook and Megan Faulkner. Uniformed officers have been passing their homes on a regular basis. Ellie, I want you to contact them and find out where they are. We need an officer outside the front of their houses at all times.'

'We've got a bit of time,' George said. 'The killings have always been committed at night. Perhaps we can set up some sort of sting.'

'Explain,' Whitney said.

'Why don't we make sure the women aren't there and instead have someone take their place. A police officer in bed and other officers hiding throughout the house? When he breaks in, we can catch him.'

'I'll have to run it past, Jamieson. You know what he's like regarding our operations. It certainly seems the right thing to do.'

Whitney left the room and went to Jamieson's office. She knocked on the door but there was no reply, so she stuck her head in. The room was empty. As she turned to leave, she saw him heading towards her.

'What can I do for you, Walker?' he said.

'I need to speak to you about an operation I'm putting together,' she said.

'As long as it's nothing to do with putting civilians in danger. You know my views on that,' he said.

'Nobody will be in danger. But we do want to place someone in the homes belonging to the women on the list of targets. We know who the murderer is. Our copycat has been working with the original Lenchester Strangler with a view to framing somebody else for the murders.'

'Sounds very complicated,' Jamieson said.

'Not really. The offender is the ex-copper, Larry Cane,

so he knows all about how we operate. We've got an alert out for him, but he's gone missing. What we'd like to do is use two female officers, and place one in each of the possible victims' houses. There will be a number of other officers there, in hiding. The actual targets will be placed in protective custody until the operation's over. We'll need officers in both houses as we don't know which he's targeting.'

'Why don't you have a huge police presence at one house, and then at the other have less of one. That should make him believe the second house is the easiest target. Then you only need to have officers inside one of the houses,' Jamieson said.

'It's a thought, but possibly too obvious.'

Leading Cane to a particular house was a good idea, but not doing it the way he'd suggested.

'Well, I'm sure you'll come up with something.'

'Yes, sir. Does that mean we have your permission to undertake the operation?' Whitney confirmed.

'I'm assuming Dr Cavendish isn't going to be involved in this. Bearing in mind what's happened in the past,' he said.

'You have my assurance on that front. I have no intention of letting her anywhere near. Do we have your approval?'

'You do. Let me know how it goes. I assume it's going to be this evening.'

'Yes, sir. If he knows we're onto him and wants to complete the job, then he's going to do it straight away, and after it's over he'll duck out of sight.'

'Okay. Off you go.'

Whitney returned to the incident room. 'The Super's approved the operation' she said to George. 'He came up with a half-arsed idea, but that's hardly surprising.'

'One day he might actually do something to impress you,' George said.

'I doubt it. Anyway, we'll come up with our own plan. Listen up, everyone. We need to direct Cane to one of the houses, so we can focus our efforts in one spot. Ideas?'

'It's possible he doesn't know we've worked out the two women at risk, which will go in our favour,' Frank said.

'I doubt that's the case,' George said. 'He doesn't strike me as someone who leaves things to chance. He's too methodical.'

'As we don't know who his victim is, we have to assume it could be either of them. I suggest we make him believe one of the women isn't at home. We'll leave one house in darkness from early evening and one with the lights on and a police presence outside,' Matt said.

'Won't the officer outside deter him?' Frank said.

'I don't believe so. If anything, it would be a massive thrill for him, and would feed his ego, if he could attack while an officer was on the property. He has complete disdain for the force following his dismissal,' George said.

'We'll lead him to the house which is easiest to access from the back, just in case he is deterred,' Matt said.

'That could work,' Whitney said. 'But we'll make sure both women are well away from their houses. I'll take the place of the potential victim and be in her bed. We'll have officers strategically placed inside the house and in the surrounding streets so we can track Cane's progress.'

'What about me?' George said.

'You're not involved in this.'

'Why not?'

'You know why not. You're not a police officer and Jamieson said you can't be there. Once we've brought Cane in for questioning, you're more than welcome to watch the interview.'

'Is that going to be sometime during the night?'

'If all goes to plan and he attempts the murder tonight, then we'll bring him in, and we'll interview him first thing in the morning.'

'Okay,' George said.

'Right. I want everyone to meet back here at eight o'clock. Go home, get some rest. This is going to be an all-nighter.'

Whitney managed to get home for a quick two-hour nap and was back in the office by six. She tried to get on with some outstanding paperwork but, as usual, began pacing, waiting for the rest of her team to arrive. They were all there by eight and she ran through their plan.

Ellie had been in touch with Greta and Megan and they were out of the way under police protection. For several hours Megan's house had been left in darkness, with the curtains open, so it appeared no one was home.

They were going to be at Greta's house waiting for Cane.

'Right, I'm going to be in the bedroom. Doug, you can be in the en suite. Matt, I want you downstairs, but you need to keep out of the way. Listen for him coming in. We're assuming he'll enter through the back door like he did previously. There's an easy way in around the back. Frank, I want you situated in your car a little way up the road so you can see him arrive and let us know.'

'Yes, guv,' Frank said.

'Be cautious with *all* cars as we have no idea whether he's still in his Toyota or using a different one.'

'Yes, guv.'

'Ellie, you can be upstairs with Doug. Sue, I want you

at the other end of the road in case he comes that way or decides to walk some of the way, rather than drive. He could park around the corner. Is everyone clear?'

'Yes, guv,' they all said.

'We'll let him come up the stairs and into the bedroom and then we'll catch him in the act. That way there's no way he can wriggle out of it. Okay. Let's go. The drinks are on me once we've nailed him.'

Chapter Thirty-Three

Whitney surveyed Greta Cook's house from a distance. The main thing was to make sure no one saw them enter, so after scouring the area to make sure he wasn't there they went around the back separately. It was only nine-thirty, she doubted he'd be hanging around yet.

Once inside, they sat together in the lounge, with the curtains closed and the light on, so it looked like Greta was there.

At eleven Whitney instructed them to go to their positions. 'It's probably a bit early to be lying in bed,' she said to Doug once they were upstairs. 'But we'll wait here just in case he's impatient. Although I doubt he will be as all the other murders have taken place after midnight.'

They sat there talking and soon it hit midnight. 'Okay, everyone, it will be any time from now. Frank, Sue, are you still awake?' Whitney said into the radio.

'Yes, guv,' came from both of them.

'No sign of anything yet, but I'll let you know when there is,' Frank said.

'Actually, there's a car moving slowly along Linden

Road,' Sue said. 'They've just gone past the end of this road and stopped a couple of hundred yards down. I'll phone in the registration plate.'

'Thanks, Sue.'

'The car belongs to a Ryan Cole,' Sue said after a couple of minutes.

'Are they related in any way to Larry?' Whitney asked.

'I'm not sure,' Sue said.

'Has it been reported stolen?' Whitney asked.

'No, it hasn't. Maybe it's a car he's borrowed from a friend, or one he's stolen that hasn't yet been noticed. Oh, they've got out of the car. Sorry, guv. It's a woman and she's heading into one of the houses. She's either visiting someone or lives there,' Sue said.

'Okay. No problem. Keep looking.'

They were in their positions for a while, when Frank buzzed in.

'He's coming guv. He's walking on the opposite side of the road. He's gone past the house and looked across at the uniformed officer out the front. He's now crossing the road and heading back up the street towards you.'

'Thanks, Frank. Everyone be prepared,' Whitney said.

'He's skirted beside the hedge running alongside the house. He's going in the back, as predicted.'

'He can climb over into the back garden easily enough. We'll be ready for him. Silence everyone,' Whitney said.

They were quiet for what seemed like an hour, but was probably only a few minutes. The sound of smashing glass came from downstairs. Presumably he'd put his hand through the back door to get in. She caught her breath as the dull echo of footsteps against the carpeted stairs rang out.

She swallowed hard. Even though she knew she was

perfectly safe and that everyone was there, her heart still pounded.

The door opened slowly, letting light leak in. She lay motionless on the bed, pretending to be asleep. Through a tiny gap in her eyelids she made out a dark shadow standing by the open door. He took two steps towards her and stopped. After a few seconds, he took two more, before again coming to a halt. He repeated this until finally he loomed over her.

Every breath he expelled reeked of stale onions.

The urge to gag almost got the better of her but she had to keep still.

She strained to listen for backup but there was nothing except her own roaring pulse and the rustling sound of fabric. Her hand tightened around her taser and she tensed every muscle in her body as the sheet was dragged from her face and a hand clamped down on her mouth.

Then all of a sudden the room was lit up.

Adrenaline flared through her body and she swept the hand away from her mouth, sending Cane flying backwards.

'Bitch,' he swore as he righted himself and charged towards her, pink chiffon scarf in one hand.

Whitney jumped from the bed and ducked out of the way of his oncoming fist. He turned and lunged towards her, his hand wrapped around her wrist. But she shook him off and managed to grab hold of his arm, yanking it firmly behind his back. He let out a cry of pain but managed to shake her off.

He made a dash towards the door with Whitney in hot pursuit, but he didn't get far as Doug came charging into the room and rugby tackled him to the ground.

'Cuff him.' Whitney said.

Doug pulled Cane into a standing position, hand-cuffed him behind his back, and held him in front of Whitney.

'Larry Cane, I'm arresting you on suspicion of the murders of Celia Churchill, Cassandra Billington, and Pamela Whitehouse. You do not have to say anything, but it may harm your defence if you do not mention something which you later rely on in court. Anything you do say may be given in evidence. Do you understand?'

'Whatever,' Cane snarled.

～

George walked into the station, the tension in her shoulders easing when she saw Whitney standing with Matt. She'd waited up most of the night for a text to say the operation had been a success and that Larry Cane was in custody.

All she'd got was an emoji thumbs up. That told her nothing. She'd no idea whether anyone had been hurt or what had transpired.

'Good morning,' she said to both of them.

'You're here just in time for the interview. Cane's solicitor has arrived. Matt and I will interview and you can observe, as usual.'

'Before we go down, perhaps you can give me a rundown on what happened last night?' George said.

'Sure. Matt, give us a minute.' They waited until the officer had left them. 'I did text you after it was all over.'

'A text which told me nothing. Was anyone hurt? Did he try to make a run for it? What exactly went on?'

'Suddenly, now you want to know the ins and outs of everything. Usually, you don't care. That's why you got the thumbs up. I thought it would be enough for you.'

Whitney was right. Normally she didn't need all the details. Why was this so different?

'I was concerned for you. You could've been in danger.'

'Says the person who seems to attract it.'

'I can see that you're fine. Is there anything else I need to know?'

'The operation went well,' Whitney said, resting her hand on George's arm. 'Thanks for being concerned. Are we okay to interview him now?'

'Yes.'

They collected Matt and headed downstairs. George went into the observation room and looked through at Larry Cane, sitting there, his brow furrowed. His solicitor was seated next to him, shuffling papers.

Whitney and Matt walked in. She set the recording equipment. 'Interview between Detective Chief Inspector Walker, Detective Sergeant Price and … State your name for the recording.' She nodded at the prisoner.

'Larry Cane.'

'William Bow, solicitor for the accused.'

'I'm sure you know all this, but just to confirm, you understand you're still under caution and anything you say may be used in evidence against you.'

Cane glared at her and nodded. 'Speak for the recording,' Whitney said.

'Yes, I understand,' he said.

'Let's start at the beginning, you were acting as a copycat murderer for Harold Skinner, the Lenchester Strangler. Is that correct?'

'No comment.'

'Larry, you know how this is going to go. Why don't you make it easy on yourself and tell us what happened?' Whitney said.

'Why don't you just do your job? You're useless. Like the rest of the force,' he snarled.

'That's your opinion,' Whitney said calmly.

'Because that's what I know. You're all totally inept, and yet I get kicked out for trying to do my job.'

'I don't think that's the case. You falsified evidence in the original Lenchester Strangler case.'

'To get a conviction, which we didn't get, even though he was guilty. And then he murdered again.'

'You've also been found guilty of sexual harassment,' Whitney said.

'It was just a set-up designed to get rid of me. If—'

'We're not here to discuss that,' Whitney said, interrupting. 'We're here about the murders. As I'm sure you're aware, if you tell us everything you know, it will go in your favour.'

'I want a deal. I'll give you information and you offer me a lighter sentence. Remember I've been in the job. I know what goes down in cases like this.'

'So you should also know that I don't have the power to authorise a deal. What I can do is let the Crown Prosecution Service know you've cooperated and that will go in your favour.'

He sighed. 'Okay. What do you know so far?'

'You tell us.'

'Jeremy Jacobs, aka Alastair Hepworth, stole money from Harold Skinner. Skinner found out I'd been kicked out of the force. He assumed I'd got no money as I'd lost my pension, so he offered to pay me to carry out the murders and frame Hepworth for them. I placed the evidence in his flat.'

'How did he know about you leaving the force?'

'I don't know. Ask him.'

'And you were quite happy to murder those innocent women for money?'

'Don't start trying to lay a guilt trip on me. I agreed to do it because I was offered a lot of money, which I needed.'

'How much?' Whitney asked.

'Half a million pounds.'

'Where did Skinner get that sort of money from?' Whitney asked.

'He had money stashed all over the place from dirty dealings he was engaged in before he went into prison. He gave me two hundred thousand down and said I'd get the rest once I'd completed the murders and Hepworth had been framed.'

'Once you'd found out Skinner definitely was the Lenchester Strangler and you'd visited his locker, why didn't you report it?'

'After what the force did to me? You must be joking. As I've just told you. Skinner offered me money and I took it. No way was I going to live the rest of my life from hand to mouth, after giving nearly forty years to the force. It might have been different if they'd treated me better. But they didn't and I don't owe them anything,' Larry said.

'I understand Harold Skinner informed you about the scarves, cable ties, and everything you needed to frame Hepworth, but how did you find out about the women buying the Drury Wilde paintings?' Whitney asked.

'That was down to Skinner. He was blackmailing the driver who worked for the gallery, because he'd been in prison and Serena Hastings didn't know.'

'How involved was the driver in all this?'

'All he did was let Skinner have a list of who had bought particular paintings and where they lived,' Cane said.

'How did you get the list of names to Skinner? There

must have been someone else involved. We checked the visitor list at Featherstone Manor and the driver wasn't one of them.'

'It was all done electronically. I was emailed the names and the addresses of the women to target.'

'Did Skinner stipulate in which order you were to carry out the murders?'

'No. He left it up to me. Once I had their details, I staked out two women at a time and then decided who was going to be first.'

'Not very methodical,' George said in Whitney's ear.

'A bit like sticking a pin in,' Whitney said.

'There was more to it than that. I'm a police officer. I do know what to do. I looked at the addresses, staked out the houses, and then I made my decisions.'

'I take it you're now pleading guilty to all offences?' Whitney said.

'I think that's obvious,' Cane said. 'Otherwise, I wouldn't be answering all your questions, would I?'

'Why were the victims all customers from the art gallery who had bought Wilde's paintings?' Whitney asked.

'Skinner wanted to do as much damage to Hepworth, and those close to him, as possible. It was the perfect scenario.'

'How did Skinner know about the art gallery and Hepworth's involvement with Serena Hastings?'

'The same as he knew about me. He used a private detective. And before you ask, no I don't know the name of the person he hired.'

'What have you done with the down payment?'

'It's at home.'

'Don't tell me, stashed under the mattress?'

'I could hardly put it in the bank, could I?' He leaned in and spoke quietly to his solicitor.

'My client isn't prepared to answer any more questions,' the solicitor said.

'Does anyone else know about this money?' Whitney asked.

'No comment.'

'I'd end the interview, if I was you,' George said. 'Judging by the stubborn expression on his face and his closed body language he's ceased being cooperative.

'Interview terminated,' Whitney said, stopping the recording equipment.

After Cane was escorted back to his cell, she went in to see George.

'Thoughts?' Whitney said.

'He showed no remorse whatsoever,' George said.

'And to think he was once a police officer. It makes me sick.'

'He wasn't an officer at the time, because he'd been fired. He probably believed he was getting revenge.'

'I don't care. He's still despicable.'

'Can we do anything about Skinner?' George asked.

'I'll speak to the Crown Prosecution Service. We may be able to arrange a psych evaluation, but even with Cane's testimony it's not going to be easy because of the dementia. We might be able to get him admitted to a secure facility, though.'

'What are we doing now?' George asked.

'We'll find the driver, Rod Kerr, and tie the rest of this up. Do you want to come with?'

'Yes, you've got me all day as it's Sunday,' George said.

They left the station and went to Rod Kerr's house. Whitney knocked on the door and he answered almost immediately.

'Rod Kerr, we're here to arrest you for being an accessory in the murders of Celia Churchill, Cassandra Billington, and Pamela Whitehouse. You do not have to say anything, but it may harm your defence if you do not mention something which you later rely on in court. Anything you do say may be given in evidence. Do you understand?'

'I don't know what you're talking about?' Kerr said.

'We've just arrested Larry Cane, who's been working with Harold Skinner, and he has informed us that you were the one to provide them with the list of women who bought the Drury Wilde paintings, and who were subsequently murdered.'

He paled. 'B-but…'

'Do you understand the charge?' Whitney said.

'Yes. But I had no idea what they were planning. I thought they were going to break into their houses. Those people were rich. They were insured and could afford it.'

'That doesn't make it right,' Whitney said.

'I couldn't do anything else. I was in danger of losing my job and we need the money.'

'You do realise that thanks to you, three women are now dead and there could have been two more. Being worried about your job isn't a good enough excuse. You're coming with us down to the station.'

Whitney handcuffed him and put him in the back of the car.

Chapter Thirty-Four

George sat in the café waiting for Whitney and Tiffany to arrive. It was a crisp, bracing day. The sort she usually enjoyed, but today she couldn't, knowing how hard it was going to be now Tiffany had finally made her decision. Whitney was going to find it very difficult with her gone.

After a few minutes the two of them arrived. They were both smiling as they came over to her.

'Hi, George. Have you ordered?' Whitney said.

'I was waiting for you.'

'I'll go,' Whitney said.

'No, I will,' Tiffany said. 'Coffee and cake all round.'

Tiffany went to the counter and Whitney sat opposite George, her brow furrowed.

A sure sign she was worried.

'How are you coping? And don't say *fine* because I won't believe you,' George said.

'It is fine. I've wrapped my head around it. I know she won't be gone forever and she deserves to have a good time. I can't live my life through her. It's what my mum told me.'

'Your mum's very wise.'

'I just wish it wasn't so soon. She's leaving in two weeks.' Whitney bit down on her bottom lip.

'She's going to have a good time. You must try not to worry about her. It will do her good to travel,' George said.

'I know, but I'm still going to miss her. At least she can return to the university once she's finished her travels.'

'Yes, but you mustn't hold on to that,' George said.

'What do you mean?'

'This is her life, not yours, and you must remember that.'

'I already told you that. It's what Mum said.'

'I wanted to reiterate, to make sure you really understood.'

'Oh, stop being all therapist over me. You know what I'm like. I'm going to miss her like crazy. But if that's what she wants to do, then I'm happy for her. What about you?' Whitney said.

'What about me?' George shook her head. How did they get on to her?

'What's going on with you and Ross? Where's it heading?' Whitney leaned forward, a mischievous twinkle in her eyes.

It was unsettling.

'I have no idea.'

'Really? None?' She tilted her head to one side.

'I'm happy as it is, and I don't want anything to change. We're in a good space.'

'You know that means now that something will happen,' Whitney said.

'Of course it won't. Don't be so ridiculous. What on earth could happen?'

'A proposal, maybe?'

'You've been reading too many romance books. That is most definitely not on the cards. I'd know if it was.'

'What if he did ask you to marry him? Would you?' Whitney pushed.

'No.'

Whitney's face fell. George hadn't meant to sound so harsh. Would it hurt her to open up a little? Whitney would appreciate it.

'It's not something I've considered,' she said.

'Well—'

'What's with the serious faces?' Tiffany had arrived back in the nick of time.

'She was about to spill the beans about her relationship with Ross,' Whitney said, winking at George.

'Really?' Tiffany's eyes widened.

'Talk about like mother, like daughter. I've got no chance,' George said, shaking her head. 'Hopeless.'

'You know you love us, really,' Tiffany said.

They exchanged a glance and all started to laugh.

Whitney would be okay when Tiffany left. George would make sure of it.

∾

GET ANOTHER BOOK FOR FREE!

To instantly receive the free novella, **The Night Shift**, featuring Whitney when she was a Detective Sergeant, ten years ago, sign up for Sally Rigby's free author newsletter at www.sallyrigby.com

A word from
Sally

Did you enjoy this book? You can make a big difference.

Reviews are the most powerful tools in my arsenal when it comes to getting attention for my books. Much as I'd like to, I don't have the financial muscle of a New York publisher. I can't take out full page ads in the newspaper or put posters on the subway.

(Not yet, anyway).

But I do have something much more powerful and effective than that, and it's something those publishers would kill to get their hands on.

A committed and loyal bunch of readers.

Honest reviews of my books help bring them to the attention of other readers.

If you've enjoyed this book, I would be very grateful if you could spend just five minutes leaving a review (it can be as short as you like).

Thank you.

Read more about Cavendish & Walker

DEADLY GAMES - Cavendish & Walker Book 1

A killer is playing cat and mouse....... and winning.

DCI Whitney Walker wants to save her career. Forensic psychologist, Dr Georgina Cavendish, wants to avenge the death of her student.

Sparks fly when real world policing meets academic theory, and it's not a pretty sight.

When two more bodies are discovered, Walker and Cavendish form an uneasy alliance. But are they in time to save the next victim?

Deadly Games is the first book in the Cavendish and Walker crime fiction series. If you like serial killer thrillers and psychological intrigue, then you'll love Sally Rigby's page-turning book.

Pick up *Deadly Games* today to read Cavendish & Walker's first case.

FATAL JUSTICE - Cavendish & Walker Book 2

A vigilante's on the loose, dishing out their kind of justice...

A string of mutilated bodies sees Detective Chief Inspector Whitney Walker back in action. But when she discovers the victims have all been grooming young girls, she fears a vigilante is on the loose. And while she understands the motive, no one is above the law.

Once again, she turns to forensic psychologist, Dr Georgina Cavendish, to unravel the cryptic clues. But will they be able to save the next victim from a gruesome death?

Fatal Justice is the second book in the Cavendish & Walker crime fiction series. If you like your mysteries dark, and with a twist, pick up a copy of Sally Rigby's book today.

～

DEATH TRACK - Cavendish & Walker Book 3

Catch the train if you dare...

After a teenage boy is found dead on a Lenchester train, Detective Chief Inspector Whitney Walker believes they're being targeted by the notorious Carriage Killer, who chooses a local rail network, commits four murders, and moves on.

Against her wishes, Walker's boss brings in officers from another force to help the investigation and prevent more deaths, but she's forced to defend her team against this outside interference.

Forensic psychologist, Dr Georgina Cavendish, is by her side in an attempt to bring to an end this killing spree. But how can they get into the mind of a killer who has already killed twelve times in two years without leaving a single clue behind?

For fans of Rachel Abbott, L J Ross and Angela Marsons, *Death Track* is the third in the Cavendish & Walker series. A gripping serial killer thriller that will have you hooked.

～

LETHAL SECRET - Cavendish & Walker Book 4

Someone has a secret. A secret worth killing for….

When a series of suicides, linked to the Wellness Spirit Centre, turn out to be murder, it brings together DCI Whitney Walker and forensic psychologist Dr Georgina Cavendish for another investigation. But as they delve deeper, they come across a tangle of secrets and the very real risk that the killer will strike again.

As the clock ticks down, the only way forward is to infiltrate the centre. But the outcome is disastrous, in more ways than one.

For fans of Angela Marsons, Rachel Abbott and M A Comley, *Lethal Secret* is the fourth book in the Cavendish & Walker crime fiction series.

∽

FINAL VERDICT - Cavendish & Walker Book 5

The judge has spoken……everyone must die.

When a killer starts murdering lawyers in a prestigious law firm, and every lead takes them to a dead end, DCI Whitney Walker finds herself grappling for a motive.

What links these deaths, and why use a lethal injection?

Alongside forensic psychologist, Dr Georgina Cavendish, they close in on the killer, while all the time trying to not let their personal lives get in the way of the investigation.

For fans of Rachel Abbott, Mark Dawson and M A Comley,

Final Verdict is the sixth in the Cavendish & Walker series. A fast paced murder mystery which will keep you guessing.

About the Author

Sally Rigby was born in Northampton, in the UK. She has always had the travel bug, and after living in both Manchester and London, eventually moved overseas. From 2001 she has lived with her family in New Zealand, which she considers to be the most beautiful place in the world. During this time she also lived for five years in Australia.

Sally has always loved crime fiction books, films and TV programmes, and has a particular fascination with the psychology of serial killers.

Sally loves to hear from her readers, so do feel free to get in touch via her website www.sallyrigby.com

Acknowledgments

First and foremost, I'd like to thank my friends and critique partners, Amanda Ashby and Christina Phillips, for their help and support in getting this book ready for publication. I couldn't imagine life without them.

Thanks to Emma Mitchell for being so much more than a fantastic editor. I still can't believe how lucky I was to find her. Thanks also to Kate Noble and my Advanced Reader Team for their input in proof reading.

Stuart Bache, once again, has produced such an evocative cover. It's one of my favourites.

And, of course, my love and thanks go to my wonderful family Garry, Alicia, and Marcus for always being there.

Made in the USA
Columbia, SC
13 January 2022

54207482R00174